T0113017

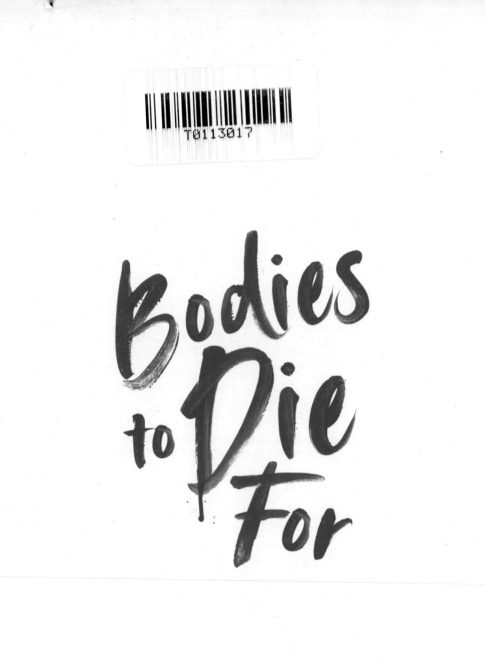

Bodies to Die For

Lori Brand

BLACK
STONE
PUBLISHING

Copyright © 2024 by Lori Johnson-Brand
Published in 2024 by Blackstone Publishing
Cover and book design by Kathryn Galloway English

All rights reserved. This book or any portion
thereof may not be reproduced or used in any manner
whatsoever without the express written permission
of the publisher except for the use of brief quotations
in a book review.

The characters and events in this book are fictitious.
Any similarity to real persons, living or dead, is coincidental
and not intended by the author.

Printed in the United States of America
Originally published in hardcover by Blackstone Publishing in 2024

First paperback edition: 2024
ISBN 979-8-212-63273-7
Fiction / Thrillers / Psychological

Version 1

Blackstone Publishing
31 Mistletoe Rd.
Ashland, OR 97520

www.BlackstonePublishing.com

For all women, everywhere

Content warning:
this book contains depictions of disordered eating,
body dysmorphia, and related conditions.

Showtime

The ceiling is dripping. That's what the guest called down.

Dale now stood in the bathroom of 651, gazing up to where a dark stain was forming. Fat water droplets collected in its belly, periodically splatting to the earth, like jumpers.

"Someone must have left the water on upstairs," the guest offered. Dale's headache, camped at the base of his skull since morning, spread out and set up satellites at his temples.

Gemma. That was the guest in the room above. Dale knew this because in the last twenty-four hours, she had lost her room key twice, misplaced the bottoms of her crystal-encrusted bikini, and run through the hotel lobby in a skimpy robe to flag down a police officer. She was one of the many crazy Olympia contestants.

For the second year in a row, the bodybuilding show was taking place at the Orange County Convention Center in Orlando, Florida. It was one of his hotel's biggest events, booking over five hundred guest rooms, as well as several conference rooms for check-ins, makeup, hair, and tanning. And it wasn't just the full house that made the Olympia so profitable. The spa was packed with competitors seeking massages and manicures.

The restaurant was jammed with sponsors devouring steaks and martinis.

Despite the Olympia being a boon to business, it was the source of many a headache for Dale. There were screaming matches between the competitors and their significant others, between the competitors and their teammates, between the competitors and the staff—really, just the competitors *at* the staff. These bodybuilders were a rather high-strung breed. Maybe they just needed carbs?

Then there were the mounds of hotel linens stained orange by spray tan. The smells: perfume layered over body odor spritzed with protein farts. And medical crises, everything from panic attacks to heart palpitations to seizures. The whole hair-raising affair dragged on for six long days.

But if last year's event had given Dale headaches, this year's was giving him a full-blown, face-numbing migraine. Earlier today, there had been a Fat Activist protest against one of the contest's main sponsors, REIGN. Somehow, while the police were rounding up the protesters, a few broke loose and went rogue. They were now at large, somewhere in Dale's hotel. DIET CULTURE SLUTS had been scrawled on a wall in black five-foot-high permanent marker. So as Dale stood in the bathroom of 651, he figured, why not a flood?

Dale looked at his watch. Tonight's Finals were about to start. That meant Gemma likely left the water on at least thirty minutes ago. Dale knew from experience that thirty minutes of running water could result in thousands of dollars' worth of damage. He assured the guest he would take care of the dripping and took the stairs, two at a time, to the seventh floor. By the time he arrived outside 751, he was out of breath and sweating.

That was another thing about this show, it always high-lighted how out of shape he was. Just this morning, he'd found himself in one of the elevators, the stench of Egg McMuffin on his breath, belly hanging over his khakis, standing next to a male Physique competitor. The man's body fat was so low that the veins on his arms protruded like bloated earthworms after a storm. The man was holding a gallon-size jug of water and dressed in athletic shorts and a tank top, likely on his way to the gym. He eyed Dale's McDonald's coffee, laden with artificial creamer, suspiciously. Dale simply nodded good morning and promised himself, yet again, that he was going to start hitting the gym just as soon as this show was over.

Before knocking on 751's door, Dale took a moment to collect his breath and straighten himself. He tucked in his shirt and smoothed his hair. Wiped his sweaty hands on his pants, leaving faint wet streaks on the fabric. Once righted, he banged on the door. "Hotel maintenance. Open up, please."

There was no answer. He stood still, listening. He could hear the shower running inside.

Again, he banged. "Hotel maintenance. We've had a report of leaking water downstairs." Again, there was no response.

After a few moments, Dale slipped his master key card from his pocket and ran it across the lock. Three green lights appeared, making a happy, chirpy sound. Dale pushed the door inward.

The beige carpet was saturated. Small currents eddied on top, reflecting light from the open bathroom ahead.

"Hotel maintenance," he said. Above him, the air conditioner kicked on, making the hair on his forearms stand up.

Slowly, Dale stepped forward, his feet squishing into the carpet. Water worked its way through his shoes and dampened his socks. He continued, putting one soggy foot in front of the other, toward the sound of the running water. As he got closer, something that looked like a yellow ribbon began to snake its way out of the bathroom, floating.

His eyes adjusted, and he realized it wasn't a ribbon at all, but a hank of blond hair. It continued its bobbing path, and Dale saw that it ended not in a hunk of human flesh, but in a plastic comb. He had seen enough female competitors carrying ziplock bags of hair around the hotel to recognize it as a hair extension.

"Hello?" Dale asked, his voice now small and hollow. He instinctively knew there would be no reply.

With the back of his neck prickling, Dale continued toward the rectangle of light spilling from the mouth of the bathroom. When there were no steps left to take, he took a deep breath and steeled himself for what was inside.

And there it was. Like he knew it would be. Floating face down in the tub before him was a body. The back of its head bashed in and matted with blood.

Two Months Earlier

Chapter 1

GEMMA

Eight Weeks Out:

122.4 pounds | 125 g protein | 200 g carbs | 50 g fat

"Our next guest found herself one hundred pounds overweight when she decided she'd had enough. Since then, she's not only shed the excess weight but transformed her life. She is now a fitness model, personal trainer, and bodybuilder. Her Instagram account, @GymmaGemma, has almost half a million followers and is dedicated to helping others get healthy. Please help me welcome Gemma Jorgenson," announces Josephine Warner, the host of *Morning Cup of Jo*.

I take a deep breath and stride out onto a well-lit set. Josephine greets me with a hug, while the audience claps and cheers. There are two other guests, both women, who have also transformed their lives (today's theme) already seated in comfy armchairs. One woman went from losing her job and moving in with her parents to launching a successful shapewear company. The other went from a college dropout to selling a meditation app for millions. We're all here to talk about how we did it. To show the way. Offer inspiration. I feel a little outclassed, since I'm likely the only one who still scrubs her own toilet.

Morning Cup of Jo is the big time—one of the top-rated morning shows in the United States. I've been trying to get on it since I was twenty-five. In the intervening three years, I've pitched ideas, emailed congratulations, and followed both Josephine and *Morning Cup* on all social media platforms. I even sent Josephine's bichon a pair of WagWellies for his birthday. But it wasn't until a photo of me leaving a Whole Foods with actress Ava Anderson appeared in *People* magazine, captioned "Ava's Personal Trainer, Gemma Jorgenson, teaches her how to grocery shop!" that Josephine finally returned my email. Not that I'm complaining.

Looking at Josephine now, I can't believe that someone who loomed so large in my mind is actually rather small. At five foot two, one hundred pounds tops, she weighs less than the amount of weight I lost. Basically, I shed the equivalent of a full human being and became an entirely different person in the process.

"So tell us your story," Josephine says once I'm seated.

Behind us, two twelve-foot-high photos appear. The first, the obligatory "Before," shows me wearing an ugly flowered blouse, my eyes peering out of a doughy mound of flesh. The second, the "After," has me clad in a hot pink sports bra and leggings, a pair of dumbbells in my hands. Blond highlights spill over one shoulder. Long lean muscles shimmer.

I take a deep breath, point at the Before, and begin. "This was me at the darkest point in my life. I had just finished college and was working fifty plus hours a week in an unrewarding marketing position, thinking, 'I went to college for this?' I was eating aimlessly: pizza, fast food, donuts. I thought I had no time for fitness—I was already tired all the time. How could I add in one more thing?"

Josephine nods sagely and addresses the audience, "Any of you ever feel like that?" The audience whoops and claps.

I continue, "One sweltering August day, I had to meet a potential client at her office. We'll call her Jess. When I got to her building, I realized the office was on the third floor of this poorly air-conditioned three-flat. There was no elevator, so I had to take the stairs. I gritted my teeth and began to schlep my portfolio up.

"By the second floor, I was wheezing and out of breath. I remember resting against this cool wall on the landing for a couple of minutes and actually wondering if I might have a heart attack, if I should turn back. Ultimately, I decided that it would be more embarrassing to turn back than to have a heart attack. At least then I'd be dead, I reasoned. So upward I continued."

Josephine gasps, "Oh my." She reaches out and takes my hand, which is warm and damp. I've told this story a hundred times, and every time I tell it, my hands still get sweaty, like they're forever trapped in that stairwell.

"When I finally got to the top, I had sweat running down my back, pooling in my bra, and—I'll just say it—gathering in various creases." I wince at the memory.

The audience laughs. Someone yells out, "I feel ya, sister."

"So I reach the third floor, completely out of breath. There's this birdlike receptionist there, and she looks up at me, totally alarmed. She says, 'Are you okay?' I'm clearly not, so I ask for a glass of water. And she brings me a Dixie cup from the water cooler. A Dixie cup! That's, like, two ounces. I drink it down in a single gulp.

"There's a mirror above her desk, and I can see my reflection. I'm a mess: dark wet splotches under my arms, my hair matted, face bright red.

"Just then, Jess comes out of her office. She's petite and

trim and wearing white tailored pants. She takes one look at me and suggests I rest a moment before we go to the conference room. So I sit on this gray leather sofa, attempting to slow my breathing and calm my racing heart. To not take giant, gasping breaths like a dying fish on the beach. I can feel Jess and the receptionist exchanging worried looks above me.

"After a few minutes, Jess says, 'Shall we?' And even though I'm thinking, 'No way,' I'm like, 'Sure.' The sofa I'm sitting on is super low, and it's hard for me to stand. I have to rock back and forth a couple times for momentum and use both hands to push myself up off of it. Then there's this horrible moment where I almost fall backward, but somehow manage to pull through and end up on my feet. I turn around to grab my portfolio and see that I've left a giant, ass-size sweat mark on the sofa. Jess pretends not to notice, and we go to the conference room.

"I give my pitch. I don't remember a thing I said, but I distinctly remember leaving sweaty fingerprints all over my beautiful presentation. The whole time I'm presenting, I know I'm not getting the account. That we're both just going through the motions. I think about asking if I should leave, but am too embarrassed, so I gut it out.

"Anyway, Jess was perfectly polite, but sure enough, my company didn't get the account. I'm certain it was because she couldn't imagine working with me, couldn't imagine me climbing those steps. It didn't matter how good my work was. She couldn't see it. All she could see were my physical limitations.

"After I left, I couldn't bring myself to go back to the office. Instead, I went home. I walked into my air-conditioned apartment and shut the door. In the past, when I was stressed out, I would eat something, sometimes a lot of something, to make myself feel better. But that day was different.

"'Enough,' I thought. I took out a garbage bag and filled it with all the ice cream, chips, and junk food in my apartment. Brought it out to the garbage chute in the hall and threw it away. I imagined that I was throwing out my old life with it.

"This was my turning point—when I realized how much my health was affecting my life. I already knew it was affecting me socially. I didn't go out with friends because of how I looked. I wouldn't join a softball team because I didn't want to run the bases. But now my health was affecting me professionally? Just: No."

I turn and address the audience. "Telling myself I didn't have time was an excuse. We make time for what's important to us. My health is important to me. What's important to you?"

The audience erupts in applause. I feel myself blush, a lump form in my throat.

I swallow it down and go on to discuss how I developed better eating habits and started walking just five minutes a day. The five minutes grew to thirty which morphed into jogging. Eventually, I added in lifting weights, and then my confidence exploded. Because I wanted to share my passion for fitness with others and believe that exercise is transformative, I became a personal trainer. Eventually, I took a leap of faith and quit my marketing job so I could dedicate my life to helping others get healthy.

Behind me, Before and After photos of some of my clients appear. The Befores show men and women stuffed into clothes that strain against their girth. Their faces are buried beneath flesh, double chins, and jowls. The Afters show the same people, barely recognizable, beaming back at the camera, eyes sparkling with life. Some are crossing finish lines of 5Ks, others are wearing swimsuits or chasing toddlers around.

The last photo is a picture of me looking fit and healthy with my hunky husband, Steve. You'd never guess we got into a massive argument that morning.

Josephine asks me a few more questions, then turns it over to the audience to ask the panel anything they want. The first question is from an apple-shaped, middle-aged woman in a pink twin set. She directs her question to me. "For someone who is overweight and wants to get in shape but doesn't know where to start, what would you suggest?"

"The first thing to get a handle on is your diet. You can't out train a bad diet. It's a lot easier to not eat that piece of chocolate cake than it is to burn off its calories. Eat lots of fruits and vegetables—mostly real foods. Start going for a walk every day. It's good for your heart and lungs. It clears the mind. Eventually, add in some strength training and take it from there."

A second woman raises her hand. Josephine walks the microphone over to her. She also directs her question to me. "Are there any foods you don't eat? Like carbs or red meat or dairy?"

I laugh and shake my head. I get asked this question a lot. "No. I eat everything!" (I say.) "The only foods I try to limit are highly processed ones, like Twinkies. Basically, if it can exist for months on a shelf, or is made out of ingredients you need a science degree to recognize, I stay away."

The questions go on from there. I am by far the favorite panelist, the one these women—the audience is almost all women—find the most inspiring. The other two panelists are self-made millionaires, but they're single and a little flabby. I lost a bunch of weight, look great, and married a hot guy. So I win.

I'm not sure how I feel about that.

Finally, Josephine says, "We have time for one last question."

Many hands go up. Josephine selects an athletic woman in her twenties with red springs for hair. The woman asks, "Gemma, what happened at last year's Olympia? You were expected to win, and . . . didn't."

The audience waits. Drops of sweat prick near my hairline.

My breathing, amplified by the microphone pinned to my blouse, bounces around the room. An audience member's feet shuffle.

I take a deep breath and force a smile. "Sometimes things don't work out. I still had an amazing time." No, I didn't. Because of her.

Deep inside me a cage door rattles. I grit my teeth and knock that bitch back down.

Chapter 2

ASHLEY

The "Before" photo of the woman on TV looks surprisingly like me. A knife to my heart, like so many others. I forget the program I'm coding, the cool celadon walls of my home office, and free-fall into the body image abyss. Again.

Look, I know I'm fat. I've tried not to be. And tried some more. I've tried until my hands shook with hunger. Until I saw black spots. Got dizzy standing up. I've tried just about every diet known: WeightWatchers, SlimFast, Jenny Craig, keto, Atkins, South Beach, and all the rest. I've gone gluten-free, dairy-free, meat-free, fat-free, and carb-free.

Every once in a while, I would make some progress and think, *This time. This time I'm going to do it.* Until something went wrong. A stressful situation at work, my boyfriend dumping me, or some other curveball of life. Then I'd lose focus on the diet for what felt like a few days, and boom: up ten pounds. I'd be so angry with myself that I'd give up and gain all the weight back. Sometimes more.

I've done this for over two decades. Two decades! I'm thirty-two now, and I've been yo-yo dieting since the fourth grade, when my mom would pack flaccid celery sticks in my Powerpuff Girls lunch box, instead of crackers or chips like the other kids got with their sandwiches. I've spent thousands of dollars and have nothing to show for it other than a damaged self-esteem.

And here is this dumb twat Gemma blaring through my TV, implying that I need to "transform" myself. Insinuating that I'm not okay the way I am.

Just when I think I can't be any more pissed, my phone rings. I don't even have to look to know who it is.

Don't do it, I tell myself. I let the phone go to voicemail. Ten seconds later, it rings again, rattling my teeth, as well as my nerves.

Because I know my mother's tactic (the wear down: keep calling, eventually show up in person, if necessary) I bite the bullet and answer.

"Hi, Mom."

"Are you watching *Morning Cup of Jo*?"

"No."

"You need to turn it on. There's a girl on the show who reminds me so much of you. She was in your same predicament a few years ago, before she turned her whole life around and became a personal trainer."

"Mom, I don't want to turn my whole life around and become a personal trainer. I'm a software engineer, and a very good one."

A sigh. Then cautiously, "Well, I'm not saying you have to give up software."

"Then what are you saying?" I sound like an angry thirteen-year-old. I feel like an angry thirteen-year-old. Why am I even asking her this?

"Oh, Ashley, I love you so, my girl, but I feel like you've given up on yourself. This girl on the television is an online trainer. She used to be overweight. I think she could help you. She specializes in working with people like you."

She specializes in fat people. Just say it. "Mom, for the millionth time, I'm not interested in another diet." In failing again.

"Ashley, I'm worried about your health. You're in the prime of your life. There is so much your weight is holding you back from."

"My health is fine. And there's nothing that being fat is holding me back from." I spit the word "fat" out. It feels powerful to hurl it back at the world. To make others squirm. For so many years I was terrified of that little word. Getting comfortable with its sharp edges, with the way it feels in my mouth, has taken away some of its power.

"Sweetie, your health may be fine now, but I worry about your future." And the husband and children you will never have because you're fat.

I could hate her. I really could. All 110 pounds of her, with her ladies' tennis and garden club. She has no idea what it's like to live in a body like mine. The thin privilege she experiences. Being able to squeeze around someone in a narrow hallway, or post pictures of herself in a swimsuit at the beach without a bunch of whale emojis appearing in the comments.

But I can't quite hate her because my beloved father, her beloved husband, died of a heart attack on their kitchen floor last year. I inherited the fat gene from him. Deep down, I think she views his dying as her failure. Despite decades of trying (and trying), she simply couldn't get him to "eat less and move more."

I am their only child, and with him gone, I'm all she has left. My health and dating life—really anything to do with procuring offspring—are hot topics.

I tell my mom that I have a deadline coming up and can't chat. I hang up and push my laptop aside, watch the audience go nuts over this Gemma phenom and get increasingly annoyed. Woman after woman fawns over her and asks her the most idiotic questions: "For someone who is overweight and wants to get in shape but doesn't know where to start, what would you suggest?" You nimrod, it's not the starting that's the problem, it's the sticking with it. "What would you say to someone thinking about starting their own business?" Um, maybe ask the panelist who built a shapewear empire and not the Instagram chick? Even the other two panelists, women way more accomplished, seem cowed by her.

I navigate to Gemma's fabled Instagram account. She has posted nearly a thousand times in the last five years. Her account chronicles her weight loss, becoming a personal trainer, meeting her husband, and getting married. Her wedding dress is beautiful, her husband gorgeous: a rakish blond with a strong jaw. They have fabulous Sunday brunches. Poached eggs, avocado toast, and fancy cappuccinos with hearts in the foam. Gemma starts competing in bodybuilding competitions, starts winning, and eventually models for fitness magazines.

Her account links to her website, GymmaGemma.com, which sells online training programs ($300 for six weeks), in-person training sessions ($100 each), an upcoming five-day Mexican retreat ($5,000, includes hotel, meals, training sessions, and swag bag), and apparel. There is a link to Amazon for products she recommends, a free downloadable exercise program (if you provide your email), an exercise video library, and clips of her appearing on various television shows.

The annoyance I originally felt starts to condense down into a tight kernel of hate deep inside me. Years of self-loathing and tears have made for fertile soil. She's one more person telling me that I'm not okay the way I am. That I need to shrink.

Chapter 3

GEMMA

"So tacky," Anita stage-whispers. She frowns, or attempts to, but there is so much Botox jammed between her brows that instead her face contorts like a funhouse mirror, the sides of her forehead going up like horns, while the center remains smooth and bland. Blond sheet-like hair hangs around it, glaring in the light.

From our REIGN booth at the Tampa FitExpo, Anita, Craig, and I look across the convention floor to Bianca, standing in her Bianca Summers Fitness booth, her middle cinched cartoonishly small by a bright pink waist trainer. Above her, a matching pink banner screams, "Cinch Me!" With her wavy blond hair and domed breast implants, she looks like a Barbie doll.

Bianca is a REIGN-sponsored athlete, like Anita and I, and was supposed to work the REIGN booth with us. Instead, she pulled out at the last minute to promote her new line of waist trainers. And Craig, the owner of REIGN, is incensed, though you'd never know it by looking at him. The consummate professional and yoga enthusiast, he nods at passersby beneath dark, closely cropped hair and well-tended facial stubble. But

I'm close enough to notice the way his muscled hands repeatedly smooth the luxury leggings in front of him. Like he wants to rip them in two.

He says, "I can't believe the FitExpo organizers let her have a booth here. Waist trainers compress your internal organs. How is that healthy? I let them know that if she's back next year, we won't be. A company like REIGN can't afford to be associated with the likes of hers."

REIGN is Craig's baby. He grew it from the ground up. It's known for its high-end fitness apparel and vegan supplements, all produced in an ecologically minded manner.

Anita sneers. "I mean, that fabric is the color of Pepto-Bismol."

Craig says, "I'm thinking of dropping her from the REIGN family."

Bianca glances our way and flushes. She seems to know we're talking about her. Regardless, she squares her shoulders and directs a customer to a full-length mirror. Bianca wraps a tape measure around the woman's waist, flicks the tape free, then wraps a demo trainer around her and remeasures. The woman appears delighted and pulls out a credit card.

Anita and Craig continue to bash Bianca while I remain silent. Yes, the waist trainers are vile, but Bianca's been nothing but kind to me. Despite being my competition—in everything from bodybuilding shows to fitness magazine spreads to coaching clients—she's helped me. She loaned me earrings at the New York Pro when I lost mine. Put in a good word for me at *Fit Gurl* magazine, where I now have a photo shoot next month. She helped me grow my Instagram following by giving me shout-outs and advice.

Bianca's also the only person who knows the real reason I bombed last year's Olympia, and she's kept my secret.

Craig stalks off to check out his competition, and I slip away to the bathroom. On the way back, I stop by Bianca's booth. "Hey, looks like you're doing great business," I say.

She looks up and smiles. "I am. And it's a good thing. Craig's going to drop me, isn't he?"

We glance at the REIGN booth where Anita glowers at us. "I think so."

"Well, that's okay. I don't want to be associated with his brand anymore, anyway."

I turn to Bianca in surprise. REIGN is a premiere brand. A real feather in one's cap. "Why?"

She looks down at her hands. Long eyelashes flutter against her cheeks. She fiddles with a tag. Then back to me, like she's made a decision. She looks both ways, takes a deep breath, and leans forward.

Before she can answer, a male voice behind me booms, "My two favorite girls!" I turn and see Rick, our coach. He's big as a former linebacker, wearing a track suit and clutching his trusty iPad. Despite approaching fifty, the sides of his head have shaved stripes, leaving the dyed-black hair on top to flop down to the left. This is a trendy hairstyle for twenty-somethings. On Rick, it just accentuates his hard mileage.

Rick is a bodybuilding legend. He's helped numerous competitors, both men and women, win all the big-name competitions. In fact, he's coached more Bikini Olympia champions than any other coach around.

The Olympia is the most prestigious bodybuilding competition in the world, and Bikini is my division. Bikini Olympia winners go on to grace all the top fitness magazine covers and get lucrative commercial endorsements.

Rick says, "Gemma, I caught your interview on *Morning Cup* yesterday. You looked great!" He turns to Bianca. "Now, Bianca, what's going on, my love? Are those dark circles under your eyes?"

Bianca shrugs and begins straightening the waist trainer in front of her. "Maybe. I didn't sleep well last night."

"Well, we can't have that! The Olympia's just two months out. You need your beauty rest. You both do."

I nod. It's easier. I leave them to discuss Bianca's sleep cycle. Rick will have lots to say. He's big into all things lunar, as well as circadian. What neither Bianca nor Rick knows, what no one knows, is that I'm pulling out of this year's Olympia. Bianca's won the last three. Meanwhile, I've had to settle for second twice, and then got blown out last year.

What happened last year? Fat Gemma happened. Fat Gemma is my inner fat girl. Always lurking in the background, biding her time, waiting for me to let my guard down. That tripe I said on *Morning Cup* about eating everything? Not true. There are many foods I won't eat. Fat Gemma foods. Deep dish pizza, birthday cake, marshmallow fluff, to name a few. Even a taste, and she's back. Raging. Out of control.

Two days before last year's Olympia, Anita and I were guests on the talk show *Fit Bodies*. That awful day happened to be their one-year anniversary. Toward the end of filming, the producers brought out an anniversary cake and offered us each a slice. At first I declined, but Anita piped up, "Seriously, Gemma? We've just spent an hour talking about moderation, and you won't even taste it?"

And so I did.

After two straight months of a calorie deficit, of not eating anything that wasn't carefully calculated and planned, that bite was like a hit of narcotics. It went straight to my head, sent a rush of endorphins flooding through my body. The cake was, in a word, amazing. Perhaps the best thing I've ever tasted. But that's what semistarvation will do to you. That taste turned into the whole piece.

It would have been fine, maybe, if it ended there. But it didn't. After I left the show, I stopped at a bakery on the way back to the hotel and bought a six-inch-diameter birthday cake. I smuggled it into the room, like a drug trafficker with a brick of cocaine, and hid it in the closet. All afternoon it called to me. I kept asking Steve when he was going to go to the gym.

Once he finally left, I locked the deadbolt and took the cake out of the closet. Out of its box. Laid it on the table before me, feeling like Gollum with his precious in *The Lord of the Rings*. Pink frosting sugar crystals sparkled like stars. I took one tentative bite. It was as good as I thought it would be. Bite by glorious bite I continued. Until the bites were no longer glorious and I felt sick. I finished it, anyway. And hated myself.

As punishment, I made myself throw it up. Somehow, through sheer willpower, I managed to wrestle Fat Gemma back into her cage. But the damage was done. That one slipup cost me. All those carbs, the ones my body frantically absorbed before I could puke them out, caused it to puff up. Not enough for the average person to notice, but enough for a table of judges at a bodybuilding competition to note, especially considering I was standing in front of them in nothing but a bikini.

It was only after my humiliating Olympia defeat, where Anita took second, finally surpassing me, that I realized something: I never saw her take a bite of that damn cake.

So this year, though I've once again qualified for the Olympia, I'm going to decline. Why risk a resurgence of Fat Gemma, especially when I know Bianca's going to win, anyway? And why see any more of Anita than I already have to?

I haven't told my husband yet. Steve won't be happy. He'll only see the lost income potential. But then, he doesn't know about Fat Gemma.

Chapter 4

ASHLEY

"Here we are, miss," the driver says, pulling up to the curb across from my apartment. "You want me to drive around?" He eyes me in the mirror, probably judging my ability to make it across the street with my carry-on.

"No, this is fine," I say. I've just returned to Orlando from a last-minute work trip and can't wait to crawl into bed. Despite the late hour, cars are zooming back and forth along the boulevard. I roll my bag down to the corner where there's a crosswalk and press the button. I check my phone. Ignore a message from my mom, send a quick reply to a client, and get sucked into an Instagram post by @GymmaGemma, the woman I saw on *Morning Cup* the other day. Stop it, I tell myself. Just stop it. Do not get sucked in again.

I force my head up and see the "walking man" signal has begun to flash. I think I can make it if I hurry. Carefully, I look both ways and step off the curb. My bag clatters down behind me.

I'm halfway across when the "walking man" changes to the flashing orange "don't walk" hand. I pick up my pace. The carry-on's wheels start to rattle, and the hand stops flashing and blasts its steady light.

A black Cadillac Escalade next to me lays on the horn. I try to move faster, but my bag feels unsteady, like it might topple over. One of the wheels seems stuck. Sweat is running down my back.

Just as I make it past the Escalade—I'm not even to the curb yet—the driver peals past me, kicking up pebbles and dust. They get in my hair, my lungs, my heart. His windows are down and out sails, "Hurry up, you fat bitch!"

I stumble to the curb and trip. My knee screams. My palms skid across the sidewalk. The Escalade must have clipped my bag, because it's lying on its side a few feet away with the zipper open. My jumbo-size underwear is in the gutter.

I push myself up to my hands and the knee that's not on fire just in time to see the driver flip me off through the rear window, above a bumper sticker that reads "Keep Honking, I'm Reloading."

———

"Obese people are much more prone to falls," says the lanky urgent care doctor, picking bits of debris out of the inch-long gash in my knee caused by a broken beer bottle.

"A man in an Escalade almost ran me over," I explain. Again.

"Yes, but if you didn't have all that extra weight, you'd have been able to move out of the way much more nimbly."

"So you're saying it's my fault?" I ask in disbelief. Although you'd think by now, I'd expect it.

He looks up at me with sharp blue eyes. "In a way, yes."

And here it comes. Like it so often does when I go to the doctor. The dreaded Fat Talk. It's one of the reasons I avoid health care. Maybe it's one of the reasons us fatties have such shitty health?

Instead of listening to him, I listen to the blood whooshing through my ears. Angle my face toward the worn linoleum tiles. With their putty and beige pattern, they remind me of sedimentary rock, the kind with fossils of long-ago creatures trapped inside.

Eventually, I sense silence and pull my attention back to the doctor. "I'm sorry, what?"

"I said, 'Have you tried eating less?'"

And then the anger. Always the anger. Warm and wet, it rises up inside me. Threatens to spew out all over this doctor's pristine white coat. His arrogant face. The entire medical establishment. *Shut up and fix my damn knee!* is caged behind my teeth. But I can't bring myself to release it.

Instead, I shrug and settle for, "Could you please just fix my knee so I can go home?" And hate myself.

He sighs, like I've disappointed him.

Once I'm stitched up, while going over my aftercare, the doctor hands me a glossy brochure with green lettering, "A New You: Weight Loss and Bariatric Surgery Center." On the cover is an average-size blond woman with bright pink lipstick and a bad perm. She's standing inside a mammoth pair of jeans that she holds up to keep from falling.

The letters start to swim; the woman's smile twists. I clutch the brochure in my sweaty hands. Its colors smear and green ink bleeds into my fingertips. When the doctor returns his attention to my chart, I drop the propaganda into the waste basket beside me. It makes no more than a whisper, but I know he hears. His ears redden as he jots down a note. I wonder if it includes the words "noncompliant" or "obstinate." From the basket, I feel the brochure pulsing.

At last, the doctor leaves me in the room to collect my things. Just before I split, I snatch the smeared woman from the garbage and bury her in the pit of my purse.

Chapter 5

GEMMA

A buzzing insect is trapped in my ear. It's the stinging kind. I know it. I swat at it and shake my head, but it keeps buzzing, drilling in deeper. I try to scream, but my throat is stuffed with cotton. Just when I'm certain the insect will pierce my eardrum, I wrench myself awake with a great whoosh of air. It takes me a moment to identify my surroundings. Then I remember that I'm at the Marriott in Tampa for my appearance on *Morning Cup of Jo* and the FitExpo, which just wrapped.

My lungs heave as I untangle the twisted sheet from my sweaty legs. Moonlight casts an eerie pall across the room. I reach for Steve, but his side of the bed is cold.

Again, the buzzing. My phone is jittering all over the nightstand. The green numbers of the alarm clock show it's one in the morning. Where is Steve? I reach for my phone, expecting it to be him. But I don't recognize the number. Is he okay? I answer just as the caller hangs up.

They don't leave a message, but I see a voicemail from Bianca at 9:02 p.m. I press play. Her voice comes out naked and afraid. "Gemma, please call me as soon as you can. It's about what I wanted to tell you earlier today. There's something you need to know. Or better yet, stop by my room. It doesn't matter how late."

The room door clicks open. Steve must be back. He kicks off his shoes in the entry, where they will undoubtedly languish as a tripping hazard, and shuffles into the bathroom. The shower blasts on.

I crack the bathroom door. "Steve, where were you?"

"I couldn't sleep, so I went down to the bar and grabbed a quick drink."

"Why are you taking a shower?"

"It was way too hot in that place. Their AC must be on the blink or something."

I click the door shut and head back to our bed but am no longer tired. Instead, I decide to get dressed and head up to Bianca's room. She said it didn't matter how late, and I'm curious about what she wants to tell me.

I'm grabbing my key card when Steve exits the bathroom, towel hanging low around his hips. Blond surfer mop dripping. "Where are you going?" he asks.

"Up to Bianca's room. She left me a message to stop by."

"Babe, it's one in the morning." He threads his fingers through mine and draws me to him. Steam rises from his waxed chest, like wet pavement in July. "Stay with me," he whispers.

Where was this earlier? Earlier this week, this month—hell, earlier this year? It's like the only time he shows me any affection anymore is when I have somewhere else to be.

Nevertheless, my traitorous body warms to his. My knees falter. But my mind pulls through. Bianca needs me.

I place my palms on his chest. Feel his galloping heart. "I'll be back in ten minutes," I say and push away.

———

Bianca's room is down a long, empty hallway that pulses with energy. The navy carpet has large gold zigzags coursing through it like lightning. There's a bucket's worth of fresh ice dumped outside her door. I step around it and raise my hand to knock, but hear a man's voice inside and freeze.

I thought Bianca was staying by herself. My fist is hovering in the air when the door swings open wide. A hairy man in a suit almost runs into me. Beyond him, Bianca, clad in a white robe, is lying on the floor. Her hair's askew. Something pink (a scarf?) is wrapped around her neck. It's the color of Pepto-Bismol. I realize it's not a scarf.

Police officers and medics swarm around her.

"Who are you?" asks the man, coming out into the hall. He quickly shuts the door behind him.

My jaw hangs open. Everything is wrong with this scene. And shouldn't *Who are you?* be my line? But I can't make my mouth work.

My knees sway, and he catches my elbow. "Here, why don't you come sit down," he says, pushing open the door of the next room over, whose deadbolt is popped out to allow for ease of access.

I rip my arm away and scream. Scramble backward into the hall and slip on an ice cube. I land on my ass. Dig my heels into the carpet and push away from him.

A police officer pokes his head into the hall, sees me on the carpet, and looks at the hairy man. He lets the door fall shut.

"Hey, hey, sorry about that. I didn't mean to scare you," says the hairy man, pulling a badge out of his jacket and showing it to me. "I'm Detective Dan Cooper."

There's a void where my thoughts should be. "What . . . what's going on?"

Detective Cooper sits down on the hallway floor across

from me. He's got bushy eyebrows, hairy nostrils, winding side-
burns. Hair everywhere except for the top of his head, which is
smooth and bare, shining under the hall light. He says, "I was
hoping you could tell me. Did you know the woman who was
staying in this room?"

Did. Was. Past tense. "Bianca?"

"Yes, Bianca."

"Yes. I know her." *Knew?*

"What were you doing here, just now?"

I tell Detective Cooper about Bianca's call. Let him listen
to her voicemail. Scroll through my messages. I tell him about
my encounter with her earlier today, how she was about to tell
me something when Coach Rick interrupted. "Is she okay?" My
voice sounds small, foreign to my ears. I already know the answer.

"I'm afraid not." His eyes probe mine and I brace for it.
"I'm sorry to tell you this, but she's dead. Likely murdered. Do
you know if she had any enemies?"

"Not really, other than the usual Instagram haters." It occurs
to me that many of Bianca's haters also hate me.

Just then the door to Anita's room, two down from Bianca's, opens and a tall, regal-looking woman exits. Her brunette
hair is scraped back into a tight ponytail. Her eyebrows pull
back with it, giving her a hyperaware appearance. She spies
me sitting on the hallway floor with Cooper and shoots him a
questioning look.

Cooper addresses me. "This is Detective Jenny Stark. She
was just talking to Anita. You know Anita?"

I nod.

He continues, "Poor girl dropped an ice bucket on her toe.
Apparently, she was stopping by Bianca's room for a drink when
I answered the door and gave her the shock of her life." He
turns to Stark. "This is Gemma. She's a teammate of Bianca's."

At the mention of my name, Stark's eyes light up. "I just tried calling you," she says.

"Me?" What could I possibly have to do with any of this?

"Yes, I got your number from Anita. She said that you and Bianca were close." Stark helps me off the floor, and we all go into the room next door. Cooper fills her in about Bianca's call to me. I let her listen to the voicemail.

Detective Stark hands me back my phone and asks, "Where were you tonight after the FitExpo ended?"

"I helped Craig—that's the owner of REIGN—and Anita pack up the booth and load it in Craig's truck. Then I went back to my room, ordered room service, and spent the rest of the night inside."

"The whole night? You didn't leave once?" Her eyes penetrate deep into my skull, like she's sifting through its inner workings.

"Yes."

"Hmm." The corner of her mouth twitches. "Anita said she saw you outside Bianca's room around seven?"

I clarify. "I stopped by Bianca's room on the way back to mine—I wanted to hear what she tried to tell me earlier—but she wasn't there. Or at least she didn't answer."

"So you *didn't* go right back to your room?" Detective Stark asks.

I squirm. "I guess not."

"Can anyone vouch for your whereabouts after you left Craig and Anita?"

"My husband."

"He was with you the whole night?"

Damn Steve and his late-night drink. "He went down to the bar sometime after I fell asleep, which was around nine. I must have just missed Bianca's call."

Stark scribbles this down in a notebook, then sits forward. Looks me deep in the eyes. "I understand you've got some sort of bodybuilding competition coming up? The Olympia? And that you've twice taken second? That's gotta be rough, always coming in second." She says it with practiced empathy. Gets the eyebrows just right.

That bitch Anita. She set me up. I lean forward, return Stark's soulful gaze. "Actually, last year I lost big time. Anita, that's the girl you just interviewed, she took second. I'm not planning to compete this year. Anita is."

Stark asks to see my hands, and I comply. They're deeply calloused from pull-ups and deadlifts. She snaps a few pictures and swabs my palms with a wipe, which she then seals in a zip-lock bag.

Chapter 6

ASHLEY

"You'll never guess who I've run into at the grocery store!" my mom trills through the phone. The brightness in her voice alerts me that the mystery shopper is with her now. I have to be polite.

I set my *People* magazine aside. "Who?"

"Mitch Riley, Jane's son! You remember him?"

Snot-nosed kid who wet his pants in second grade. "Not really."

In the background, she says, "She remembers you fondly!" Then to me, "Well, he's all grown-up now and is a urologist! He's offered to take a look at your knee!" Ugh. This again. She's trying to set me up with poor Mitch, who's too polite to tell her to buzz off. I'm sure he'd have no interest in someone like me.

And why would I see a urologist about my knee? Especially considering it's already stitched up? I'm about to ask but stop myself. There's no point in arguing with crazy, it will just prolong this conversation. I glance at my knee, green and purple, propped on a pillow on my sofa. "No thanks. It's almost better."

"Oh look, the Lean Cuisines are on sale! Can I bring—" I hang up.

The silence in my apartment is deafening. I pick *People* back up, see the glamorous actresses with their gorgeous successful dates. They're going to galas, ballgames, for walks in the park, while I sit on my sofa in grubby sweats, alone.

I'm so tired of being alone, of never having anyone in my corner. But that's practically impossible when you're my size. It's like having a target on your back.

I think about the way the Escalade man treated me. The way the doctor treated me. The way the whole world treats me. How they only see my repulsive body. Not the person inside all this flesh.

Maybe it's time to try, again, to lose some weight.

Seeking inspiration, I idly scroll through Instagram, checking out posts with the hashtags #weightlosstransformation, #transformationtuesday, #weighinwednesday, #dietjourney. I drool over other women's Before and After weight loss pictures like I imagine some men drool over porn. It's the fantasy: What would it be like? What would it feel like?

Then reality lands: What would it take? That's the part where I get hung up. I know it will take months of hunger. Months of restriction. A lifestyle overhaul. And for what? So the world treats me better? Is that a good enough reason? I'm not sure.

There's a post from @GymmaGemma. She's banging on about her new weight loss program. Could I do it? I click *Follow* and consider signing up.

Then have second thoughts. I've gone down this rabbit hole before. Gotten a little too invested in an influencer or two.

Instead, I pull out the pamphlet the doctor gave me and read about all the ways A New You can help me, which include bariatric surgery. I've thought about this surgery before, but always viewed it as a last resort. Well, maybe it's time to break the emergency glass.

I flip the pamphlet over and see A New You has monthly informational seminars. And it just so happens that the next one is this afternoon.

Before I can change my mind, I go to their website and fill out the form. Take one last breath and click *Register*.

———

I look around the seminar room and see only one other attendee. A mousey-haired woman about my size, reading the same FAQs sheet that's on the table before me. I reassure myself that more people will arrive soon. That it won't just be the two of us. There are still seven minutes until the presentation starts.

As if I've been granted a wish, the door swings open, and a raven-haired woman built like an opera singer sweeps in. She's clad in a black Lycra catsuit and red patent thigh-high boots. It's early afternoon.

Despite there being about a dozen chairs in the room, she plops down next to me. Picks up the FAQs sheet in front of her, leans back in her chair, and kicks her boots up on the table. She starts reading.

I pick up my own FAQs sheet and begin to skim the benefits of this surgery. I'm on *improved blood pressure*, when Red Boots rocks forward. Her boots thunk the floor. She snatches the sheet from my hand, flips it over, and slaps it on the table in front of me. Taps *Risks* with a red fingernail. "Bowel obstruction, dumping syndrome, vomiting, malnutrition, death. What the fuck are you thinking?"

Mousey turns around and stares at us.

I hesitate, then answer evenly. "I know the risks. I've been thinking about this surgery for years." I pick up the sheet and turn it back to the front. With my bare fingernail, I tap the

Benefits section. "Remission of type two diabetes, improved cardiovascular health, relief of depression—"

"Are you depressed?"

"Um, that's sort of a personal question, don't you think?"

"If you're depressed because of your weight, it's because Diet Culture has brainwashed you."

"If you're not interested in this surgery, why are you here?"

"To save you." She turns to Mousey, whose jaw has come unhinged. "And you."

Mousey gets up and speed walks out of the room, as an overweight couple file in and take a seat.

I ask Red Boots, "You're like one of those antiabortion crusaders who harass women outside abortion clinics?"

"Yes, exactly. Except I'm pro-choice."

The door flings open and smacks the wall. The couple jumps. Their heads swivel toward the entrance, where a blond woman, all angles, strides in. Mousey trickles in after, clinging to the wall, as far away from Red Boots as possible. The blond declares, "I've called the police."

Red Boots rolls her eyes. "Third time this month." Then to me, "Come with me. Let me set you free."

"Um, I'm good, thanks. I think I'll just hang here."

Her face sags. She crumples up the FAQs sheet and whips it at the blond as she stalks to the door, where two other heavyset women are entering. She yells at them, "Run for your lives!" She gestures to the blond. "She'll brainwash you."

The new participants stand stock-still, their mouths agape. "Run!" Red Boots screams. They take a step away from her. Red Boots throws up her hands and storms out the door.

The room is suddenly very quiet.

The blond addresses us. "I'm so sorry. That woman's clearly

mentally unstable. I'm Renee. Please stay for the seminar and learn about all the ways this surgery can transform your lives."

I'm so shell-shocked I couldn't stand if I'd wanted to.

For the next hour, I see impressive Before and After pictures of surgery recipients. Hear about all the ways this surgery can improve my life. I'm also told of the aforementioned risks, plus numerous others. But the thing that gets me is Renee keeps saying that many of the risks can be reduced by lifestyle modifications, such as not overeating. See, that's the whole problem. If I could control that, I wouldn't be in this mess in the first place.

I look around to gauge the body language of the audience and see if anyone else is feeling as frustrated as I am. From what I can tell, they're buying what Renee is selling. Sheep, all of them.

I leave A New You feeling discouraged and begin the slog back to my car, parked four blocks away. As I limp along, I become aware of a car rolling behind me. I glance over my shoulder and it stops. It's a vintage Lincoln Continental, dark as night. I return my attention forward and continue my journey. After half a block, I sense it creeping and peek behind me. It stops again.

The sidewalk's empty. The building to my right is a Pilates studio. I consider going inside to hide from the polished Lincoln's tinted windows but can't bring myself to face the stares I'd surely get.

I pull out my cell phone, and the Continental starts creeping forward once more. Afraid to turn my back on it, I punch in 9-1-1 and keep my finger hovering over the dial button.

The Continental glides up and the passenger window rolls down. It's Red Boots. "I see you're limping. Can we give you a ride? My name's Lydia. This here's my driver, Tony." Tony's lean and wiry and wearing a Metallica T-shirt. Veins run down his forearms like ropes. He doesn't look like a driver.

Somewhere in the back of my mind *Don't get in the car with strangers* rings out. It mingles with Renee's assessment that Lydia is *clearly mentally unstable.*

But maybe Lydia really is here to save me. What was I thinking, considering a surgery that has dumping syndrome and even death as possible risks? Besides, my knee is killing me, and my car is still three blocks away. How dangerous can Lydia be? She's fat, like me. Plus, I'm curious about her. A little in awe. And I really love those boots.

So against my better judgment, I accept their offer and introduce myself. Tony swings the Continental's suicide doors open. The interior is cavernous. The seats, floor, and ceiling, bloodred. Like the insides of an animal. I crawl in, expecting to feel its heartbeat, the rise and fall of its breath.

When a bag isn't thrown over my head, I ask Lydia, "So you go around to surgery centers and talk people out of bariatric surgery?"

"Oh, sister, I do *so* much more than that."

"Like what?"

"I fight Diet Culture in all its forms." She points out the window to a bus stop, where a meal replacement advertisement screams, *Shake your way to a better body!* A skinny model is stepping out of her old fat body. It falls to the ground like a deflated balloon. "For instance, take that ad. How does it make you feel?"

"Sad."

"Why?"

"Because I am the bad thing to be shed."

"See, that is exactly how Diet Culture wants you to feel. But a skinny body isn't better, and a fat body isn't worse. They're both just bodies. That ad shouldn't make you sad. It should make you angry."

I sigh and shrug. "Why bother?"

"Why bother?" she shrieks and grabs my shoulders, as if to straighten me out. Instinctively, I shrink away, but she holds tight. Levels her gaze at me. "Because anger is good. It motivates. Empowers. Revolutions are born from anger."

"Uh-huh. Okay." My eyes slide to the window. To the world drifting past.

"Ashley, look at me. I'm serious. You need to learn to fight back, metaphorically and physically. In fact, Tony's got a boxing club. You should check it out. Once you get comfortable throwing a punch, there's no stopping what your mind can unleash."

Me take up boxing? That's preposterous. Nevertheless, I answer, "Sure." She's not someone I want to argue with.

Tony's studying me in the rearview mirror. Self-consciously, I shift closer to the door. A moment later, we roll up next to my car.

Lydia pulls out a business card. Jots something on the back. "Here, take this. I wrote Tony's club info on it. Like I said earlier, I'm here to save you."

On the back is the address of Antonio's Boxing Club. The front of the card is shiny red with black lettering:

LYDIA'S FED UP!
Join the Revolution
Fight Diet Culture
Insta: @Lydia_Fed_Up
Lydia_Fed_Up@gmail.com
888 875 5764

While I appreciate Lydia's point of view, the only revolution I want is over my own body.

Chapter 7

GEMMA

The flight home to Chicago is smooth, but my thoughts are a mess. Threatening to bubble over like lava.

When I got back to the room last night, I woke Steve and freaked out about Bianca's murder. The pink waist trainer around her neck. Detective Stark's insinuation that I might have killed her. Steve assured me that he was only gone for thirty minutes. That my alibi was tight and everything would be okay.

Well, nothing feels okay.

The moment our front door closes, I drop my bag and announce, "I'm not competing in this year's Olympia."

Steve puts up his hands, like he's trying to stop a steam engine. "Hold on. I don't understand. Why?"

"Why do you think? Because Bianca was murdered!"

"What does Bianca's murder have to do with you competing in the Olympia?"

"She was strangled with her waist trainer. Everyone's saying it's some kind of message." Thanks to Anita, who posted to Instagram about Bianca's murder the second Detective Stark left her room, the news is all over social media.

"Whoa there, babe," Steve says, resting a hand on my arm. "Don't you think you're overreacting?"

I knock his hand off me. "Steve, Bianca is dead. She was in the same line of work as me, had the same sponsors as me, and was the three-time champ of the contest I'm scheduled to compete in. So in a word: No. I don't think I'm overreacting." I rip the hair tie off my ponytail. Shake out my hair and let it fly wild. "Any one of us could be next."

"Her death could have nothing to do with any of those things. It could have just been some random event."

I take a step closer, so he can feel my heat. "There's nothing random about someone strangling Bianca with her waist trainer."

Steve sighs and looks up, like he's searching for patience. His face brightens. "You know, this could work in your favor. This could finally be your time to shine."

"Tell me you're not suggesting Bianca's murder is an opportunity."

"How can you not see it? She's shut you out the last three years running. Now, this year's wide-open." He spreads his hands, like he's making me an offer.

I shudder.

Steve continues, "Besides, think of all the potential business opportunities you'll be giving up."

What would he know about business opportunities? Steve is a bartender. *And actor*, he would correct. He's had two auditions in the last year. No ambition whatsoever. "They won't matter if I'm dead!" I abandon the luggage in the living room and stomp off toward our bedroom.

I make it as far as the dining room, when a breeze tickles my cheek. Startled, I stop and look for its source. "The window is open. Jesus Christ, we've been gone for almost a week, live on the first floor, and you leave the window open." My eyes leap to Steve's enormous flat-screen television, but it's still here. So is his PlayStation.

"I didn't leave it open," he says as I bang the window shut.

I ignore him and stalk off to our room. Slam the door and wait. And wait and wait for him to come and apologize. To tell me that if I don't want to go to this year's Olympia, he'll support me.

My body throbs with anger. And not just at Steve. I'm angry at myself. For missing Bianca's call. For finding her voicemail too late. For not being there for her. She sounded so urgent. So scared. What did she want to tell me? It's been eating at me since I found out she was dead.

I pull up my last Instagram post, made from the plane. It's a picture of me and Bianca, taken earlier this week at the FitExpo. Both blond, both attractive, both hiding something. Below it, I've written, **Bianca, I will miss you so. Thank you for your friendship and support. #RIP.**

The first comment, like usual, is from @hedgefundguy1, my superfan who buys all my products. Even my elastic glute bands. He writes, **Stay safe! So terrible what happened to Bianca.**

So even a virtual stranger is more concerned about me than my husband. Go figure.

There are more comments below my post, then one from Craig. **What a tragedy. Thank you, Gemma, for all your hard work and support this week.** I hesitate, then hit the like button.

Craig direct messages me, "Thank you again for everything."

"Of course," I answer.

I sulk in the bedroom, killing time on my phone, waiting for Steve. Eventually, I arrive at the conclusion that he's not coming. That he's not going to apologize. That the luggage still needs to be unpacked and put away, the laundry done, and the refrigerator restocked. And that if I want any of these chores done, I'm going to have to do them myself. Which means leaving this room.

Accepting defeat, I exit and hear Steve talking to someone in the next room. He says, "It feels so much better."

I hover in the kitchen and eavesdrop. Catch another snippet, "So much faster."

A deeper voice, "Graphite shafts are the best, man."

It's Steve's annoying friend Todd. Steve and I haven't even been home for an hour and Todd's already over. He's becoming a fixture in our apartment. In our lives. His favorite Wheat Chex Snack Mix (made with partially hydrogenated soybean oil) is in our cupboard.

I stomp into the living room, eyes on the luggage.

"Hey, Gemma," Todd half-heartedly calls out.

"Hey, Todd." I barely glance at him.

Todd is a digital attorney—he'd be more than happy to tell you all about this exciting field—and self-righteous tool. But for whatever reason, he's Steve's best friend. They both have an incessant need to watch and play all sports imaginable. Baseball (longest season ever), football (college and pro), basketball (March Madness is intolerable), NASCAR (just, why?), and (God save me) golf. In a pinch, they will even watch eating contests (disgusting) and poker matches (ridiculous commentary). So if nothing else, Todd serves the purpose of someone for Steve to engage in this bizarre behavior with.

There's a commotion as Steve drags his golf clubs out of the hall closet. Hangers clang. A few fall to the floor. Winter coats thud about. It sounds like the floor gets scratched. Steve starts rummaging around for his golf shoes. They must be going golfing. After we just got home. But then, things like laundry and groceries aren't really priorities for Steve. Why should they be? He's got me to take care of that.

Chapter 8

ASHLEY

Beneath the glass, the guns are inky black, soaking up all the light.

"May I see that one, please?" I ask, pointing to a medium-sized gun in the corner of the case. The man behind the counter of Orlando Pawn & Gun, nametag: Tim, bends down to retrieve it. Tufts of white hair curl out of his ears like smoke.

Tim places the gun in my hand. "This here's a Smith & Wesson nine millimeter." He continues to talk but I don't listen. I focus on the gun. Cool and heavy, like a sinking stone.

Ever since Escalade man almost ran me over, it's like something inside me has snapped and floated away. Only darkness remains. Ugly and corrupt. It frightens me. Excites me. It causes me to do things like enter gun shops and hold weapons of destruction in my hands. Revel in their power.

I tell myself that I'm considering purchasing a gun for self-protection. After all, the whole world seems to hate me. To enjoy knocking me down.

But it's the fantasies that give me away. Holding the smooth black weight in my hands, I imagine shooting out the Escalade's tires. Its windows. The driver's teeth. Watching his head explode like a watermelon.

Then reality hits. While exploding heads are lovely to imagine, in real life, they'd be messy, their consequences final. Realizing that I don't have what it takes to pull the trigger, I give the gun back to Tim, my hands now empty and powerless.

I leave the pawn shop, disappointed in my inability to defend and stand up for myself. I continue my shuffle along the sidewalk, avoiding eye contact with passersby. They stream around me like they're in a hurry, like they have important places to be. I drift closer to the storefronts and try to stay out of their way.

Walking is supposed to help my wound heal and my body lose weight. Each day, I set off in a different direction, becoming more familiar with my neighborhood by foot than I ever did whizzing past it in my car.

A sidewalk sign catches my eye. "Antonio's Boxing Club. Learn to Fight. Take Back Your Power!"

The name is familiar. Isn't that the boxing club Lydia's driver runs?

I peer inside Antonio's plate-glass window, where a pair of tattooed fighters spar in a ring, feet dancing, sweat dripping. Around them, other fighters punch heavy bags hanging from the ceiling, still more skip rope. Some walk out the door carrying training bags. Others have boxing gloves hanging from their shoulders. All are men. All look a bit feral.

I'm about to turn away and continue my walk—this isn't really for me—when a wiry man with salt and pepper hair spies me through the glass and waves. He starts making his way to the door. Shit, it's Tony.

The door opens. "Ashley?"

"Hi, Tony."

"It's great to see you. I was afraid you weren't going to come."

"Actually, I was just walking by. I'm on my way to a dentist appointment," I lie.

"Well, as long as you're in the neighborhood, why don't you let me give you a quick tour. It'll take less than five minutes. I'm a pro." He winks.

His confidence is magnetic. Plus, he's standing there holding the door, and I don't want to be rude. So I cross the threshold and enter another world. One where the air is soupy and smells like gym socks.

Tony leads me around, pointing out equipment and giving me the lay of the land. Posters of fighters cover the walls. My eyes are drawn to one of a dishwater blond, her corn-rowed hair pulled back in a tight knot. She's in a ring throwing a punch, bleeding from her nose and eyebrow. There's a dogged determination in her eyes. Something inside me stirs. Like a seed germinating, reaching for the light.

Tony follows my gaze. "That's Ronda Rousey. First woman inducted in the UFC Hall of Fame."

I wonder what that's like. To throw a punch. To land it. To turn one's aggression outward, rather than swallow it down.

Tony's moved on, so I tear my eyes off Ronda and catch up. He introduces me to staff and fighters, and they're all warm and friendly. No one seems the least bit surprised that a fat woman is in their club.

When the tour is complete, Tony turns to me. "So what do you think?

"It's great. But I don't get it. You own a boxing club, and you're also Lydia's driver?"

Tony laughs. "Nah. I'm more of a rent-for-hire bodyguard / driver / whatever-Lydia-needs-me-to-be type of guy. I used to do more work for her years ago, but now I've sort of gone straight. I just help her out from time to time. What can I say? She pays well. She's an heir to some sort of wallpaper fortune. More money than she knows what to do with. So you gonna let me teach you to fight?"

"Did you teach Lydia to fight too?" I wish I was more like her. She's practically a mythical creature: a fat woman who's confident and not on a diet.

"I did. A long time ago. And I've taught quite a few of her recruits over the years."

"Recruits?"

Tony rubs his neck, glances away. "Forget I said that." He trains his eyes back on me. "Let's talk about you. You want to learn to fight?"

I look around the club again. Feel its pull but hesitate. "I don't know. I mean, look at me."

Tony scrutinizes my face. "I am looking. And I think you're a fighter. Saw it in your eyes the moment we picked you up."

He's so earnest that I can't help but smile. "We'll see."

"No, Ash. This isn't a 'we'll see' type of situation. It ain't the weather. This is something you have complete control over. Say, 'Yes, Tony, I'll do it.'"

I look at him and blink.

"Waiting," he says.

"Yes, Tony, I'll do it." I sound more sure than I feel.

Before I know it, Tony's fitted me with a pair of gloves and wraps. "I got a six p.m. Thursday. You free?" he asks.

Wow, this is all moving so fast. Nevertheless, out of my mouth pops, "Yes."

What am I getting myself into?

I try to pull out my wallet to pay, but Tony won't hear of it. Which means that now I can't back out. Because he has invested in me.

Chapter 9

GEMMA

Seven Weeks Out:

122.1 pounds | 125 g protein | 200 g carbs | 50 g fat

I snatch Steve's ugly amber bong, its fetid water-breeding bacteria, off the coffee table and toss it in the trash. It cracks. The sound gives me satisfaction. I'm on a cleaning bender. It's how I process my emotions.

Steve and I argued about me going to the Olympia again last night. Not only does he still think I should go—strangled former champion notwithstanding—but that it could "generate new revenue streams." I nearly spit out my Diet Coke at that one. He insists that I'm letting my imagination run wild. Oh, and hey, he can't join me in Orlando, so I'll have to go alone. Why can't he join me? Because, apparently, he has to work that week. I find it hard to believe that a bartender can't find someone to cover for him, and that Steve doesn't feel the slightest need to protect his wife while there is a killer on the loose.

But that would take responsibility and consideration. Characteristics that Steve, I failed to realize when we were dating, has

in limited supply. Instead, I chose to focus on how handsome
he was, with his broad shoulders and strong jaw. How fun he
was to hang out with. How great we looked as a couple. When
I started posting pictures of us doing couple things, like going
for walks at sunset, lolling about on blankets at picnics, and
laughing while picking apples at the local orchard—this last
one took a lot of cajoling and a blow job—both my likes and
followers noticeably went up. The post where I announced we
were engaged generated, according to Instagram analytics, the
most engagement with my account that year.

I was so busy living a life in pictures, that I failed to notice all
the things I left out of them. The mess that trails Steve wherever
he goes. His inability to plan or pay bills on time. His dwin-
dling interest in me, other than as a cash cow.

And now, here I am. Handling the finances. Making sure
the bedding gets washed and the garbage gets taken out. All
while trying to act sexy, look desirable, and be fun. Be sponta-
neous. It's fucking exhausting.

As if summoned by my irritation, Steve wanders into the
room carrying a box wrapped in plain brown paper. It's about
the size a man's shirt would fit in. He eyes the sparkling clean
room warily. "Hey, I was about to run to the store when I saw
this outside. Looks like it's for you," he says, handing it to me.
My name and address are spelled out in block letters with black
marker. There is no return address.

I slip my finger under the paper at one end. As the postal
wrapping pulls away, a white box with gold lettering, *La Perla*,
is revealed. All thoughts of the Olympia fall out of my head.
My heart plummets into my stomach.

"What the fuck, Gemma?" Steve says flatly.

I don't answer. Instead, I lift off the cover. Inside is a white
silk bra and panty set, decorated with ethereal ivory lace, nestled

amongst layers of diaphanous tissue. Without picking them up, I can tell the panties are thong. I set the box on the glass coffee table. I'm about to put the lid back on top, when Steve reaches out and grabs the panties with his big, thick hand.

"Gemma, what the fuck?" His voice is rising.

"I don't know." I reply, quiet and dry. I look away from the panties that are now dangling before me.

"You have no idea where these came from? Who sent them?"

"Maybe there's a card?" I squeak.

Steve picks up the box and dumps it out. There is no card anywhere inside. He lifts the discarded wrapping from the floor and inspects it, in case we missed the return address. We didn't.

He snatches my phone up off the coffee table and starts scrolling through it. Scoffs at a few of my posts. Checks my texts and email. Apparently finding nothing of interest, from shoulder height, he drops my phone on the glass table, where it clatters. I momentarily fear the screen will shatter, but it doesn't.

The corners of his mouth curl into a smirk. "You know, a Detective Cooper contacted me to confirm your alibi. I told him I was gone from twelve thirty to one. But now that I think about it, it could have been longer. In fact, I have *no* idea what you were doing that night. Fucking another guy? Murdering someone? I don't know what goes on in your world anymore."

With that, he turns and storms off. The slam of the front door reverberates through our home. Traces of sweat and testosterone linger in the air.

Is Steve saying he was gone longer than half an hour, or is he just threatening to say that?

And who could have sent me an anonymous package like this? My mind goes to @hedgefundguy1, the follower who comments on all my posts. But he doesn't have my address. At least, I hope he doesn't.

I pick the bra up and look at it more closely. It looks oddly familiar. With a punch to the gut, I realize why.

I close my eyes and pull the scene into focus: Bianca in my hotel room the evening before the Pittsburgh Pro, trying on a top she was thinking of ordering. Me remarking upon her gorgeous bra. The same white silk, the same ivory lace. So delicate against her caramel skin. Her blushing, saying it was a gift, and changing the subject.

I yank myself back to reality. This is ridiculous. It's highly unlikely that Bianca's and my lingerie sets are exactly the same. There must be a million companies out there that have something similar. And even if hers did happen to be this same La Perla set, so what? That doesn't mean anything. Maybe Steve is right? Maybe I am becoming paranoid?

Regardless, I don't have time to dwell on this now. I bury the box in the back of my closet, this incident in the back of my mind, like I have with so many others. I have a free phone consult with a former client of Bianca's at noon, which is in ten minutes.

Kylie (@queen_kylie), according to the online form she filled out, wants to lose five to ten pounds. She is five foot five and weighs 142 pounds. Five to ten pounds seems like a reasonable weight loss goal for a healthy twenty-three-year-old, but there's something about her that trips my senses. First, she contacted me within twenty-four hours of Bianca being murdered, wanting to sign up for a program, which I found a bit off-putting. Then, when my first available time slot was two weeks away, she direct messaged me, begging me to fit her in. She said it was urgent. Fortunately, I had a cancellation and was able to accommodate.

I study the photo she sent: not a lot of muscle tone, mediocre highlights, eyelash extensions. She's sticking out her tongue.

At 11:55 my phone rings. "Hi, this is Gemma."

"Oh, thank God. I need to sign up for one of your programs right away. I tried signing up online, but all I could click was this Free Phone Consult button. There's, like, something wrong with your website."

"Is this Kylie?"

"Yes!"

"Oh, sorry, you called a bit early. Anyway, my website's specifically designed that way, so you can learn more about me and I can learn more about you before either of us commits to anything."

"Look, I want to commit. Like right now. I need a coach. I already checked you out online and I'm good. What more do you want? I mean, I filled out your whole form. I would have left more information, but the 'Anything Else I Should Know' box has a limit of one thousand characters. If you want to know more, you shouldn't have a character limit. Seriously, what else do you want to know?"

"How about what you would have written on the form if there was no limit?"

She sighs dramatically. "Well, that I'm, like, super anxious to get started. Now that Bianca is gone, I don't know what to do. I feel, what's that word . . ." I'm thinking *unhinged*. "Like, when a balloon gets let go?"

"Untethered?"

"Yes, exactly that."

"Okay, well, let me tell you a bit about how I work. And at the end of our call, if you wish, you can sign up for one of my plans. I would suggest my six-week plan for three hundred dollars. It comes with a custom workout and meal plan, as well as weekly check-ins. It also includes a welcome packet with additional information, tips, and meal/snack options." I'm only suggesting the six-week plan because it's my shortest one. I'm not getting a good vibe here, but I'm cutting her a break because I figure that it must be stressful to have a coach you depend on die unexpectedly.

"Okay, done. Where do I sign up?"

I wonder if I'm going to regret this.

Chapter 10

ASHLEY

"I'm scared every time I go into the ring, but it's how you handle it. What you have to do is plant your feet, bite down on your mouthpiece, and say, 'Let's go.'" I study the words on the Mike Tyson poster. Isn't he the guy who bit someone's ear off? He was scared?

My first boxing lesson starts in five minutes. I wait on a bench, clad in a ratty T-shirt and sweats. Savage-looking men with tattoos walk by. *Bite down*, I tell myself.

"Ashley, you ready?" Tony asks.

"Yep, let's go." I plant my feet and get off the bench.

It's not long before I start to doubt myself. Tony has me warm up by jumping rope. Easier said than done; I'm not very coordinated. I wasn't even good at this in fourth grade. I stumble over the rope and try not to trip.

From there, we move on to shadow boxing. This involves me staring at my lumbering body and beet red face in a mirror while I dance around and throw ill-timed punches. I look ridiculous.

We do footwork. It's confusing.

I'm thinking about quitting when Evander Holyfield's words

leap off another poster: "A champion shows who he is by what he does when he's tested. When a person gets up and says, 'I can still do it,' he's a champion." I soldier on.

But then during bag work, something happens.

My arms are heavy and tired. My heart is thrumming. Tony's voice echoes from far away, "Jab, cross, hook." Over and over. I blindly do as he says, sweat streaming down my back, breath heaving through my lungs, not knowing where I get the strength.

And in that blur of punches, something moves through me. Something strong. I catch a glimpse and it's gone. Leaving me to wonder if I imagined it.

When we're finished, I sit on the bench panting. Sweat dripping off my forehead onto the mat, like I've been baptized.

"Well, what'd you think?" Tony asks.

"That was amazing," I whisper.

Chapter 11

GEMMA

There's something large and gray, the size of a body, curled up outside my front door. I stop in my tracks, still damp from the gym, and look around. The neighborhood is eerily quiet for this time of day. Not a soul in sight. A breeze snakes across the back of my neck, lifting escaped hairs from my ponytail.

I consider getting back in my car and driving away. Away from my apartment, from Steve, from my life. But responsibility tugs me forward.

The gray object comes into focus, and I realize that it's my old canvas duffel bag. The one I loaned Bianca after the Chicago Pro.

We had been working the REIGN booth together, and it was slow. That was when I told her about Fat Gemma, and that I was considering dropping out of this year's Olympia. Bianca didn't think I should. She said she'd be there for me. That we could share a room if I wanted. That she would be my accountability partner and help keep me from slipping up like I did last year. In fact, she thought that my winning the Olympia might actually help me conquer Fat Gemma. I said, "Why would you want to help me? Then you'd lose."

She smiled. "Who says I'll lose by you winning?"

And then awful Anita walked up and ruined the moment.

Anyway, Bianca mentioned that she bought so many items, she was afraid she wasn't going to be able to get them all home. Because the Chicago Pro is only thirty minutes from my apartment, it was easy enough for me to loan her my duffel bag. I wasn't even that fond of it. It's worn and battered, a relic from my college days. In fact, I forgot all about loaning it to her until now. What is it doing on my doorstep? And who would leave it here?

I bend down to pick it up, but hesitate. Like it might infect me.

Just as I'm reaching out my hand, my phone shrills and I jump. Kylie. The muscles in my neck tense. We're not even through our first week yet, and she's already called me over twenty times. A sampling: "Can I substitute hazelnuts for walnuts?" Yes, please see the substitutions list you received as part of your welcome packet. "Is it okay to substitute farm raised salmon for wild?" Sure. "Since I did sixty minutes of cardio instead of thirty, can I eat the extra thirty minutes' worth of calories that I burned if I want?" That's fine. "How many calories are burned during cowgirl-style sex?" Maybe one hundred.

And it's not just the barrage of questions, I'm starting to feel like her therapist. She's rung me from her work to vent about her manager. Called me from her car to gloat after sleeping with an acquaintance's boyfriend. (See: cowgirl-style sex, calories burned.)

As a result, yesterday I reinforced some boundaries. Told her to save all non-urgent questions, such as substitutions and calories burned, for our weekly check-ins. Because today's not our weekly check-in, this must be urgent.

I leave the duffel bag on my stoop and step inside. "Hi, Kylie."

"Gemma, you've got to help me." She's hyperventilating and sounds like she's pacing all about.

"What's wrong?"

"There's a half quart of cookie dough ice cream in the freezer." I hear what may be a freezer door slam in the background.

"Uh-huh?"

"It's not mine. It belongs to my boyfriend, Miles."

"Okay."

She whispers, "I'm afraid I'm going to eat it." I hear a door creak open.

"Well, first of all, I wouldn't put this in the 'urgent' category."

"It damn well is, and you know it! It's fucking terrifying." The door slams shut.

My palms start to sweat in sympathy. Fat Gemma stirs. I smack her down.

"Kylie, terrifying situations are things like discovering an intruder in your home or finding out that you have cancer. I mean, even if you eat the ice cream, so what? It's a recoverable situation." I feel like a fraud but plunge ahead. "Now, I'm going to go. I'll talk to you at our weekly check-in." I hang up as she's starting to say something.

Heart pounding, I return to Bianca's bag and drag it inside. I examine the paper tags hanging off it. It looks like Bianca recently went to China and the airline lost her bag. When they found it, because my name and address are prominently displayed, they must have sent it back to me.

With a creepy sensation, like Bianca's sending me a message from beyond the grave, I unzip the bag, holding my breath, as if I'm expecting to find severed body parts inside. Discovering mostly clothes (no La Perla lingerie), shoes, and makeup, I breathe a sigh of relief. There is a loose receipt from a Starbucks at the Grand Noble Hotel in Dongguan, China. I look at the receipt closely and note that it's dated six days before the Tampa FitExpo, the event she was killed at. What was she doing in China six days prior? Then I remember, this was the same week she went dark on Instagram.

Searching for answers, I open every makeup case. Check every pocket. Uncap every lipstick. (So many lipsticks.) The last lipstick is called Victorious. It's in a shiny silver tube and is the most amazing shade of red. Deep and rich, the color of blood on a sword. I hesitate, then glide it across my lips. It's thick and luxurious. Fortifying. My lips tingle.

I replace the cap and set it on my coffee table. I'm going to keep it to remember her by.

I'm about to give up my search, when I see a zippered pouch on the inside of the bag. It appears empty, but I thrust my hand inside and feel around. Way down in the bottom corner, I feel something hard and pull it out. It's a USB drive. It's likely mine, left over from my college days. I mean, what would Bianca be doing with this?

To be sure, I plug it into my laptop. There is only one file. I open it and see some sort of Excel spreadsheet. I'm certain that this isn't my USB—I've never seen this spreadsheet before—but something about the data looks oddly familiar.

The leftmost column is labeled "Item." Under it are rows with letters and dashes, like "WH – L – s" and "WH – L – m." There are more columns to the right, labeled things like "Production," "Scrap," "Cost," and "Net." These columns contain numbers in the thousands and tens of thousands.

I should probably let the detectives know about this duffel bag, but don't want to stir up any more of their suspicion. I had hoped to never have contact with them again. But I owe it to Bianca, so I call Detective Cooper. He seems the lesser of two evils.

"Hi, Gemma, I'm glad you called. We haven't been able to confirm the timeline for when Steve claims he was in On the Rocks. Apparently, he paid with cash and talked to no one other than the bartender, who doesn't remember seeing him."

How is that even possible? On the Rocks is the hotel hub where many of the FitExpo promotors and staff gather to socialize. Someone there would surely have recognized Steve as my husband. And even if they hadn't, Steve's still a memorable guy. He looks like a *GQ* model and talks shop with every bartender he meets.

What if Steve wasn't in the bar? What if he's lying about everything? I can't bring myself to go down this path, so I sigh and say, "Well, I don't know what to tell you. Steve says he was only gone from twelve thirty until one."

Then I change the subject and tell Cooper about Bianca's bag. I hope that offering this up might cancel out my shaky alibi.

Detective Cooper says, "Thank you." I hear him shuffling something around. "You know, I'm going to be in the Chicagoland area later this week. Why don't I stop by and pick it up?"

This seems incredibly coincidental. I must still be a suspect. I croak out, "Sure."

"Say, what was Bianca's relationship like with your coach, Rick?"

I'm relieved he's asking about other potential suspects, but I think Rick's a dead end. "It was good. She was his best Bikini competitor. Not only did she win a lot of competitions, she had a huge social media following which brought him a lot of recognition. He'd be the last person who would want her dead."

I hear Cooper scribbling. "One would think, but I understand that he's somewhat . . . erratic. In fact, he's got a charge of domestic assault against him from an incident with his ex-wife,

Megan Miller. Did you ever witness any violence from him, either against you, or another competitor?"

"I've never witnessed anything personally. Just heard rumors."

And man, did the rumors fly. During their divorce, Megan told anyone who would listen that Rick dragged her through their home by her hair. She was left with bald spots on her scalp from where her hair extensions were ripped out in the process. She also alleged he kept their refrigerator chained and padlocked and only let her eat what, when, and how much he deemed acceptable. If he was angry with her, she might go an entire day without sustenance. The final straw, however, was when he shook her by the shoulders and screamed at her so loudly that he damaged her left eardrum. She was one of the top IFBB Bikini competitors, but she became so fearful of him during their divorce that she left bodybuilding completely. She's now the head trainer of the hit reality show *Shrinking*.

Cooper asks, "And what about Bianca's relationship with Craig, the owner of REIGN?"

I take a deep breath. This one's trickier. "To be honest, it was a little tense. Bianca was supposed to work the REIGN booth at the FitExpo but pulled out to work her own booth and promote her new line of waist trainers. So not only was she not helping REIGN, Craig felt like she was sullying his brand by association." I quickly add, "But he would never kill her. He's all about doing no harm. To people, animals, even the environment. He won't even eat meat."

Detective Cooper answers, "Genghis Khan was a vegetarian. So were Adolf Hitler and Charles Manson."

Chapter 12

ASHLEY

The shiny red card glows like an ember from the depths of my purse.

I unearth it. The corners are sharp. Its words, *Join the Revolution*, beguiling. I run my finger over its thick edges. Scrape them across my palm.

I recall the elusive feeling of strength that came over me at Tony's. Like I was tapping into some secret force. Maybe it's the same force flowing through Lydia. Maybe it got turned on when Tony taught her to fight.

She said she was here to save me.

I navigate to Lydia's Instagram account, @Lydia_Fed_Up. She has almost fifty thousand followers. Her posts tend to center around fat shaming, fatphobia, and how the medical establishment has fucked over fat people. Some takeaways: She hates Jillian Michaels. Like, totally hates her. Thinks Adele's weight loss was a sellout, but doesn't hate her for it, just feels bad for her, because it must have been a result of low self-esteem, which caused poor Adele to succumb to Diet Culture. And that the people commenting about how great Adele looks now are implying that she didn't look great before, which she deems fat shaming.

Her latest post is a picture of her in a red bikini. Frolicking on the beach for the whole world to see. Below it, she's written:

> Yes, I'm fat. And guess what? I'm happy! I have bid farewell to trying to shrink my body to a size that is acceptable to society. To trying to fit it into a shape it does not want to be. Instead, I am embracing my body as it is. I am wresting my life back from Diet Culture. And I'm loving it.
> #fuckdietculture #fatacceptance #takeupspace #fatactivism

And then it hits me. Why Lydia's strong and confident. Why she can do the things she does and dress any way she pleases. It's because she's happy the way she *is*. Right now. She's not waiting for a future size to start living her life.

Maybe I could do the same. Maybe I could finally make peace with my poor body.

Suddenly, it's like I have been in a prison my entire life and now realize that I've been holding the key the whole time. Tentatively, I unlock the door. Step out into the light, blinking like an albino mole in the wide blue open.

I add the comment, I met you at A New You the other day. Thank you for the ride back to my car. Btw, I love this post. I've been on a diet for most of my life and failing miserably. Maybe it's time to fight back. I've started boxing lessons at Tony's.

A few minutes later, Lydia replies, That's great! Once you break the shackles of Diet Culture, your life will go from small and gray to wide-open and technicolored.

I press the Follow button, and she follows me back. Then

she sends me a direct message. "Hi, Ashley. Thanks for reaching out. I recall that you're a software engineer. I could actually use some help in that area. You see, I have started a movement with some like-minded warriors. We have some ideas. Some very novel ideas. After years of defensive play, we're going on the offensive. Change doesn't happen in comfort. It happens through pain. Bloodshed even. What do you say, are you in?"

She wants me to join an *actual* movement? Not just some Instagram group? Is that what Tony meant by training her recruits? While a movement sounds exciting, there's a bubbling current of unease snaking through my stomach. It's all that business about pain and bloodshed. Coupled with Renee's *She's clearly unstable.*

I tell myself that I'm being ridiculous. That Lydia's just dramatic. That maybe some drama is exactly what my boring life needs.

And I'm flattered that she wants me to join her group of "like-minded warriors." Could I be a warrior? I remember how I kept swinging at Tony's, long after my body said it couldn't.

I think about all my failed diets. All the years down the drain. The false promises. The being kicked around. For once, I'd like to be the one doing the kicking.

Before I can change my mind, I navigate back to my own page and change my handle from @always_ashley123 to @fat_and_fabulous, and reply: "I'm in!"

Chapter 13

GEMMA

Six Weeks Out:
122.2 pounds | 125 g protein | 200 g carbs | 50 g fat

Not everyone who is fat wants to lose weight. And not all fat people are unhealthy, just like not all thin people are healthy, reads the comment from @fat_and_fabulous. It's in response to my transformation post.

I navigate to @fat_and_fabulous's account and see this bio:

FAT and FABULOUS!
Fight Diet Culture ✊
Fat Activist, Revolutionary,
and All Around Badass!

There are no pictures of the owner, but it's clearly a "her" (an old knitting post precedes a recent spate of Fat Activist screeds). I click on the comments section of her last rant and see, "Comments on this post have been limited." In other words, I can't comment on her posts, but she can comment on mine. I'm sure it's easier to be an "All Around Badass!" when you don't have to face criticism.

I navigate back to my page and reply, I agree that not everyone who is fat wants to lose weight. Those people should ignore my fat-loss posts and take advantage of my exercise and nutrition tips. My account is for anyone who wants to be healthier.

@fat_and_fabulous fires back, Your account and your appearances on shows like Morning Cup of Jo are contributing to the culture of body shaming.

I respond, How?

By implying that thin is good and fat is bad.

Being significantly overweight IS bad for your HEALTH. It does not make YOU bad, I type. I hesitate before posting because of the all caps. Usually, I try to stay away from them, unless it's the word "AMAZING," which I have a weakness for. After a moment of deliberation, I decide *fuck it* and press Post.

———

For the rest of the afternoon, I turn over what @fat_and_fabulous wrote. The uncomfortableness it triggered in me. Is my account a form of body shaming? I don't think so. It's well established that being overweight is bad for one's health. Not that long ago, the smoking industry denied the health risks of its product. And look how that turned out.

Am I upset because @fat_and_fabulous doesn't like me? Not a chance. I'd have been out of this game years ago if I needed everyone to like me.

Nevertheless, our exchange niggles at me as I prepare for my weekly check-in with Kylie. I review my notes and am reminded of the weather wheel in my second-grade classroom. Each day, a different student would look out the window and set the dial to the day's weather. Stormy, sunny, windy, snowy, cloudy, or rainy. What will Kylie's mood be like today, I wonder.

At five p.m., bang on, my phone rings.

"Hi, Kylie."

"I tried to call you, like, three times," she informs me as the storm clouds roll in.

"Yes, I saw that. I was reviewing my notes so I could be fully prepared for our time together. How's everything going?" Inwardly, I cringe and await the onslaught.

"Awful. I weigh a hundred and forty-three pounds. That's more than when I started. Once you abandoned me, I ate all the ice cream. And then it really spiraled out of control. I've eaten pizza, a tube of cookie dough, and three donuts at work. I don't even like donuts that much, but they were there, so I ate them. Now I'm fat and everyone hates me. I hate myself. It's all your fault. You're the worst coach ever. I wish Bianca was here." Sobs strangle her voice.

"Oh, Kylie, I'm sorry. I miss her too."

"No, you don't. You're happy she's gone. You get her clients and have a better chance of winning the Olympia . . . Well, maybe not you." My molars grind. *Two years ago I took second!* "I mean, let's face it. You're no Bianca. I saw your earlier pictures. And you weren't just fat. You were, like, morbidly obese. Underneath your veneer, you're more fucked-up than I am."

I'm speechless. She didn't just call me obese—a word I can't stand, a word that makes my breath shallow—she called me morbidly obese, a term I pretend doesn't exist.

And she's right.

I remember the first time a doctor told me that my weight put me in the morbidly obese category. I simply nodded, like I understood what that meant. As soon as I got home, I googled it. "Morbid obesity" is defined as being more than one hundred pounds overweight, or having a BMI of forty or greater. Then I looked up the word "morbid," which means unhealthy or diseased. In other words, I was so fat that I was diseased. No wonder the whole world was revolted by me.

Even though I know I was those two words put together, I like to pretend that Fat Gemma was someone I used to know, like a high school acquaintance, or a former coworker from a long-forgotten job. Someone I've outgrown. But that's not true.

She is me.

Suddenly, it's clear why @fat_and_fabulous got under my skin: She is my former fat girl. Out of her cage.

The hand holding my phone starts to sweat and tremble.

Kylie continues, "So maybe you're not the right coach for me after all." She hangs up.

I feel like I'm on a stage set, somewhere in the middle of the second act. And Fat Gemma, from the long-forgotten first act? Turns out she's been lurking backstage the whole time. Waiting to return.

And she's really fucking hungry.

Steve's at work and won't be back for hours. I could order a whole pizza and eat it all. My mouth starts to water at the thought, my nostrils recalling the heavenly smell of oregano. Deep dish pizza was one of my favorite foods, back when I was fat. Bready, gooey, Chicago-style, with extra cheese and sauce. I would order a large and promise myself that I would only have one piece, maybe two. Knowing, even as I placed the order, that I was lying to myself. I'd order a six pack of ice-cold Coca-Cola to go with it, the crisp carbonation the perfect foil to the thick, heavy pizza.

I'm begging Fat Gemma not to order it. As soon as the order is placed, it's all over. I remember telling Kylie how binging on ice cream wasn't a terrifying situation and feel like a hypocrite.

It *is* terrifying. The loss of control. The raging hunger. Once you start to feed it, it becomes all-consuming. Swallowing whole pizzas, whole evenings, whole lives.

I look down at my phone and see that Fat Gemma has googled the phone number for the nearest Giordano's pizza. I don't even need to dial; I can just click on the link.

I beg, "Don't do it. Please don't do it."

Fat Gemma: "Don't be ridiculous. It's only pizza. We'll have one piece and save the rest for Steve."

"No, we won't. We never do."

While Fat Gemma is looking over the menu, distracted by all the options, I spin through my arsenal of weapons: call a friend (who?), make a healthy substitute (Fat Gemma will not be fooled), get out of the house (I remember suggesting this to Kylie when she was craving ice cream and how it failed). Nevertheless, I'll give this last one a try. Before Fat Gemma realizes it, I've grabbed my purse and fled.

I head to the bar where Steve is working. I need to see him. Remind myself that this is my new life. That it's real. That I have a real husband who loves me.

I careen into the lot, hastily park my car, apply lipstick, and exit. Heat and sunlight bounce off the asphalt. On shaky legs, I make my way inside.

It's like entering a cave. Dark and cool. My eyes blink as they adjust. It's a moderately sized establishment with two bars. From where I stand, I can see that Steve's not working the main bar, nor the smaller one in the back. Maybe he's coming in for a later shift? I rush to the main bar and ask the nearest of two bartenders if he knows when Steve will be in.

"Sorry, doll, Steve's not working tonight."

"Are you sure?"

"Yep, I'm covering his shift for him."

I stand stock-still, like he's slapped me. Then squeak a thank-you and stumble out the door. Somehow, I manage to find my car and crawl inside. It seems to steer itself home, like a giant capsule drifting through space.

I arrive at our apartment half expecting to find Steve draped on the couch, the Bears on TV. To find that this has all been a misunderstanding.

The apartment is empty.

I drop onto my white cloud sofa. Without thinking, I call Steve.

He picks up after two rings. "Hey, babe. Really busy right now. One of the bartenders called out. I'm manning the main bar myself."

My breath rattles in the mouthpiece.

"Babe? Are you okay?"

"Oh, sorry, butt dial." I hang up.

I sit alone, perfectly still in my pristine white living room. For once, I have nowhere that I need to be. Nothing that I need to do. I'm about to google *my husband is cheating on me*, but when I open the app, there is the link to Giordano's pizza.

I sit for a full minute looking at the link, then click the X and close the site. Fuck Fat Gemma. Pizza is not the answer. Pizza can't fix this. Nothing can.

My marriage is a farce. Sleek and pretty on the surface. Rotten and hollow at its core.

Just like me.

Fat Gemma's finally gone, for now, but the realization hits me: I can't keep doing this. She's getting stronger. Consuming me from the inside out. Somehow, I need to destroy her before she destroys me and everything I've worked for. But how?

My eyes roam the room and land on Bianca's lipstick, Victorious, on the coffee table.

Epiphany strikes. Of course. Fat Gemma's been feeding on my fear. Dropping out of the Olympia would be submitting to her. But you don't beat a bully by submitting. You beat her by fighting back.

Bianca was right: The way to vanquish Fat Gemma, once and for all, is to win the Olympia. The ultimate body war.

Chapter 14

ASHLEY

My new burner phone trills. I jolt to attention.

Into my old phone, I say, "Jacob, your new website will be great, but I have to go. An emergency has come up."

He starts to speak, but I end the call. I pick up the burner. "Hi, Lydia."

"Ashley, what's going on with Walter Jameson? Why isn't there an article about him up yet on Media Bigots?"

Lydia sent me an unflattering picture of editor-in-chief Walter, along with his personal information, at eight this morning. I'm supposed to create a story about him for her website, media_bigots.com. The site is devoted to turning the tables on fat shamers. The people behind the curtain. Photographers, editors-in-chief, and chief operating officers of magazines have all found themselves pictured here, the details of their appalling deeds on display for the world to see.

"I've been in meetings with clients. I was going to work on it this afternoon." It's not quite ten o'clock.

"This afternoon? That's ridiculous. If it's going to take you that long, I might as well do it myself." Lydia doesn't have the skills, or even a basic working knowledge of how to do this. We both know it.

I eye the time: 9:52 a.m. Now that I hung up on Jacob, maybe I can finish the Walter story before my ten o'clock? I was already working on it while I was on the phone with Jacob anyway. It's almost done.

I tell Lydia, "No, that won't be necessary. I'll do it now." I hang up and go to my second screen, where crimson letters scream "BIGOT!" over Walter's head, like a weight about to crush him. I hope they do. He looks out at the camera, at the world, as if caught by surprise in the middle of scratching his balls.

I increase the letters' chroma so they pop even more against the tasteful cream cedar siding of his home. Below the photo, I type, "This man, Walter F. Jameson, of 437 Old Orchard Road, Kettleworth, Florida, is the editor-in-chief of *Latest Celeb Scoop*. He plays racquetball at Neilsen Racquet. His daughters (!) attend Holy Faith. Meanwhile, his rag is responsible for articles such as 'Baby Weight Battles,' 'From Waif to Whale,' and 'She Can't Stop Eating,' that document celebrities struggling to maintain their rail-thin figures. It also includes shots of everyday fat women going about their lives—until one of Walt's henchmen leaps from a bush and photographs them. These women then appear as body fails in his magazine, with black rectangles over their eyes. How does it feel, Walt, to have your personal life on display for all the world to see?"

I vacillate over calling out where his daughters go to school. It's not their fault they have a shitty dad. Maybe I should leave that part out? But Lydia must want it in, or she wouldn't have included it. I glance at the time and see it's 10:02. A bead of sweat trickles down my forehead. I pull the trigger and post the article.

My client is already waiting by the time I dial into our

meeting. "Hi, Rob, give me a second to pull up your file." It takes me over a minute to locate it. In the background, I hear Rob drumming his fingers.

The burner rings. I ignore it.

I open Rob's file and share my screen. "So this is what I was thinking for the landing page. What do you think?"

A text comes through from Lydia, "There's a typo."

While Rob talks, on my other screen I scan Lydia's article. I find the typo and fix it.

"Just fixed it," I text her.

I think of my new phone as the bat signal. Whenever Lydia calls, I drop what I'm doing and respond. It's been a challenge, sure, but I'm rising to meet it.

Frankly, my work with her is just the opportunity I've been searching for. I first entered the realm of hacking a couple years ago as a hobby, learning the techniques and browsing the dark web. It wasn't long before I started picking up odd jobs and growing in reputation. But lately, I've been yearning for a chance to stretch myself. To see what I'm capable of. I've fantasized about doing some hacking for the greater good.

And here it is, offered up to me on a platter. It's almost too good to be true.

Since meeting Lydia, I've done all sorts of exciting things. I've installed ransomware on TeenTemptationsApparel.com. Lydia then gave them the option to pay in Bitcoins or make bigger sizes. They chose to pay up. I've also shut down a pro-anorexia site, hacked an Instagram Diet Culture account, and signed up for a free phone consult with Gemma under the alias Amy Giuseppe (more to come!).

Lydia keeps alluding to something bigger. I envision a multi-leveled organization with sweeping projects of global impact. But then, I've always been a dreamer. When I ask her for details, she tells me to be patient. That first I need to prove my allegiance through hard work and loyalty. I don't know how much more allegiance she needs. Already, I'm putting in three or more unpaid hours a day, on top of my respectable day job. I'm teetering dangerously close to the edge of not being able to keep up. It took me years to build my company. I can't afford to let it slide now.

Chapter 15

GEMMA

Five Weeks Out:
120.2 pounds, 130 g protein, 140 g carbs, 35 g fat

So. Fucking. Hungry.

Since committing to the Olympia, I've cut my calories by three hundred fifty-five a day and added in an hour on the elliptical in the evenings. This is on top of the fifty minutes of strength training and thirty minutes of cardio I was already doing in the mornings. I check the clock on my laptop, for the third time in the last twenty minutes, and see that I'm not due to eat for another hour and a half. Unbelievable. My stomach pinches in upon itself. I briefly close my eyes, rest my head on the desk.

"So what do you think?" asks my free phone consult. I jolt to attention and realize that I've missed the last bit of what she was saying. This is inexcusable during any phone check-in, but especially so with a potential new client who is testing out my services.

"I'm sorry, can you repeat that, please?" I ask.

"I said, what is your success rate? Like, what percentage of people who sign up for your programs actually achieve their goal?"

I hedge. "I've never run the numbers, but I'd say most of my clients do lose weight." Almost all lose a few pounds, at least initially. It's not my fault if some drop out or lack the discipline to hit their goals. At least, that's what I tell myself.

There is a long pause, during which she seems to process everything I didn't say, and I'm sure I've lost her. I look at her contact form: Amy Giuseppe, thirty-two years old, five feet and six inches tall, weight of 230 pounds. She doesn't have any known allergies or health risks, other than her weight. She didn't submit a Before picture with her application. And I can't find her on any social media. Weird.

She is someone I could help. In fact, she is exactly the type of client I live for.

I speak up. "Look, Amy, I can help you. I used to be overweight too. I lost over a hundred pounds, and I can show you how. Hold your hand. But you're the one who will have to do the work. You contacted me for a reason. I think you're ready to make a change. What do you say?"

To my surprise, she answers, "Okay, let's do it," and signs up for my six-week program.

———

I've just wrapped up with Amy, when Detective Cooper stops by to pick up Bianca's bag. I have it ready in the foyer and hand it over. I'm about to shut the door when he says, "Actually, I was hoping to talk to Steve if he's around."

Steve's around, and I suspect he knows this.

My stomach flutters as I remember Steve saying that he

has no idea what goes on in my world anymore. That for all he knows, I was fucking, or possibly murdering, someone the night Bianca died. I try to reassure myself that he was just upset about the mysterious lingerie, that he'd never throw me under the bus like that, but my stomach's not having it.

I never confronted him about his lie about working the other night. I just can't deal with it right now. If I'm going to win the Olympia, I need to stay focused. Keep my eyes on the prize.

With a shaky voice, I call over my shoulder, "Steve, there's a detective here to see you."

Steve appears beside me, hair rumpled, clad in shorts and a Weezer T-shirt. "What's up?"

Detective Dan says, "May I come in? It may be easier."

I step aside and walk him to the living room. "Have a seat," I say.

I'm about to join them, when Cooper says, "You know, Gemma, I was hoping to talk to Steve in private."

My heart catches. What doesn't he want me to hear? I look to Steve, but he's looking at the floor. "Oh. Sure, I'll go do some dishes." I wipe my trembling hands on my leggings and head to the kitchen, letting the kitchen / dining room door swing closed in my wake.

There is exactly one cereal bowl and a spoon, both Steve's, in the sink. It takes less than a minute to rinse them and put them in the dishwasher. Unsure what to do with myself, I hover near the door and strain to hear the conversation.

Detective Cooper says, "Look, we know you weren't at On the Rocks on Saturday, August fourteenth. We've got their security footage, and footage from the lobby, as well, and you don't show up anywhere."

Steve's deep tenor rumbles, but I can't make out what he's saying.

Cooper says, "There are serious penalties for lying in a situation like this."

Steve rumbles some more.

Cooper sounds incredulous. "Now, why would you think that?"

Steve's voice rises. I catch, ". . . didn't want her to . . ." and lose the rest.

"If there's anything else you forgot to tell me, now would be the time to remember it."

Steve says emphatically, "No, man. That's it. I'm telling the truth."

"Can anyone substantiate that?"

Steve says something.

Finally, Cooper says, "Well, I'll be going now. If you think of anything else, please contact me."

The front door shuts. I spin around and am pouring soap in the dishwasher when Steve enters the kitchen. His face is red and shiny, like he's run a mile, hard.

"How'd it go?" I ask.

"Fine, fine. Hey, I'm going to the store. Want anything?"

"Which store?"

Steve appears startled by the question. It takes him a moment to answer. "Um, the grocery store."

"No, that's okay. I went yesterday." We are in need of absolutely nothing.

Five minutes later he's gone, and I'm reeling. If he wasn't at On the Rocks, where was he the night Bianca was murdered? And what do I do now? What if he was gone for two, or even three, hours? There goes my alibi.

Chapter 16

ASHLEY

My email chimes. Bingo.

After I signed up for Gemma's program, she emailed me her welcome packet, filled with glossy Before and After pictures of her clients. The packet contained a meal plan, link to an exercise video library, weight/activity tracker, and a Frequently Asked Questions document. The meal plan was ridiculous. It included a suggested snack of seven almonds—seven! No wonder she didn't give me the percentage of her clients who met their goals. With a plan like this, I'm sure most failed.

Nevertheless, I emailed back thanking her and asking for her opinion on the article, "Are the Dangers of Obesity Overblown?" that I attached.

Well, she just replied. She doesn't agree with the article, commented that it's over a decade old, and wrote some other gibberish that I won't read. Because what do I care? What's important is that she opened the attachment. And now I'm in.

I take a look around her PC and can't believe the state of affairs. Her antivirus software is outdated. Her firewall weak, her browser security settings low. Does she not watch the news?

It's almost too easy. I take a look through her email inbox. It's rather banal stuff. The biggest shock is that most of her clients seem to love her. They blame themselves when they go "off track." On their behalf, I make a $200 donation from Gemma's bank account to the National Eating Disorders Association.

I'm about to log out, when up pops an email from rachel@ fitgurlmagazine.com, subject line: "Friday's Photo Shoot."

Hi Gemma,

We've decided to take this Friday's shoot outside for our Sweat It Out series! Therefore, instead of coming to our studios, please go to Sturges Park, at 463 Green Street.

We're also pushing the shoot up by an hour, from 9 a.m. to 8 a.m.

Soooo looking forward to seeing you Friday at 8 a.m. SHARP! It's going to be hot, Hot, HOT!

Stay fit,
Rachel Ballaster
Editor-in-Chief, *Fit Gurl*

Chapter 17

GEMMA

"Think: Inferno," Craig declares, with a sweep of his hand.

We're seated outside at Shanghai Terrace, the restaurant atop The Peninsula in downtown Chicago. Japanese maples, stone sculptures, large ferns, and views of the skyline surround us. Inferno is the last thing I'm thinking.

Craig is in town for business, some sort of meeting in the garment district, and wanted to see me to discuss REIGN's new line, Bombshells Only. The sports bras are low cut with spaghetti straps. The leggings' butt seams gathered. Sizes cap out at large—a rather small large, at that. Aptly enough, the line will be available in all the colors of exploding bombshells. Per Craig, "Explosions are sexy."

He pulls a stack of fabric samples out of a black Bottega Veneta messenger bag and begins to lay them on our table in a neat grid. There are five colors: Red Flame, Orange Glow, White Hot, Smokin' Smoke, Banging Black. Each is available in multiple fabric options, everything from lightweight and shiny to heavy and matte.

While he's busy ensuring all the swatches are evenly spaced

and their edges parallel, I look around. And spot Detective Cooper in the corner. The air drops out of my lungs.

"Did you see the detective?" I whisper.

"Of course. I see everything." Craig waves his hand dismissively, keeps his focus on adjusting the samples.

Is Cooper here for me or for Craig? For us both? I haven't heard from him since he left my home with Bianca's bag yesterday. With a shaky hand, I take a sip of water.

Once the fabric squares are perfect, Craig hands me one from the top right corner. "This is Red Flame in the Cloud fabric. Check out the four-way stretch."

I dutifully stretch the fabric in different directions.

Craig continues, "Every one of these fabrics is anti-microbial and moisture-wicking. They're all made with low-water dyes, which is so important for maintaining a small eco-footprint."

"So important," I echo.

One of REIGN's founding tenets is to be a good global contributor. Their headquarters are solar powered, with electric-car charging stations (Craig drives a Tesla) and a Zen garden. They have an open-door pet policy that does not discriminate—you can bring your dog, cat, or orangutan, doesn't matter. And at noon, everyone, from the lowest employee to Craig, rolls out their mat for a thirty-minute yoga session led by REIGN's own in-house yogi master.

I return the fabric swatch, which Craig places back in position. He continues to hand me fabrics, one at a time, and I *ooh* and *ahh*. But it's hard for me to focus. Out of the corner of my eye, I track Cooper. He doesn't appear to be watching us. Could he simply be here for lunch?

Finally, the waitress arrives with our food. Craig has her set it on the empty table next to us. "Gemma, there's one more fabric option I want to show you." He reaches back into his bag and pulls out a last stack of swatches in the same color palette. "Now this," Craig says, holding up a thick double-knit in White Hot, "is going to be a game changer. It's engineered to not only lift and sculpt, but to smooth, contour, and compress. It's super soft. Feel." He hands it to me.

It's heavy and opaque. Soft as cashmere. I rub it against my cheek. "Amazing."

Craig continues, "We're calling it Marvel. With fabrics like this, there's no need for those tacky waist trainers that are all the rage right now." He wrinkles his nose, like he smells something repulsive.

A cold current winds through my stomach. Suddenly, our food doesn't smell so good. The colors on the table start to blur.

"Gemma, what's wrong?"

"Nothing."

"Oh, I'm sorry. I didn't mean to criticize Bianca and her waist trainers."

I nod and stare at the bleeding colors.

"Well, I've got just the thing to cheer you up." Craig reaches into his bag and pulls out a Bombshells Only Banging Black workout set in the new Marvel fabric. "You get to premiere it at your *Fit Gurl* photo shoot this Friday! I've talked to Rachel and cleared it."

He leans in close. "Between you and me, Anita won't be happy. She indicated that she wants to be the one to debut the Bombshells Only line, but Rachel and I agreed you were better suited. Don't worry, Anita will come around."

I don't feel cheered up but attempt a smile. It wobbles. I glance away.

"Gemma, look at me. You know how much you mean to our REIGN family. You're our number one girl."

I look up into Craig's sincere blue eyes. "Thank you." It comes out dry, and I hope it doesn't sound as hollow as it feels. After all, their last number one girl is dead.

Chapter 18

ASHLEY

Orange County Corrections flashes across my caller ID, accompanied by a ring. It's my regular phone. The one I get calls from my mom and clients on.

I blink my eyes a couple times, in case there's something wrong with them, but it happens again. My eyes shift to my burner phone. It remains dark and silent.

Cautiously, I pick up. An automated voice states, "This is a call from . . ."

Lydia's voice, "Lydia Wright . . ."

The automated voice continues, "at Orange County Corrections. Will you accept the charges? Press one for yes. Two to decline."

I press one. "Lydia, what's going on?"

"I was arrested. That's what."

"For what?"

"They think I spray-painted '*All* bodies are beach bodies!' over a Get a Beach Body advertisement on the side of a bus."

I am about to ask, *Did you?* when the automatic voice

returns, "This call is being recorded," and think better of it. Instead, I ask, "How can I help?"

"I need you to bail me out of jail."

No *please*. No *would you be able to?* Just expectation. Never mind that it's a weekday at two p.m., and that I'm already behind on a few clients' projects. Yet, despite all that, I answer, "Okay, where are you?"

"Ashley, where do you think? Orange County Corrections!"

"Oh, right, right. I'll leave right now. What do I need to bring?"

"One thousand dollars cash and your ID."

———

Thirty minutes later, I find myself in my Toyota on the way to the jail, ten crisp hundreds in a bank envelope in my purse.

Lydia called *me*. I've seen the cop shows. I know she got one call. And she chose me. This signals a certain level of trust, demonstrates that I've finally worked my way into her inner circle.

Maybe soon I'll get to meet the rest of her team. Be part of the resistance. Then all these disruptions, all my efforts will have been worth it.

Once I get to the jail and pay the bail, I wait in an uncomfortable plastic chair for Lydia's release. I surreptitiously snap a few photos for posterity. Eventually, my excitement dies down—it takes a surprising amount of time to bail someone out of jail— and I scroll through my Insta feed and land on a post by Gemma, where she offers her services as an "accountability partner."

And just like that, my good mood evaporates. Why do I even follow Gemma? In fact, my pointer finger has hovered several times over the Unfollow button, but I never see it through. I suppose it's similar to how one's eyes are drawn to a car crash.

Her post was only put up a couple hours ago and already it

has 512 likes. How can there be so many brainwashed people out there? There are also 42 comments. I read through them and not one asks the obvious question, so I do:

> **@fat_and_fabulous:** Why would anyone want to be accountable to someone else for their body? To be "accountable" is to have an obligation to report on, explain, or justify. No one should have to answer for their body.

> **@hedgefundguy1:** @fat_and_fabulous, read the fucking post. There were three reasons given. Hint: See the bullet points.

> **@queen_kylie:** @hedgefundguy1, What @fat_and_fabulous is pointing out, is called Another Point of View. You should try it sometime.

I like @queen_kylie's comment and navigate to her page. She's an average-looking girl who wears too much makeup and takes too many selfies. She has photos of herself sticking out her tongue at Starbucks, making duck-lips at restaurants, and checking out her abs in bathroom mirrors. The captions are mostly forgettable things like, **Monday morning!** and **Date night!** However, every now and then, there will be a rant, such as a recent one directed at the Costco in Tampa. In it, she discusses, with limited punctuation, the incompetence of the staff, the harsh store lighting, the poor store layout, and their shitty return policy. The rant hits the word limit, so she continues it in the comments section. I read through the entire ramble, and near as I can tell, her dissatisfaction originated when she was unable to return a tablet with a cracked screen four months after she bought it. She is certain the tablet was defective to have broken so easily.

The latent rage lurking below her screeds is compelling. She seems rudderless and alone. Like she could use some direction. A friend. I add a comment to Kylie's tablet post, like several others, and follow her. Right away, she follows me back.

I create my own post and tag Gemma:

I keep seeing all these accountability posts. I don't understand. The last thing women need is more accountability. Society already expects us to answer for our bodies in so many ways:
Why aren't you pregnant?
Why can't you have kids?
Why don't you want sex?
Why do you want sex?
Why don't you masturbate?
Why do you masturbate?
Why can't you orgasm?
Why don't you want a cock in your ass?
Why are you eating that?
Why aren't you eating that?
Why are you so hungry?
Why aren't you smaller?
Why don't you look like a model?
Why would you cut your hair?
Why don't you cover your gray?
Why don't you shave your legs?
Why don't you wax your pussy?
Why are you dressed like that?
Why aren't you dressed like that?
WHY DON'T YOU ALL JUST FUCK OFF.
#fuckaccountability #riotsnotdiets #fuckdietculture
#fatliberation #fatactivism

Right away, @queen_kylie comments, You complete me.

"So you ready?" Lydia asks, startling me.

"Yep." I jump up like a servant, ready to be of use.

"Okay, let's go." She leads me out the door, despite not knowing where I parked.

Once we get to my car, I toss my training bag, boxing gloves peeking out, from the passenger seat into the back.

Lydia climbs in. "How's it going with Tony? I try to send all my warriors his way."

I start the ignition. "It's going great! I can actually feel myself getting stronger. Not just physically, but mentally. Punching something is so satisfying."

"Excellent." She buckles her seatbelt and we hit the road.

"And he's such a great coach. So patient. He really goes the extra mile, you know? He's been staying late to work with me one-on-one. Giving me assignments to practice at home. When my car was in the shop earlier this week and I was going to cancel, he swung by my place and picked me up."

Lydia's quiet. I glance her way, and she's staring out the windshield. Her face immobile. Finally, she says, "That seems a little excessive for a coach, don't you think?"

My face gets hot. "Well, maybe it sounds that way. But not if you know him. That's just the way he is."

Lydia snaps, "For fuck's sake, Ashley, I *know* him! Jesus, I'm the one who introduced you to him."

"Oh, right. Sorry. I didn't mean it like that."

She takes a deep breath. Then another. "Anyway, I wouldn't get too close to him. He's got a . . . colorful past."

I laugh. "Says the woman I just bailed out of jail. So did you really spray-paint the side of a bus?"

Lydia smirks. "Of course."

"In broad daylight?"

Lydia waves her hand dismissively, "Oh, honey, please. Don't look so surprised. That was child's play."

I want to ask what the grown-up games are, but I'm not sure that I want to know.

Once we're on the freeway, I say, "I've been wondering, what were you doing at A New You that day we met? Like, I get it, you hate Diet Culture, but what's so special about that place? There must be a zillion other medical centers like that to save people from."

Lydia turns her head and looks out the window. My Toyota skims across miles of road. The air-conditioning hisses. Just when I think she's not going to answer, that I've overstepped my bounds, she says, "They killed my mother."

My brain goes empty. I didn't see this coming.

Lydia takes a shaky breath and continues. "She didn't die during the surgery itself, but from complications after. The week of my high school graduation."

It's quiet. Only the tires hum. Eventually, I say, "I'm so sorry." Because, really, what else is there?

Chapter 19

GEMMA

Four Weeks Out:
119.3 pounds, 130 g protein, 140 g carbs, 35 g fat

Shrill words leap out of my car speakers, "Where are you? I've got makeup, photography, and an assistant, but no Fit Gurl!" It's Friday morning, and I'm in my car, ten minutes from *Fit Gurl* studios. My shoot isn't scheduled to start for another thirty.

"Rachel?"

"Who else?"

"I'm sorry, you caught me off guard. I'm on Grand. I'm only ten minutes away."

"What are you doing on Grand? If you're on Grand, you're not ten minutes away."

Trying to get my bearings, "Your studio is on Grand?"

A scream of frustration. Dual ice picks stab my ear drums. I adjust the volume and refocus on the road. "You're all such idiots. Every. Single. One. Of. You. Do you not read your email? Did you not see that the shoot got moved up to eight and that the location is now at Sturges Park?"

There's a sinking in my stomach, like a torpedoed submarine falling to the bottom of the ocean. I can't check my email because I'm driving, but I take her word for it. I've been so hungry for so long, my brain is literally running on fumes. This morning, I couldn't even remember if I brushed my teeth.

I whip a U-turn and head for Sturges Park, which is at least twenty minutes away. At every stoplight, I scroll through my email, trying to figure out how I missed Rachel's update. I don't find it anywhere. I try searching by her name, by Fit Gurl, by Sturges. Nothing.

When I finally get to the shoot, everyone is sitting around looking bored and waiting for me. Except for Rachel, who is pacing back and forth. I rush up to her. "I'm so sorry, but I never got your email. Are you sure you sent it to me?"

She turns her phone to face me. Taps the screen with a lime-green manicured finger. "Right here. Sent 8:02, Wednesday morning."

I'm speechless. Indeed, there is her email.

She continues with exaggerated patience. "Now, if it's not too much to ask, can you please get to work? I'm paying three people by the hour."

I'm rushed through makeup and hair. Not introduced to the assistant. The test shots are abbreviated.

Once the actual shoot begins, the photographer tries to lighten the mood by joking with me, but Rachel glowers at him and points out everything I do wrong: I'm angled the wrong way, sweating like a farm hand (I'm to *glisten*), and I don't look like I'm having fun. ("For fuck's sake, Gemma, have some fun!")

The sun continues its ascent in the cloudless sky. My Banging Black outfit absorbs its heat, the thick Marvel fabric doesn't let it escape, doesn't let me breathe. The humidity is relentless. Makeup runs down my face as I climb ladders and swing from monkey bars. My hair sticks to my face and back. At one point, my slick hands slip from the monkey bars and I fall to the sand.

"Makeup!" Rachel screams. A tattooed makeup lady clad in pilled black leggings rushes up. Rachel flings her lime nails at me but speaks to the lady. "Jesus Christ, can you please do something about this?" The makeup lady starts to pad my face with an absorbent sponge. Rachel taps her foot, checks her phone, and announces, "I don't have time for this. You guys finish," and storms off. She hops in a white BMW and squeals away.

After she's gone, the rest of my shoot goes okay, but I don't know that it will ever see print. And I'm certain *Fit Gurl* will never ask me to work with them again.

As I'm leaving, head hanging low, the photographer calls out, "Hey, don't feel bad. It's the Sweat It Out series!"

I'm driving home when Craig calls. I put him on speaker. "What's this I hear about you messing up Rachel's photo shoot?"

Word travels fast in this industry. "She rescheduled our time and location, but somehow I never got the email."

"Gemma, this is unacceptable. We need our athletes to be known for their professionalism, to be in all the best magazines, to be a source of inspiration for young women everywhere." They need us to sell lots and lots of leggings.

"I know. I'm sorry."

"I'm going to call Rachel back and try to patch things up. Tell her you'd be happy to do another shoot of her liking, for free, whenever she wants it. Okay?"

It's not a question. "Okay."

His voice softens. "Don't worry, we'll work it out. You're still our top girl."

Before I can thank him, Craig hangs up.

I park outside my apartment and scroll through my email

again, slowly, line by line, wondering how I missed Rachel's update. It's not there. Finally, I check my trash folder. And there it is. The only email in my trash folder. Despite being a sweaty mess, I get chills. Could I have deleted Rachel's email by accident? Doubtful. My thoughts go to the laptop on my desk. How I never shut it down. Never sign out of my email. How Steve is often there alone with it.

I enter our home, my pores jammed with layers of makeup. Hair flattened to my head. Steve looks up from his video game. "Yikes, what happened to you?"

"I just had a shitty photo shoot, that's what. Turns out the email alerting me to a change in time and location was somehow mysteriously deleted from my inbox." I stab him with my eyes.

"What? You don't think I had anything to do with it?" Steve rocks back, like I physically stabbed him.

I sigh, realizing that he would send me out into the desert for a photo shoot, even with a fever of one hundred and two, for the right price.

I hear a truck rumble by outside and realize it's louder than I would expect. I walk toward the sound and see the dining room window open. Again. "Steve, for the love of God, why can't you ever shut and lock this fucking window!" I stomp over and slam it so hard, a hairline crack appears in the vintage glass. "Fuck!"

"Gemma, relax. I didn't open it."

"Are you serious? Or are you lying to me? If you're lying, you better tell me now. Because if you didn't open it, who did?" I lean over the dining table, brace my palms on the shiny wood, and start to hyperventilate.

There's a knock on the front door, and without waiting for a reply, Todd walks in. He looks from me, sweaty and hyperventilating, to Steve, frozen on the couch, his eyes bugging out, and says, "What's going on?"

"Todd, did you leave this window open?" I frantically gesture toward it.

"No. Is that okay? Was I supposed to?"

"No! Don't ever open this window again. Neither of you. Do you understand?"

They both nod.

There's a roll of duct tape on the hutch. Because of course there is. I snatch it up and tape over the crack. Then I tape a giant X across the window. Sill to dash. Rub the tape down firmly.

Steve says, "Babe, you need to relax."

"I do NOT need to relax. Someone is coming in our house. Deleting my emails. Leaving this fucking window open. It could be the same person who murdered Bianca, and you don't seem to give a shit." I slam the tape down. "And put this fucking duct tape away!"

Chapter 20

ASHLEY

"Come on, Ashley. One, two, three. Jab, cross, hook," Tony says.

Despite Lydia's warning about not getting too close to Tony, for the third time this week, I'm at his gym.

I don't care about Tony's colorful past, whatever that may be. I need this place. It's become an oasis, of sorts. The other boxers seem to accept me. No one snickers, no one sneers. It's like we're all here to work out our own issues.

And it's not only this club that I need. It's Tony. He's helping me get stronger. I can feel it.

But I worry about Lydia finding out how much time I'm spending here. About disappointing her. My life has been so much more exciting since she entered it. So much more meaningful.

Tony and I have finished pad work, and he's putting the pads back on the shelf. I ask, "So what's up with you and Lydia? How did you guys meet?"

Tony pauses with a pad midair and thoughtfully examines it. "You know, it's been so long, I don't remember." He uses his shirt to rub a spot off.

"She told me that you have a colorful past."

Tony throws his head back and laughs, like I've told him a whopper. Then tosses the remaining pad on the shelf. "Well, if that isn't the pot calling the kettle black."

"I know it's not any of my business, but did you guys used to date or something? Or are you dating now?" I feel my checks redden.

"We dated a long, long time ago. What can I say? It didn't work out. We're better off as friends."

I want to ask more but don't want to pry any more than I have. He's confirmed what I suspected. Lydia doesn't want me hanging around him because she used to date him. Maybe she even still has feelings for him.

Tony turns to me. Gets serious. "You know, Ash, be careful with Lydia. I know she's dazzling. A modern-day siren, and all. But listen to her song too long, and you might wind up crashing against the rocks."

"Okay." I say it to keep the peace. I'm a big girl and can make my own decisions.

We ditch the subject and move on to heavy bag. I punch a black leather sack, hanging from the ceiling. There are streams of sweat running down my back. My legs feel like Jell-O, but my mind is laser focused. Jab, cross, hook. Jab, cross, hook. While one hand delivers, my other stays up, protecting my face. Jab, cross, hook.

"More power. More speed. Excellent. On the hook, pivot in the direction of the motion. There you go. Use those hips," Tony says.

I drive my hips into the hook. Jab, cross, hook. I'm panting but I keep going. Jab, cross, hook.

"Excellent, Ashley. Excellent. Okay, last set."

The hanging bag is the world at large. All its taunts. All its scorn. I strike. I pummel. I go ballistic, and the faceless world starts to converge. Condense down and come into focus. A single face emerges: Gemma. Smiling out at me from today's post, titled, "Don't Give Up."

> Have you given up on yourself? Decided that you're simply meant to be overweight? That your body likes it this way? Guess what? It doesn't. When you're overweight, your body is inflamed. It's under siege from the damage you're causing it. That extra fat makes you more likely to have a heart attack, experience high blood pressure, develop diabetes, and get cancer.
>
> It doesn't have to be this way. Fight for yourself! Fight for your health! I can help you. I've been right where you are. Look at me now. Let me show you the way out. #transformationtuesday #youreworthit #gethealthy

It's such a slick, slimy proposal, with its wholesome promise of "health" packaged under a veneer of bubblegum pink lipstick and spray tan. It's not "giving up on yourself" to reject a societal ideal. To reject making your needs small. Shrinking. Plenty of thin people develop all of the ailments Gemma fearmongers about. And plenty of fat people don't. I'm way outside of society's ideal, yet here I am in all my fatness, sweating up a storm and embracing my body. I imagine pummeling that smug-ass smile off her face.

Jab to the face. Cross to the jaw. Hook to the ribs. Jab, cross, hook.

"All right, Ashley. That's a wrap." I hear Tony, but he's far away. Jab, cross, hook. "Ashley, come on, enough already."

Jab, cross, hook. Jab, cross, hook. I don't want to stop. I can't stop. Jab, cross, hook.

"Ashley!" Tony barks.

I stop. Tony never raises his voice. My breath comes in big, gasping waves, rolling through my body. I double over and brace my gloved hands against my thighs. Sweat, and maybe tears, drip off my face and splat on the mat. Tony rubs my back. "Hey, you okay?" His voice is deep and resonant. Masculine. Yet, there is a gentleness to it.

My throat closes up. "Yeah, I need a minute," I choke.

After a moment, he says, "Someone giving you hell? You want, I'll go take care of him for you." Tony appears to be serious. Like, after he closes for the evening, he'll just go fuck someone up before going home and putting a frozen pizza in the oven. It's so like Tony to assume it's a guy doing this to me. That this is something that can be taken care of in a few minutes with brute strength and sharp words.

The fact that Tony would "take care of" someone on my behalf makes my vault of a heart crack open a tiny bit. Built-up emotions start to escape, like ghosts from the ark in *Raiders of the Lost Ark*. My shoulders shake and I swallow hard, try to drive them back down. My voice is hoarse. "No, Tony. It's no one person in particular. It's the whole world."

"Well, it ain't the *whole* world, because you got me in your corner."

I look at the swinging bag, now just a hunk of leather.

Tony continues, "Look, Ashley, you're a great girl and a natural fighter. You're going to be okay. Plenty of rounds left in the fight." He winks at me and gives my shoulder a friendly punch.

Chapter 21

GEMMA

Three Weeks Out:

118.1 pounds | 130 g protein | 140 g carbs | 35 g fat

I sense it the minute I walk into my closet. Something's off. The air smells musky. My sweaters are slightly askew. My underwear drawer is open an eighth of an inch. Steve's and my framed wedding photo is face down on the shelf. Someone's been in here, invaded the most personal space in home. The only room completely mine.

Yet, when I check my jewelry box and comb through the room in greater detail, nothing appears to be missing. Could I have knocked our photo over by accident? Could I be imagining that someone was here?

I reset the frame and walk to the dining room to see if the window is shut. It is. I confirm that it's locked. That the duct-taped X is still secure. The stress must be getting to me.

Out of habit, I check my Instagram account, but my eyes have trouble making sense of what I'm seeing. A grid of photos swims before me. After a few seconds, my eyes adjust and focus

on the bio. Indeed, it says GymmaGemma at the top. This is
my account. But below the bio, there is a photo tile that I don't
recognize. It has a white background. Against this, big, blocky
black letters announce, "Diet Culture Slut." Below the tile, the
caption reads:

> If you follow this account, know that you are being
> brainwashed by Diet Culture. This account, and all
> accounts like it, are designed to make you feel like there
> is something wrong with you. Then these charlatans
> will sell you their snake oil to "cure" you. Guess what?
> You're perfect the way you are! Free yourself from the
> shackles of Diet Culture and unfollow this account.
> Come to the light side.
> #fatphoic #fatactivism #fatacceptance #freeyourself
> #riotsnotdiets

Beneath it, @hedgefundguy11 has the first comment, Whoever wrote this is a COWARD! And a fat, ugly bitch.

Light encroaches at the edge of my vision. Black spots
dance before me. I realize that I'm not breathing. I've forgot-
ten how. I force a shallow inhale. Squeeze it through a crack in
my stopped-up throat.

Then all at once, the dam breaks, and my breath comes
crashing in, fast and furious. I lean over and plant my hands
on the table. My breath washes over me. Through me. I sur-
render to it until it finally slows, and I sink into a chair. Rest
my head in my hands.

I cannot afford this. This account took me years to build.
Thousands of hours have been invested. With shaking fingers, I
attempt to google, *what to do if your Instagram account is hacked*,
but my sweaty fingers slide all over my phone. Just when I think

it can't get worse, a client's text buzzes, "Hey, I think your email's been hacked." Shit, I never got around to updating my email to use multi-factor authentication.

I go to my inbox and every subject line reads *Gemma is a Liar*. I scroll down and see row after row of the same. Meanwhile, more texts buzz through, all alerting me to the hack.

A shrill ring. I recognize Coach Rick's number and ignore it. He calls two more times before finally leaving a voicemail. "Gemma, what the hell's going on? I can't have girls on my team with shit like this on their Instagram accounts! Clean it up. Stat."

As I'm listening to Rick's message, Craig calls. He leaves a carefully enunciated voicemail, "Gemma, it's Craig. We need to talk. This is bad for business. When we pay you to post our ads, we expect you to take proper cybersecurity measures. This is simply unacceptable. Call me immediately."

I can't. It's all I can do to breathe. I set my phone aside, where it continues to buzz like an angry hornet. With every reverberation, my anxiety rachets up, until it gets so high that it explodes like fireworks and the remnants drift back to earth.

Could this be it? Could it all be over? No more Instagram, no more REIGN sponsorship, no more Olympia. No more influencer income. Would Steve leave me? In a way, it's strangely appealing. I could eat whatever I want. Wear sweatpants all day. Steve would surely dump me then. Like I said: strangely appealing.

A shroud of darkness falls across the room and the temperature drops. There is a greenish tinge to the air. A taste of electricity. Everything gets eerily still.

Thunder rumbles in the distance and rain starts to splat the windows.

The *Jaws* ringtone that I recently assigned to Kylie sounds. Incessant. Demanding. Like the gnashing of teeth.

A large figure outside. A banging fist. I scream.

Todd calls out, "You okay in there?"

Annoyance squashes fear, which says something about how sick of this guy I am. He is way too enmeshed in my life. "Yep, thanks. What do you want?"

"Is Steve around?" Todd's shadow looms outside the door.

"No."

"Okay. Can you tell him I stopped by?"

Jesus. Text the guy, for fuck's sake. "Yep."

Jaws continues to play. I answer my phone simply to shut it up.

"You know, Kylie, this isn't a good time. My email and Instagram account both got hacked."

"Yeah, I saw that. But this is important. I'm no longer hungry! Food is immaterial. So I modified our plan and cut out all the carbs. I kept your exercises but added in an hour run in the afternoons. I feel phenomenal. Like I'm made of light and air. And it's over with that asshole Miles and I'm moving in with Jim tomorrow and he dumped Shanna, who I never really liked anyway because she's always such a whiny, skanky bitch, and her ass is the size of a Mack truck, and I don't know what he ever saw in her in the first place, he was so unhappy with her, and he's crazy about me and I don't know why I was even wasting my time with Miles, who was so unsupportive of me and everything I was going through, and it turns out it was really ADHD and all I really needed was medication and now I'm on Adderall, and I can see my abs, and I'm killing it at work and—"

"I need to go," I say, and hang up.

Chapter 22

ASHLEY

Red envelopes me. I'm tucked in the womb of Lydia's Continental, its purring engine lulling my nerves. My driver today is a Rubenesque redhead with a tattoo of crossed pistols above her ample bosom. She doesn't seem interested in talking.

It's hard to believe that ten minutes ago I was at my desk getting ready for a meeting. Then the bat phone rang.

"It's wheels-up at three p.m.," Lydia said.

I was like, "Wait. That's half an hour from now. And what are you talking about?"

"You're flying to Chicago. There's a car waiting for you outside."

"Why am I flying to Chicago?"

"Details will be delivered once you're in the air."

"I'll never make it through security in time."

"There is no security. You're flying private." Then Lydia hung up.

So I guess it was settled. I canceled my meeting, apologizing profusely, and here I am.

We roll through the city streets. Past the Skinny Soda model painted on the side of a building, her legs two-stories high. Past the bus stops with their life-size advertisements featuring hungry adolescent models draped in expensive designer bags and clothes.

Twenty minutes later we pull right up to a small jet. I'm whisked on board, and at three o'clock, indeed we are wheels-up.

What a difference from flying commercial, which I haven't done since a flight attendant couldn't locate a seatbelt extender for me. This resulted in a plane full of people being delayed twenty minutes, along with a chorus of grumbling and hostile looks. Flying private, there's ample seat room, leg room, and privacy. In fact, I'm the only passenger.

A flight attendant, pretty as a china doll, brings me a crystal dish of pomegranate seeds and a sparkling water. I notice her ring. A phoenix with a black onyx belly, glittering rubies for eyes, and more rubies on either side.

"Where did you get that ring? It's amazing."

"My godmother," she says, and winks at me.

"Lucky you."

Less than three hours later, we land in Chicago. The attendant hands me a set of keys for a gray Honda Accord that is waiting for me.

Lydia has assigned me a mission: perform surveillance on *Fit Gurl* editor-in-chief Rachel Ballaster. I don't know what Rachel has done to wind up on Lydia's radar, I just know I need to point and shoot. If I do enough of these small missions, and do them well, Lydia has promised to introduce me to her team. If a small mission includes flying private across state lines, what does a big mission include? Lydia says I'll have to wait to find out.

I drive the Accord through wide-open suburban streets. Past three-car garages and professionally landscaped lawns bursting with phlox and sedum. Eventually, I glide to a stop under a leafy oak. I roll down my window and check the time. Five twenty-five. Perfect.

I pull out my Nikon with its zoom lens. Train it on the front door of an immense new construction across the street. The home swallows up most of its lot and is a smorgasbord of stone, brick, and wood. It somehow, though not well, manages to include a turret, Corinthian columns, plantation shutters, and Palladian windows.

It doesn't take long before a pudgy preteen girl in a ballerina outfit stomps out. Her arms are folded tightly over her chest. Her face is red. "Rachel! I'm out front," she hollers and plunks down on the front steps. She uncrosses her arms, rests her elbows on her knees, her chin on her hands. Her shoulders slump.

I momentarily panic that she is being picked up, or that she might notice me. I lower the camera and wait. Several minutes go by. Eventually, the girl gets back up, sighs dramatically, opens the front door, and yells, "I don't even want to go! I hate these lessons."

Shards of a female voice answer. A woman with cut-glass cheekbones and a high blond ponytail emerges. She's wearing white leggings, a white sports bra, and a cropped, lime-green cardigan. I marvel that there are people who actually wear white leggings.

Into her phone, she barks, "Just tell them to run it. I don't care what ANAD says. Are they buying our ads? Look, I need to go. I'm taking Alex to dance." She drops the phone in her lime-green bag—how many bags must one own to justify splurging on a lime-green one?—and heads to the white BMW parked in the driveway, where the girl now waits. Neither notice as I snap several pictures.

The BMW drives away. I'm about to roll up my window when an older woman with gardening shears approaches. "I hope she bleeds him dry," she announces.

"Pardon?"

"Alex's mom. The soon-to-be-ex-wife. I hope she takes Alex's dad for everything he's worth. You're a private investigator, right? I saw you snapping photos."

"I'm really not at liberty to say." My heart is galloping.

"Imagine leaving your wife of almost twenty years, the mother of your child, for a tramp like that." Her mouth turns downward, emphasizing her marionette lines. "Rachel could practically be his daughter."

Suddenly my heart aches for that reluctant ballerina. I flash back to a zoo field trip when I was in first grade. Our class was leaving the lions' den, a smelly place, thick with the stench of beasts, when up ahead, I thought I saw my father holding a blond overall-clad toddler up to see the dolphin show. The child was laughing as the dolphins leapt through brightly colored hoops. I was about to call out when the man leaned over and kissed a young blond woman in a macrame halter top. Even at age six, I knew this wasn't right. But my group kept moving, and so did I.

For weeks after, I would lie in bed at night and imagine what disaster awaited me. Might I end up with a new stepmother, like my friend Emily? Someone to soak up all my father's energy, steal my mother's light? The stepmothers in fairy tales were scary. Snow White's commanded a huntsman to kill her and bring her heart back as proof. Rapunzel's locked her away in a tower. After weeks of little sleep and escalating fears, I summoned the courage to ask my father about the woman at the zoo.

He was in his study working at his computer. My mother was out in the garden. I hesitantly pushed open the heavy door, cheeks burning, eyes cast to the oriental rug. Crimson and navy swirls like the remnants of a bloody sea battle. In a whisper, I recounted what I'd seen.

There was silence. Then a big guffaw.

I looked up, startled. I didn't think this was funny at all.

"Ashley, my love, what an imagination you have! I don't know who you saw, but it sure wasn't me. I adore your mother and you. Come here. You look like you need a hug." I went to him. Found refuge in his big, strong arms, in his familiar scent of books and oak. I don't remember much of what happened next, but I know he took me out for ice cream. I distinctly remember the ride home, the ice cream sitting in my stomach like a block of ice.

Somehow, I've managed to suppress this. Until today. What an evil bitch that Rachel is. Tearing up Alex's home. Leaving her exposed and vulnerable. Someone should do something about that.

Chapter 23

GEMMA

One Week, Two Days Out:
117.5 pounds | 130 g protein | 120 g carbs | 35 g fat

I'm draped on my sofa, swilling Diet Coke, and liking Flex Friday Instagram posts, when *Fit Gurl* editor-in-chief Rachel pops up on my feed. Bloodred stilettos and sports bra. Charcoal blazer and micro-miniskirt. Slim briefcase and red lollipop.

Soda shoots out my nose. Below Rachel's picture, my REIGN teammate Anita has written:

OMG Fit Fam, Rachel Ballaster, Queen of the Fit Gurls, is dead!
For those of you who don't know, Rachel is a former Bikini Olympian and fitness model who, through hard work and determination, rose to become the editor-in-chief of Fit Gurl magazine, the most influential women's fitness magazine of all time. (In which yours truly has been featured! September 2020 issue.)

Rachel was known for being kind and personable, and recently became engaged to the love of her life. She was on the cusp of becoming a stepmother. This is tragic! #TheQueenIsDead #FitGurl #RestInPeace #crying

From the Comments:

@fitpantsgirl99: She's not just dead, she was murdered! Found locked in the sauna at her house. #SweatItOut

@Heather_Hottie_101: Another fitness girl murdered by something she was promoting. I hope the police are looking into this. #suspicious

Hands trembling, I google for more information. Indeed, Rachel's body was found in her sauna yesterday. The door deadbolted from the outside. Her fiancé swears the deadbolt is new. That he's never seen it before. "Why would we have a deadbolt on the outside of a sauna?"

Rachel was last seen leaving Power Yoga yesterday morning around eight. Her body was discovered by her fiancé that evening, by which point she had been dead for several hours. Both fiancé and his daughter have alibis: performing open-heart surgery and school/theater, respectively. Neither is a suspect. The home was unlocked. Much is being made of the Sweat It Out series, and if her murder is related to Bianca's. Again and again, the question is posed: Is there a Fit Girl Killer out there?

The print starts to swim. I can't breathe.

That's two fitness girls, both connected to me, both dead. A chill runs down my spine as I realize both are connected to Anita, as well. I return to Anita's account and scroll back through her posts. I don't know what I'm looking for, mostly signs of psychopathy, I suppose. (So, so many: narcissism, insecurity, shallowness.) But one post makes me freeze. It's a video of Anita hawking REIGN gear at the Tampa FitExpo, the same event that Bianca was killed at. And who do I see in the background but Kylie. I'm not one hundred percent sure it's her, the person is wearing a gold lamé Gucci baseball cap, but I'm 90 percent.

Kylie and I have our last weekly check-in today, and it can't come soon enough. Usually at my last check-in with a client, we review what went well, opportunities for growth, and how much I enjoyed getting to know them. I tell them that if they renew in the next two weeks, they can get 10 percent off and that if they refer a friend, that friend gets 10 percent off and my client will receive a $30 Amazon gift card. None of that will be going down today.

Throughout our call, Kylie's weather wheel twirls maniacally. There's the blinding sun of unsustainable weight loss, the blowing winds of a work crisis, and the gathering storm clouds of suspicion that her new boyfriend, Jim, may not be over his last girlfriend, Shanna. I observe it all from far away and wonder if she's not just unstable. If she's actually a murderer. Toward the end of our call, when she's back on sunny—she thinks Shanna's gained weight—I ask, "Hey, were you at the recent Tampa FitExpo?"

She doesn't answer right away. I sense a drop in barometric pressure. Then brittle as glass, "Why do you ask?"

"I thought I saw you in the background of a video taken there."

Her voice rachets up an octave and comes out with a forced lightness. "Nope, wasn't me." Several breaths rumble through the receiver.

I try another angle. "Hey, we've talked a lot about your early week. What did you do yesterday?" The day that Rachel was murdered.

More breathing. Then, with umbrage, "Gemma, that is none of your business."

Dial tone.

———

Rachel, luminous and beguiling, beckons me in the dark. Clad in red stilettos and sports bra, charcoal blazer and micro-miniskirt, she sucks a cherry lollipop. Twirls it round and round. She curls a witchy lime-green fingernail at me. I don't want to go to her, but somehow I do.

I get closer and closer. Colder and colder.

She pops the lollipop out of her mouth. Her red lips form a perfect O. Then blood spews out like a fire hose.

I wake up all at once. Something woke me. I lie still and listen. From the other room comes a flapping sound. A cool, curling breeze strokes my cheek. I travel toward it. Out of the bedroom, through the kitchen, and into the dining room.

It's cooler here. My nightgown billows all around. There's more flapping. My eyes adjust, and in the moonlight, I see duct tape fluttering.

I turn on the light. The window is wide-open. Outside, the rain is warm and soft. Unable to stop myself, I walk toward it. Toward the wet floor.

And see footprints.

I scream. I scream and scream.

Steve is in the dining room asking me what's wrong, but I can't stop screaming. I point at the footprints. They only go into our apartment. Toward our bedroom.

The killer is here. They've come for me. To drag me into oblivion with Rachel and Bianca.

———

Now the police are in the dining room and I'm wrapped in a blanket. There's a cup of tea in my hands. I am no longer screaming. I can't speak. I rock back and forth on the couch while my teeth chatter.

A male police officer is talking to Steve, while a female officer rubs my back. I want to fall into her, rest my head in her lap, but I can't stop rocking. "Here, take another sip," she coaxes. I oblige.

The male officer snaps some pictures. Asks if he can take a look around. He goes through the apartment. Confirms there's no one else there. Comes back to the dining room and says to Steve, "Do you mind if I ask what size shoe you wear?"

Chapter 24

ASHLEY

I lie belly down on the grassy knoll. Binoculars pressed to my face. Through the lenses, I watch the new *Shrinking* recruits, fat as me, doing burpees inside a track. The *Shrinking* campus is in Daytona Beach, and the unfortunate souls are drenched in sweat.

Celebrity trainer Megan Miller screams at them through a megaphone. "Don't you dare slow down. Blow up your metabolism!" Her tagline, "Blow up your metabolism," is pretty rich, considering that many former contestants have had their metabolisms damaged by *Shrinking*'s extreme measures.

The hit reality show begins each season with eight contestants, fat as me, vying for a chance to win $100,000. Week after week, the ones who lose the least amount of weight, or are voted off by their fellow contestants (in a very *Lord of the Flies* manner), are eliminated. Essentially, the show exploits poor and desperate people.

Lydia despises *Shrinking* and has sent me here to gather intel. Although her excursions can be difficult to juggle with my work, they're one of my favorite activities. They get me out into the world. Out of my comfort zone. They make me feel like a secret agent.

I've been here for over three hours. So far, I've seen the contestants walk/run around the track multiple times and perform kettle bell swings, jumping jacks, push-ups, walking lunges, a bunch of exercises with dumbbells, and tire flips. Their faces are beet red. Their movements choppy. Now on burpees, they stagger to their feet and drop to the ground, over and over. Several are bleeding from their knees.

"Look how out of shape you are. How fat you are! Look what you've done to yourselves," Megan continues.

One middle-aged man with a heavy beard gives up—or rather, collapses face down on the earth. "Get up, Adam!" screams Megan. "You're going to die. You're going leave your kids fatherless!"

Adam tries to get up, places his palms on the ground, gets his feet under him, but his legs give out. He rocks back and sits on his ass. Tears roll down his face.

"Get up, you fat fuck!" Meagan screams at him.

Adam rests his head on his knees, and his shoulders shake.

While Megan continues hurling insults at him, a blond female bends over and vomits.

A man's voice behind me. "What are you doing here?"

I flinch and drop the binoculars. He pulls away the leafy branch camouflaging my head. It scratches my face and takes several strands of hair with it. I stand and face my interrogator.

The man is midthirties and ruddy faced. His red Shrinking Staff T-shirt is stretched tightly over bulging biceps and thick shoulders. A golf cart idles behind him.

I answer, "Bird-watching. But I'm done. Not a lot of birds out today." I pick up my bag and tuck my binoculars inside it.

Ruddy scoffs, "You don't fool me. You're a reporter. You all say 'bird-watching.'" He snatches my bag and starts rummaging through it.

"Hey, give that back!" I reach for it, but he out maneuvers me.

He dumps my bag out on the grass. The binoculars and my Nikon camera bump into each other and make a terrible clinking sound. Like something inside broke.

"Stop! Those are fragile," I shout, but he ignores me. He picks up my Nikon and starts examining it.

What if he confiscates it? All of today's hard work will be gone.

"Give that back!" I scream, and lunge for my camera.

Ruddy shakes me off. What am I going to do? I hear Tony's voice in my head: *Act like a fighter, become a fighter.*

I take a deep breath and with everything I've got, I throw a left hook.

Ruddy easily catches my fist in the air. He hangs on to it with one hand, while I flail about with my other. My arms are shorter than his, and he keeps his body just out of my reach.

"Give me my camera!" I scream. I kick at his shins, but I can't reach those, either. I add spitting to the mix. Tears stream down my face, hot and wet.

Ruddy holds my fist calmly. With his free hand, he uses his thumb to pop the camera open, press a button, and dislodge the memory card. It falls to the soft green grass, where Rudy uses his big black boot to crush it.

I sink to the earth, amongst the scattered remnants of my mission. My shoulders heave.

Ruddy drops the empty camera next to me. Hops in his cart and drives away.

———

Back home, I take a shower. Wash the dirt off my hands and out of my hair, watch it whirlpool down the drain. I put on clean clothes. Gargle with mouthwash.

But it's no use. Like Humpty Dumpty, I can't seem to put myself back together.

I'm about to grab a pint of Ben and Jerry's and watch the movie *Frozen* when Lydia texts. "Call me."

I don't want to. I want a few more minutes of this fantasy I've been living, before it disappears.

"Call me," she texts again.

I let out a sigh. Might as well get it over with.

"Hi, Lydia." My voice is hoarse and jagged.

"How did it go at *Shrinking* today?"

"Not well," I whisper.

"How so?"

I take a deep breath and give her the rundown, including my impotent punch and the destroyed memory card. My utter failure of the mission. "I don't know, Lydia, maybe I don't have what it takes." I close my eyes. Tears swell beneath the lids. "It's okay if you don't want me in your group anymore."

Lydia's quiet for a beat. Then, "Let me ask you this. Do you like being in my group?"

"Yes." It escapes like air from a balloon.

"Why do you think that is?"

"Before I met you my life was boring. I hardly left my apartment. Now I'm flying in jets and trespassing. I have a burner phone. But more importantly, I feel like my life has purpose. For years I let Diet Culture roll right over me. Now I'm finally fighting back." I feel my face flush. My heart, bare and open.

"You know what you need to come into your own? A special project. You've shown yourself to be very good with the website hacks and cyberattacks. But there's something bigger that

I've had in mind for a while now. I just haven't found the right person to execute it. The project owner would have to be someone not only with the requisite skill set, but someone I could trust implicitly. Ashley, I think you could be that person. What do you think? Are you up for the challenge?"

Relief floods through me. "Yes. I most certainly am." I stand and walk to the window. Outside, the wind is whipping through the trees, exposing the leaves' pale undersides.

Lydia says, "Oh, by the way, you didn't mention that *Fit Gurl* editor mission to anyone, did you? Those pictures you took of Rachel at her home?"

"Of course not! I never tell anyone about our missions."

"Excellent. I knew I could count on you. Listen, I need you to delete the pictures."

"What? Why?"

"I think we need to lie low for a bit."

"Do you want me to save backup copies somewhere?"

"No, Ashley. Delete everything."

"Why?"

"It's not important. And if anyone asks, I was over at your place all day Thursday binge-watching *Downton Abbey*, okay?"

An imaginary centipede crawls across the back of my neck. I rub it away. "Why?"

"Never mind. It's not important."

She says this a lot. I'm getting tired of Lydia keeping things from me. But then again, I'm keeping a few things from her too.

Chapter 25

ANDREW

Andrew Lawrence, a.k.a. @hedgefundguy1, is not a hedge fund guy. Though he did take some business classes at Lake County Community College last year. But after a mishap or two there with the fucking social police—and real police, campus security, and the dean—he's taking this semester off.

All because of crybaby Sara Conley and her "I don't feel safe" bullshit. Acting like she owns the whole damn campus. That it's more than coincidence that she frequently ran into Andrew at the grill, outside of her classes, and in the parking lot. Guess what? Andrew needs to eat, likes to study in different classrooms, and has to park his car too.

And that whole mess at the library was blown way out of proportion. If Sara didn't want to help people find books, or talk to people about books, maybe she shouldn't have been working at the library help desk. It was completely unnecessary for that asshole to ask him to leave, to threaten to call campus security. Maybe Andrew felt threatened and emotionally injured? Did anyone ever think about that? How should Andrew know how that guy's tires got slashed a couple nights later when he was parked off campus under some trees, away from any security cameras?

So for now, Andrew's living in his parents' basement and working as a pizza delivery guy. He's not allowed to drive by Sara's home. But it doesn't matter anymore. She's moved away and left no forwarding address.

Delivering pizzas isn't so bad. Andrew gets to meet lots of new people, and there's a hot waitress who's been eyeing him up. The money's all right too, considering that he doesn't pay rent, and his parents gave him their old Chevrolet Malibu. In fact, he feels rather flush. He's living a life of abundance. So he may as well be a hedge fund guy.

Andrew doesn't need to leave for work for a few hours, so he's passing time playing *Grand Theft Auto*. He loves this game. The strippers, movie producers, gangsters, and souped-up cars. There is a whole other world inside *GTA* that he can immerse himself in. Today, after shooting a venture capitalist and making an impressive getaway, he ultimately goes down when a SWAT team swarms the sleek condo he's hiding out in.

Andrew tosses the controller aside and is a bit surprised when he looks around. Instead of the condo's glass walls overlooking LA, he sees brown shag carpet, fake-wood-paneled walls, and the Baker plaid couch he is camped out on (another hand-me-down from his parents). He blinks a few times, trying to ascertain which is reality—the sleek glass walls or the brown shag carpet. With a sinking heart, he realizes it's the brown shag carpet.

He's been so caught up in *GTA* that he hasn't checked on his girls for a couple of hours. Andrew follows twenty-two different women on Instagram. Most are involved in fitness in some way. There are yoga instructors, personal trainers, and fitness models. Andrew himself has no interest in exercise or healthy eating. He just likes to watch the fitness girls exercise, squat test their leggings, and drink protein shakes.

Andrew maintains a private Instagram account and has no posts. He simply has the account so that he can follow and interact with his girls.

@bianca_summers_xo used to be Andrew's favorite. He read every single one of her posts. Committed several to memory. He bought most of her products and signed up for her Twelve-Week Lean Out program, despite weighing 165 pounds at just over six feet tall. The Lean Out program came with weekly fifteen-minute one-on-one virtual sessions, after which Andrew would immediately jerk off. Andrew thought he and Bianca might have a future together. Unfortunately, that didn't work out. Andrew doesn't like to think about that.

Then there was @FitGurlEditorRachel. Now she's gone too.

Gemma is his new favorite. She's nicer than Rachel. More wholesome than Bianca. And she has the most amazing tits. Hard kernels of corn pressed up against her spandex. He scans her latest post, "Finding Your Purpose." Something about busting your ass.

He likes it then adds the comment, So true. I worked harder the year I started my own hedge fund than I ever have before. But it was worth it. He adds three money bag emojis for effect.

Gemma responds with a thumbs-up. He feels himself blush. She's not like so many of those other Instagram attention whores. She's a genuine good girl.

He looks at the photo she posted. She's wearing tiny white shorts that barely cover her ass and a matching white sports bra. Andrew likes the color white. It makes her look clean and pure. He imagines if he were to look closely, at just the right angle, the fabric may be a bit see-through.

The photo is taken from the side. She's doing a bent over

row with a dumbbell in one hand, while the other rests on a bench. Her blond hair is up in a ponytail.

Andrew can imagine coming up behind her and rubbing his dick on those white shorts. He imagines she might like that, though she'll pretend she doesn't at first. He imagines peeling those white shorts down to about midthigh. She would be shaved, he's certain of it. He imagines fucking her over that bench. Maybe even grabbing her ponytail with one hand. But not too rough.

Andrew takes his swollen cock out of his stained sweatpants and begins to stroke himself. He focuses intently on Gemma's picture as he jerks himself off, imagining the sounds she would make, the way that athletic cunt of hers would grip his cock. Yep, Gemma is his new favorite.

"Andrew! You didn't take the garbage out," his mother yells, opening the basement door. Andrew scrambles to pull up his sweats and hide his ramrod cock beneath a floral throw pillow.

Peak Week

Chapter 26

GEMMA

One Week Out:
117.2 pounds | 130 g protein | 100 g carbs | 35 g fat

"Everywhere. I want cameras everywhere," I say to the technician installing my security system.

"Even in the bedroom?"

"Even in the bedroom."

He looks at me for a beat, like he might have more to say, then appears to think better of it. Smart guy.

I'm splurging on the most badass security system around. Every window. Every door. Motion sensors, video cameras, the works. If whoever is coming in my home tries it again, I'm going to catch him dead to rights. Lock him up. I'm almost looking forward to it.

Steve's not home right now. That's by design. I specifically scheduled this installation for when he had to work. Ever since the break-in, when the police officer asked what size shoe Steve wears, my mind's been churning. Could Steve be leaving the window open just to mess with me? It seems unlikely, but those shoe prints only went *into* the apartment. And they did look about his size.

It's not like he won't notice the cameras. But I plan to tell him they only activate when we set the system to Away. In fact, these cameras will roll non-stop and send me a live video feed, day or night. I don't know what's going on around here, but I'm about to find out.

Once the installation is well under way, I call Coach Rick for my check-in.

It's Saturday, and I've just entered Peak Week—that much revered week before a bodybuilding competition when, despite looking great going in, we suddenly change everything that got me here—and Rick is in the zone. He's yammering on about immediately cutting my carbs to a paltry fifty grams a day and stopping all food seasoning, salt, and sweeteners. I'm not even allowed to chew gum. Cardio will be heavy for the next couple of days, then taper off as the week progresses. Monday, we'll begin increasing my carbs, the exact amount to be determined by the daily photos I'll be sending him (and his mood swings). Thursday, we'll add water pills to the mix. On Friday, I'll start reducing water and sending him photos three times a day so he can judiciously adjust my carbs in tablespoon increments of white rice.

We've done this every Olympia. And, in my opinion, I've come out looking the same or worse. Feeling miserable. Often with a headache. Sometimes sick. It's taken my body days to stabilize after. In fact, I believe last year's particularly brutal Peak Week was a contributing factor to Fat Gemma's resurgence.

Because I don't agree with Rick's coaching methods or ethics, and believe he's dangerous, once this year's Olympia is over, and we're in different states, I plan on parting ways with him. ("It's not you, it's me." "You were the best coach ever, and I will always look back on our time together fondly." "I just need some space.") Since I won't be leaving him for another coach, but will instead be going out on my own, I think he'll handle it okay. At least I hope so.

Rick is known for being a hothead, bipolar nutcase. Lore has it that Men's Physique contestant Russel Marks, who had just held center stage during Emerald Cup Prejudging, fired Rick right after stepping offstage. In the time between Prejudging and Finals, while Russel was on his way back to the hotel, someone came up behind him and cracked him in the head with something hard, possibly a pipe. Then, while Russel was unconscious, kicked him in the face and shattered his nose. No charges were ever filed, but pretty much the entire bodybuilding community believes it was Rick who beat him up.

So for this week, to be safe, I'm sending Rick my daily check-in pictures and pretending to listen as he makes his sage announcements.

He continues his soliloquy while I put him on speaker, chew my gum, and watch @Cats_of_Instagram. Finally, he says, "You got all that?"

"You bet," I say, and hang up.

I'm about to throw in a load of laundry when my phone rings.

"Hi, Gemma, this is FBI Agent Sean Newman." An FBI agent? This just gets worse and worse. "I'm investigating the murder of Rachel Ballaster and its possible connection to Bianca Summers. I understand that you also knew Rachel and was wondering if you could come in for a chat, please?"

Am I a suspect for this murder too? Of course I am. I consider declining Newman's invitation, but don't want to look any more guilty than I already do. Plus, I owe it to Bianca to help find whoever murdered her. Rachel, not so much.

Thirty minutes later, I find myself in a small cinder-block

room, seated at a metal table that's bolted to the floor. The words HELP ME scratched in its surface. There is a large mirror, which everyone knows is a one-way window, on the wall. I wonder if I've made a mistake. Agent Newman is seated across from me, barrel-chested and buzz cut, tree-trunk legs scrunched beneath the table. As my head swivels around taking in my surroundings, he waves a dismissive hand. "Don't mind the room. It's the only place that was relatively quiet." I can smell the pine scent of his deodorant.

He continues, "I understand there was a break-in at your apartment a couple nights ago. That, to the best of your knowledge, the intruder didn't take anything, and the only sign they were even there were wet footprints and an open window. Is that correct?"

"Yes." I shudder at the memory.

"That's rather unusual. That nothing was stolen. Any idea who might break into your home?" He glances inside a folder. "It says here that you're a fitness influencer. Do you think it could have been an overzealous fan or potential stalker?"

"I've been racking my brain on this and can't come up with anyone. I mean, I've got one follower, @hedgefundguy1, who seems a little overly involved, but he's never contacted me outside of Instagram, or said anything to freak me out."

He makes a note of it. "Okay. Now, regarding Rachel's murder, we've interviewed several people at *Fit Gurl*'s headquarters. I understand your last shoot with *Fit Gurl* didn't go well. Were you aware that Rachel put you on their Flop Girl list?"

"They have a Flop Girl list?" I ask in disbelief, then close my lower jaw.

"Yep, all the girls Rachel refused to work with again."

"How many were there?" I imagine an endless list. My name lost on it somewhere.

"I'm not at liberty to disclose that. Have you ever been to Rachel's home?"

"No, I don't even know where she lives."

"About fifteen minutes from you."

The air in this room is stagnant. Thick and hard to breathe. I will myself to return Newman's steely gaze, to not fidget or touch my face. I really want to touch my face.

He continues, "Where were you last Thursday between ten a.m. and six p.m.?"

It occurs to me that I should be asking for a lawyer. That I should quit talking. But isn't that what guilty people do?

Instead, in a daze, I pull out my phone and check my calendar. I breathe a sigh of relief when I see how heavily booked with clients I was that day. Not to mention that I met Craig, who was in town for business again, for lunch at noon. I also posted live to Instagram from the gym at three p.m. So I guess there are some benefits to being a workaholic. I show him the details of what I now realize is my alibi.

"Thanks, Gemma. Do you know anyone who didn't get along with Rachel or might want her dead?"

About a dozen people. "No. She could be demanding, but so can a lot of people in this business."

"How about anyone else who was closely connected to both Bianca and Rachel?"

I tell him about Anita and her *Fit Gurl* spread, continue to answer questions, but he tires of me once he realizes I don't know much. As I'm about to leave, I ask, "Do you really think Rachel's death is connected to Bianca's?"

"Frankly, I don't know at this point. I wish I could tell you more, but I can't. All I can say is: Be careful. We have not ruled out that these crimes are connected and that there is a Fit Girl Killer out there."

Chapter 27

ASHLEY

The angry black eyes of the lobster stare at me accusingly from its bed of crushed ice. Around it, other spiky crustaceans poke out menacing pinchers and claws. Lemon wedges adorn them, like a pocket full of posies.

Lydia and I sit on her bluestone terrace, overlooking the lushly landscaped grounds. A pair of fat peacocks waddle by. Lily pads float atop a koi pond.

I'm at her home today to learn about my exciting new project. A housekeeper finishes pouring our iced tea, and Lydia, regal in a red kimono, dismisses her.

"Now, Ashley, I can trust you, can't I?"

I nod vigorously. "Absolutely."

"Because this is a very delicate project. Certainly not for everyone."

"No problem. I love unique opportunities." I keep my eyes glued to her. I barely breathe.

"I can see that. You've shown yourself to be quite cyber-savvy. That's a real skill, you know. So hard to find." Lydia swallows. Her voice gets raspy. "And you know how I feel about A New You, the place where we met."

Again, I nod. Lydia told me about her mother's last days, thanks to that vile place. The medical complications. The operations. How her skin wrinkled. How her face became gray. How one day she never woke up.

Lydia leans forward. Looks both ways and lowers her voice. "I'd like you to break into their system, steal their patient files, and wipe your tracks."

I rock back. This is not what I expected. My mouth is dry. I reach for my iced tea. The sweating crystal glass is slippery in my hand. I take a gulp and a large floating chunk of lemon smacks me in the lip. "Lydia, that's, like, super illegal."

"So is everything else I've had you doing for me. The ransomware attacks. The website shutdowns. The Instagram hacks. Don't get all holier-than-thou on me." Lydia crushes a crab claw with a pair of metal pliers. Juice runs over her hands.

"Yes, but those were against apparel and media websites, against social media accounts. A New You is a *medical center*. You're talking about violating the privacy of thousands of innocent patients. Not to mention breaking HIPAA laws."

She waves a hand. "HIPAA schmippa. The laws only matter if we get caught. And with your skill set, that's not going to happen." Her eyes beseech mine. "You need to believe in yourself. And trust me. The only people who are going to see those poor patients' files are you and me."

It's still wrong. I know it is.

She points a ragged claw at me. "Ashley, this is our chance to really make a difference. I want to go through those records and identify how many people had their health compromised because of that place. If it's a lot, I'll have an attorney initiate a class action lawsuit." She uses a metal hook to extract soft crab meat from the shell, places it in her mouth, and chews.

I counter, "But you could do that without actual patient

records. You could initiate the lawsuit on your mom's behalf, publicize it, and then anyone else who was injured could self-identify and join if they were interested."

Lydia sighs and looks down at the pile of empty exoskeletons on her plate. "Ashley, I also want to find out what really happened to my mom." Shrugs her shoulders. "But, if you feel like this isn't for you, just say the word, and I'll find someone else." She looks back up at me. There's a piece of flesh hanging from her lip.

"I'll think about it," I say, only to buy time. I'll call her later and tell her no.

"Well, think fast. I've got some of the troops coming out tonight to meet you. I've told them many good things. I'd hate to look like a fool."

We spend the afternoon feasting on dead sea creatures, drinking wine, and swimming in Lydia's too-warm pool. My skin puckers and my brain goes soft.

When the golden hour arrives, three women emerge from Lydia's large Mediterranean manse, like the Fates in Greek mythology. I immediately recognize Heather, the tattooed redhead who drove me to the airport. She's joined by Tina and Merribeth.

Tina is the ghost of beauty-past. Tall and emaciated, her cheeks sunken, her eyeballs bugged out. I can see the contours of her skull beneath the downy fuzz covering her face. Her ponytail is dry and bristly. Despite it being a warm day, she's wearing a sweatshirt.

Merribeth looks like a former college gymnast, coiled with energy. Like she could spring into a series of backflips. An all-American girl—until I notice her ragged, discolored teeth.

The sun catches Heather's hand and unleashes a spray of red sparks. I look more closely, and see they're from rubies on a phoenix ring, just like the one Lydia's flight attendant was wearing. Tina and Merribeth are wearing phoenix rings, as well.

Lydia waves a hand in my direction. "Ladies, this here's Ashley, whom I've told you all about. Let's go inside and get her up to speed."

It's cool in Lydia's home. The pool water evaporates off my skin and I shiver, pull my borrowed kimono tighter around me. We travel through a terra-cotta-tiled hall, past gilt mirrors, fresh flowers, and tapestries, and into a paneled dining room. Heavy jacquard drapes flank Palladian windows, rough-hewn beams support a plastered ceiling. A dark wood table is set with Tuscan chicken, French bread, fresh fruit, and wine.

"Help yourself, ladies," Lydia says. Then, to her housekeeper, "Sheena, this all looks marvelous. You can leave for the evening. Thank you."

I pop a fat grape in my mouth. So firm it crunches and squirts the back of my throat. I pour myself a generous glass of Chablis, sit back, and relax, while Lydia fiddles with a laptop.

My eyes are drawn to an eight-foot-long painting based off Michelangelo's *Last Supper*. However, in this painting the table is laden with foods like cheesecake, ice cream, and pasta. The artist has replaced the disciples with a dozen luscious, sexy fat women, and placed Lizzo at the center, where one would expect Jesus. Chocolate syrup drips decadently off a sundae, pooling on the pristine white tablecloth. A raven-haired woman feeds a blond with four inches of cleavage a bite of cherry cheese-cake off the tines of an ornate silver fork. A redhead slurps eighteen-inch-long spaghetti noodles between bright red lips, splattering tiny flecks of marinara sauce across her cheeks. The women are clad in clothes suitable for clubbing—spandex, hot pants, and leather. Lizzo, table center, is crowned with a tiara that glows like a halo.

At the table head, Lydia picks up a remote control, points it at a large flat screen on the wall, and starts a Zoom meeting. Three other women join us online, each in their respective rectangles. Lydia's rectangle shows our group gathered round her table.

Lydia says, "Ladies of The Phoenix, thank you all for joining me this evening. Our group, like the phoenix, is reborn from fire. Through destruction and pain we rise, stronger and more powerful.

"I'll get us kicked off with some exciting news from Florida. I'd like you to meet Ashley." She nods in my direction. "Ashley's been helping me with all things IT and is quickly becoming my right-hand woman. In fact, she may soon be working on a top secret cybersecurity project that's near and dear to my heart." The women all look at me with respect. This job is going to be so much harder to turn down now.

Once they've welcomed me, Lydia continues, "Now, Brittany, what's going on in Texas?"

Brittany speaks up. "The Texas Bariatric Center has been bombarding the public with radio and TV ads. Billboards everywhere. I mean, you can't even go a day without hearing about how their surgery can help improve your health. Meanwhile, they're covering up a mega-high death rate. A lawyer from my team just filed a class action lawsuit on behalf of some of the victims' families. She is starting her own barrage of advertising this Monday, seeking others who have been harmed by this nasty place."

Lydia nods. "Excellent. Let's hear from Sandy in New York."

"Brooklyn's Cosmetic Dental Clinic has been installing metal magnets on people's teeth so their jaws lock and can't open more than two millimeters. These willing victims then live on a liquid diet. It's all the rage. Our building inspector stopped by their clinic the other day and found a couple building violations. She plans to shut them down tomorrow, tie them up in paperwork for the foreseeable future."

Lydia claps her hands. "Wonderful. Let me know if you need any help. How about Nancy in Los Angeles?"

"*Teen Magazine*'s got a new article coming out, 'Don't Let Puberty Make You Pudgy.'"

Lydia asks, "So what are you going to do about it?"

Nancy smiles. "Correction: What *did* I do about it? Lit the magazine's warehouse on fire last night."

There's silence all around. Everyone looks to me. Waiting. Testing. My mouth is suddenly dry. My brain buzzy. I pick up my glass of Chablis, swirl it around a bit, watch the light play off the buttery liquid. I take a gulp. "Wow. That's fucking fantastic," I say, flushed with wine. Flushed with amazement.

Lydia nods her approval, turns her laptop to face me. There is a Zoom poll open. One question only: *Ashley Shermer, in or out?* One hundred percent of the respondents have voted *In.*

"You're in," she says and slides a small black velvet box across the table to me. I open it, and inside is my own phoenix ring, its ruby eye twinkling at me.

Chapter 28

GEMMA

Six Days Out:
116.0 pounds | 130 g protein | 100 g carbs | 35 g fat

I'm going to vomit, is my first thought on waking. Currents of acid slip through my stomach like cool, clammy eels. I've let myself get too hungry.

Steve is sound asleep, his back to me, a foreign country across a yawning stretch of percale. We've barely touched since the break-in. I no longer trust him, and he seems to sense my reticence.

I throw off the covers and stumble to the kitchen. Make myself some oatmeal. As soon as it's ready, I slide to the floor and scarf it down, right out of the pan. The first few bites burn my tongue.

The food in my belly is a relief, and I'm suddenly exhausted. I set the pan aside and lie down on the kitchen floor, where I notice splashes of long-forgotten coffee on the toe kick under the cabinets. I couldn't care less.

Thirty minutes later, I wake up with a tile imprint on my

cheek. Figuring that I could use some coffee, I make a pot, but the back of my throat revolts at the first swallow. I gag it out in the sink and dump the rest.

I must be getting sick, like I do almost every Peak Week. Although usually it's not a stomach bug. But then I've never been under this much stress before. Not only is my marriage falling apart, there's a possible serial killer on the loose.

Despite feeling lousy, I head to the gym and cut my workout to just the essentials. But even so, I'm spent by the time I finish. I sit on the shower floor and let the water pummel my back. When I finally stand up and turn around, the force of the spray against my swollen breasts is too much to take, and I have to turn away. Maybe I'm finally going to get my period, after all. It's been at least a couple months. But that's not uncommon during competition season, when my body fat drops this low.

I would go home, but I'm training my favorite in-person client today. Dorothy is sixty-five years old and doesn't have any social media accounts. She confuses Instagram with Facebook and Snapchat. She's not worried about how she looks or losing weight. She simply wants to get stronger. One day I want to be Dorothy.

Despite trying to stay focused during our session, there is one instance where I forget if Dorothy's done two or three sets of dumbbell bench press. There's another where I stand up quickly, get dizzy, and have to sit back down. I apologize and tell her that I didn't sleep well, about falling asleep on the kitchen floor.

She gives me a critical once-over, and says, "I bet you're pregnant."

"No way!" But even as I say it, I'm not sure.

"Yeah, I thought that once too. He turned thirty last week."

It's all I can do to get through the rest of our session. My mind keeps turning over this morning's events: the nausea, the revolting smell of coffee, the exhaustion, the sore breasts—it all sort of clicks.

As soon as I'm done training Dorothy, I run to Walgreens and pick up a pregnancy test.

Once home, I sit in my car and check my messages. My last security alert shows someone opened and shut the front door at 11:40 a.m. That's when Steve would've left to work the lunch shift. No other windows or doors have been opened or shut since I left this morning. I love this new system.

Satisfied that my home is secure, I go inside. As a precaution, I check the dining room window. It's still locked. The duct tape adhered. I rattle the window in its frame to be sure. Then I check all the windows. The kitchen door. The front door again. All are locked. I exhale.

I open the pregnancy test kit. Read the instructions once through. Then a second time, more carefully. I use a highlighter. It doesn't seem to be too complicated.

Minutes later, I'm staring at a deep blue line. Like permanent ink. I consult the instructions in case I misunderstood. I didn't. I'm pregnant.

My first thought: This isn't a good time. I can't get fat. It's finally my chance to win the Bikini Olympia. But then I wonder: Is there ever a good time? Could I have this baby and the title?

I've worked so very hard to leave Fat Gemma behind. Tracked and calibrated every bite. Trained even when I didn't feel like it. Even when I was exhausted. A baby would change the equation for the next nine months. But not for the next six days. I just need to get through six measly days. I can still track. Still train. Still proceed as planned. My weight shouldn't increase before the Olympia, as long as Fat Gemma doesn't rear her ugly head.

But then I imagine standing on the scale, week after week,

month after month, and watching the number climb. My heart constricts like it's losing a lover.

Fat Gemma's breath tickles my neck. She's peering over my shoulder, looking at the blue line, delighted. It's the perfect excuse to emerge from her cage. A Get Out of Jail Free card. Thick gooey pizzas, dripping chocolate sundaes. All for the betterment of another life. How noble. How fucking delicious. She is so very hungry. She wants to start right now.

I must stay the course until the Olympia and win. Only then will I be free of Fat Gemma forever. Able to have my baby and finally live my life, victorious.

I just need to stay alive to do it.

Chapter 29

ANDREW

It's Andrew's day off. He's played so many hours of *GTA* that he's got a headache, so he decides to relax with a bit of Instagram. He can usually count on a new post by Gemma and is looking forward to jerking off. He's hoping for a picture where she's hip thrusting or squatting. But even a close-up of just her face would be great. Then he can picture what her mouth would look like, how her eyes would open wide, as he jams his cock down her throat. '

He scrolls through his feed until he comes to her new post. But what the hell is this? It's some lame-ass stock photo of a bunch of women's hands in different skin tones, all reaching to the center, like they're making a pact. Below it, she's written:

Body Shaming Comes in All Forms

There's certainly been a lot of buzz lately about "Body Shaming." Body Shaming is often thought of with regards to fat shaming. What is often overlooked, however, is the other end of the spectrum: fit shaming.

"I made this pie just for you, and you're not even going to eat one piece?" to "You're skin and bones!" to "Your muscles are too bulky." Or how about, "Quit posting about healthy diets and exercise because it makes me feel bad."

Listen, the world does not revolve around you. It doesn't revolve around any of us. We all have a right to our own interests, to do whatever we feel like doing with our bodies, without someone else's opinion being thrown in our faces.

Throwing shade won't help you shine more brightly. #strongwomenlifteachotherup

This was *not* what Andrew was looking for today. In fact, it's a completely useless post. Of course, he knows why Gemma wrote this. It's all because of that @fat_and_fabulous bitch who keeps making cunty, jealous fat-girl comments on all of Gemma's posts. And though Gemma's ignoring her comments, probably hoping to discourage her, she's not really ignoring them, because now she's dedicating whole posts to tripe like this. This is not why Andrew follows Gemma's account. He wants her to get back to the business of squatting in booty shorts.

He navigates to @fat_and_fabulous's page to find out more about this wretched person who's fucking up his life. He has to create a new account (@calm_and_happy_111) to do this, because she blocked his @hedgefundguy11 account after his recent "everyone knows you're an ugly, fat bitch" comment. Her latest post has a photo of a fat "model" in a camouflage swimsuit holding a machine gun, staring down the camera. Like the woman's not offensive enough simply existing, she has to wear a fucking swimsuit and burn out Andrew's eyeballs with acid. Below it, she's written:

> Fat shaming doesn't just hurt fat women. It hurts all women. It subtly lets us know our place. That we best not get too big. Too substantial. That we best conform.
>
> Fat shaming has become so prevalent, it's like air pollution. It impacts our physical and emotional health, leading to chronic stress, anxiety, and depression. Some common examples of fat shaming are snarky comments on social media, fat photos in magazines with a black rectangle over the woman's eyes, and unsolicited advice under the guise of concern. Fat shaming reeks of moral superiority and elitist healthism. It reeks of hate.
>
> Not only is fat shaming cruel, it's counterproductive. But then again, it's not meant to help. It's meant to subvert. To knock down.
>
> Rise the fuck back up.
>
> #fuckdietculture #riotsnotdiets #fatactivism #bloody_ but_unbowed

"Elitist healthism"? Well, this is getting ridiculous. Are Gemma and this nut going to keep going back and forth exchanging dueling posts? Andrew tries to leave a comment telling @fat_and_fabulous what an ugly, fat, hairy (he just knows she is), feminist cunt she is, but the comments are turned off. He scrolls through all of her posts, trying to determine where she lives or her real name. He scrutinizes every single one, looking for landmarks or errant pieces of mail, but can find none. He'd love to show up at her door and have a talk. It's so easy to hide behind the anonymity of posts and say anything you want. (Andrew does not see the irony here.) He decides to follow her. Eventually she'll slip up. Then maybe he'll pay her a visit.

Chapter 30

ASHLEY

I'm scanning A New You's networks and systems, looking for a vulnerability. And questioning my sanity.

After last night's meeting at Lydia's home and being accepted into The Phoenix, I couldn't bring myself to turn this project down. I just need to knock it out and be done with it. Who knows when another opportunity like this will arise?

You see, The Phoenix has ranks: candidate, lieutenant, captain, general. Unbeknownst to me, I started off as a candidate. According to Lydia, over half the candidates are never accepted. Once I passed the trial period, I became a lieutenant and earned my ring. The women on the Zoom call were all captains. They each lead their own cell and have voting rights. Lydia, of course, is the general.

I want to be a captain. Usually, that takes at least a couple years. First, one needs to prove oneself with fidelity, creativity, work ethic, and impact. There's an actual rubric.

I've got fidelity (I've kept all Lydia's secrets), creativity (my hacking skills), and work ethic (I've been putting in twenty-plus hours a week for Lydia, despite already having a full-time job).

What I don't have is much of an impact in the fight against Diet Culture.

That's about to change now. I grit my teeth and scan on. All I need to identify is a single point of entry, and like a mouse finding a tiny crevice in a fortress, I'll be in. I've been at it for hours and am considering taking a break, when I spot it.

My fingers jerk back from the keyboard like it's zapped me. I look around my office, as if waking from a dream. The cool celadon walls. The photo of five-year-old me and my dad in the backyard, counting the rings on an enormous tree stump. Outside my window, the sun is bright, the sky blue. Wisps of white clouds drift by. *There's still time to change your mind*, some shred of sanity begs.

No, I told Lydia I'd do this, so I will. This is a one-time thing, a means to an end. Plus, it's for a good cause.

I return my eyes to the monitor, click a few keys, and voila: I'm in.

I escalate my privileges, get root access, and download all of the patient files and databases. My heart is in my throat. My gut is screaming at me to stop, but I ignore it. I move quickly, fearing that if I pause, I may never finish.

Once I have everything I need, I cover my tracks, replace the log files, and get out of A New You's system. I upload their patient data to The Phoenix's repository on the dark web and spend the next several hours cracking the encryption and deciphering the data. And at last, patients' heights, weights, mental health histories, number of abortions, and previous surgeries are all laid out before me. Naked and exposed. I imagine someone pawing through my health history and shudder.

For the rest of the day, I sift through terabytes of data. Flagging patients whose procedures resulted in medical complications, whose procedures resulted in death. I don't know which one of these records belongs to Lydia's mom—Lydia never told me her name—and it's just as well. This whole endeavor is overwhelming enough as is.

I'm almost done when the file of a Megan Miller catches my eye. Could it be *the* Megan Miller? *Shrinking* star, terrorizer of fat people, owner of the "Blow up your metabolism" tagline? It is.

It seems that Megan's been an on-and-off-again patient of A New You for some time, and a heavy user of stimulant diet pills. So heavy that Dr. Berlin is concerned about her high blood pressure and elevated heart rate, and that perhaps she may be becoming addicted. He recommends she reduce her intake and discontinue use. There are months of documented arguments, her begging, threatening to take her business elsewhere. Which, judging by the gaps in her history, she appears to have done, before eventually returning to A New You and starting the process all over again. Interesting. I flag this file, too, and set it aside for Lydia.

Finally, I log out. Slump back in my chair and exhale, relieved that it's done. My face is hot and grimy. I head to the bathroom and splash cool water on it from the sink. Over and over, I splash. The water creeps into my hairline, runs down my neck, and dampens my collar. I let it fill my mouth. Swish it round and round.

When I finally come up for air, I see my dripping reflection in the mirror. I hardly recognize myself.

Chapter 31

GEMMA

Five Days Out:
116.2 pounds | 130 g protein | 110 g carbs | 45 g fat

The Olympia takes place this Saturday. To make sure I have plenty of time and don't feel rushed, I'm flying out today. At least, that's the reason I give Steve.

The minute the plane's wheels touch down, I take my phone off airplane mode and check my messages. The last one is from my home security system and indicates that the front door closed at 7:20 a.m. That was me leaving to catch my flight.

I apologize, again, to the young mother sitting next to me, who had to witness me vomiting into a barf bag on takeoff. She gave me a bag of Goldfish, overriding complaints from her toddler. She also clued me in that "morning sickness" is really a misnomer. Turns out, it can strike any time of day. Good to know.

I check in to the hotel under the alias Jane Doe while repeatedly scanning the lobby. When the manager, Dale, finally hands me my key, I lean in close and whisper that he must not,

under any circumstances, give out my room number to anyone.
He nods solemnly.

My room is in a good location. It's on the seventh floor, so
I don't have to worry about windows, and about halfway between two stairwells, for ease of escape.

Once inside, I deadbolt the door, then shove a towel along
the floor crack. I close the curtains.

I hate to do it, but I pull out my phone and video the
scene. I pan over my bikini, heels, and jewelry. Continue the
arc over the hotel room while speaking, "Hey there, Fit Fam!
Guess what? I just arrived at the Hyatt Regency in Orlando,
Florida, where I'm scheduled to compete in the Olympia this
Saturday! There are competitors here from all over the world,
and I'm super pumped! Come and meet me at the Meet the
Olympians event this Thursday at seven p.m., or this Friday at
the REIGN booth at one p.m. at the Orange County Convention Center!" I reassure myself that with the curtains drawn,
no one can tell what floor I'm on, and that the hotel has hundreds of rooms.

Nevertheless, I hesitate before posting it, realizing that I will
be letting hundreds of thousands of people know where and
when they can find me. What if one of them is the serial killer
who murdered Bianca and Rachel? Then I argue with myself
that each of their deaths could be a separate tragedy. That it
could just be sensationalism that has linked them. That even
the FBI isn't sure if they're related.

I need to keep posting to stay relevant. This is my livelihood
and I need to be able to support not only myself, but a baby. I
spent yesterday googling how much it costs to raise a child, and
it was hair-raising. So I suck it up and hit Share.

Next, I check the video feed to my apartment on my laptop.
I'm not exactly sure what I expect to find. Steve engaging in a

torrid affair? Him moving items around the apartment to make me question my sanity?

Instead, he's sitting solitary on the sofa in his boxer shorts playing video games. Oblivious that his wife is spying on him. That she's pregnant. That his life's about to blow up.

Confirming that home and hotel room are secure, I finally relax.

I flip on the television. *Dish with Debbie* is due to start in a few minutes, and I've been looking forward to this episode. Debbie is scheduled to interview Craig, who's in town as one of the Olympia sponsors.

I settle into bed as Craig is welcomed to the stage. His gait is loose and confident, his smile warm and friendly.

Debbie starts out by lobbing him a softy. "My, Craig, you've been busy! In the last few years, REIGN has taken the nation by storm. Can you tell us a bit about how you arrived at where you are today?"

Craig discusses how he started REIGN six years ago as a side gig while he was working in IT. He had recently switched to a vegan diet and was concerned that he wasn't getting enough protein. He started researching vegan protein powders and was disappointed in the options available. Many of them tasted horrible, contained cheap fillers, or both. Because he couldn't find what he wanted, he decided to produce it himself. And a business was born.

His vegan protein powder was so successful that REIGN expanded into virtually every supplement line imaginable. From there, REIGN branched into fitness apparel, and then his company exploded.

REIGN uses only beautiful, quality fabrics that are thick and soft. Their designs are flattering, their engineering has been called a "feat of wonder." It's said that his leggings provide at least one inch of lift to the average wearer's tush. All their apparel is organic, ethically sourced, and sweatshop-free.

Debbie says, "Your fitness apparel is often considered a status symbol. Not only is it expensive, but celebrities and influencers are frequently photographed clad in it." Photos flash of Taylor Swift, Emma Watson, and Kendall Jenner going about their daily lives, walking their dogs, and leaving yoga and Pilates studios, wrapped in the latest REIGN attire. "However, some have pointed out that your apparel is also coveted because it only goes up to a size large—a rather small size large. What do you think about that?"

Craig replies, "Well, we certainly do have some of the highest quality workout attire around. All of our fabrics have four-way stretch and are engineered to be moisture-wicking and anti-microbial. We are still a fairly small company, and we don't have the means to expand into the plus-size market yet. It's not like we can just make bigger versions of the sizes we carry. It doesn't work like that."

"It doesn't?"

"Not at all. The shape of an overweight person is not the same as the shape of a standard-size person only larger. It's not like going from a small circle to a big circle. It's like going from a small circle to a large ellipse. New patterns would need to be created. We'd have to make sure the new pattern is right and that the garment fits comfortably. For instance, do the straps need to be wider? Should the fabric under the arms come up higher? What about the lining? We're not going to just slap something together. This is our reputation."

"But isn't this a lost opportunity? Especially considering that sixty-eight percent of American women are considered plus-size?"

"I don't know. Is there the same demand for fitness apparel

in larger size women that there is in standard-size women? And if there is, are they willing to pay the same price points? We're a small company. You're talking about a big gamble."

The audience, which I now notice is made up of many larger women, boos.

Debbie asks, "You don't think there's much of a demand for fitness apparel in plus-size women?"

"Look, I go to a lot of gyms, and I don't see many plus-size women."

Debbie fires back, "Maybe that's because they don't have decent gym attire." The audience erupts in applause.

Craig smiles wryly. "If you want to go to the gym, you find a way. You wear a T-shirt and shorts, if that's all that's available. You don't skip the gym because you don't like your outfit."

I shut the television off. I can't bear to watch any more. I remember when I was fat. When I was too embarrassed to go to the gym. I felt like I wouldn't fit in, that people would stare. Not having the right clothes was part of that. It was one more hurdle.

When I started losing weight, I promised myself that once I got under two hundred pounds, I could join a gym. That was the reward: lose weight and you can join a gym. How messed up is that? Not: Join a gym to help yourself lose weight. At my fattest, I felt like I didn't belong at the gym, that I didn't deserve to be there.

Eventually, I made it to 199 pounds and was in "one-derland." I was so proud of myself, but still had nothing to wear. I remember buying my first leggings and sports top, black of course, online from Athleta. The set arrived at my door a few days later, like a Christmas present. The fabric was so soft. The cut, so flattering. To have workout clothes that fit felt like a luxury. They were a luxury.

That outfit made me more confident. It made me feel like I fit in, if only just a little.

Now look at me. I have drawers full of workout clothes in every color under the sun. I'm paid to model gym attire by a company that would never have sold to the likes of me five years ago. Craig makes some good points. He does have a small company. It would be a risk. It's his business on the line, not mine. I tell myself all of this. Yet, as I sit here in my Bombshells Only REIGN attire, I can't help but feel a bit ashamed.

I glance at my apartment's living room video feed again and notice Steve's no longer there. My heart skips a beat. I pull my laptop closer, switch the display from single room to grid and see all the rooms at once.

Steve's in our bedroom, his carry-on bag open on the bed. I zoom in and watch as he deposits pants, shirts, underwear, and socks inside. Toiletries. Until the bag is crammed and he has to press down on its leather exterior to zip it shut.

He checks his wallet. His phone. And then he leaves.

Oh my God.

Chapter 32

ASHLEY

I'm watching *Dish with Debbie*. The host, Debbie, seems like someone I could be friends with. She's got broad, substantial shoulders, an ample bosom, and hips that could knock you into next week. While her demeanor is warm and sincere, she's not afraid to ask hard questions. Today, she is interviewing the owner of REIGN, the company that sponsors some of Gemma's posts.

Lately, every time I pick up a *People* magazine or *InStyle*, I see a starlet clad in REIGN leggings strolling down the sidewalk, Starbucks in hand, or meeting a friend for lunch. The fabrics are supposed to be luxurious, the fit "like a glove." I would love to own a pair of REIGN leggings. Unfortunately, I don't think I could get them over my knees.

The owner, Craig, seems okay at first. But once Debbie starts grilling him about his refusal to make larger sizes, his arrogance becomes apparent. He keeps using the phrase "standard size" for the women he designs his apparel for. At one point, Debbie asks her producer to pull up dictionary.com and find the definition for "standard." Turns out it's something that is "regarded as the usual or most common size or form of its kind."

Debbie asks, "If sixty-eight percent of American women are plus-size, doesn't that make them the standard?"

Craig explains that the word "standard," with regards to clothing design, means something very specific. He googles "standard-size clothing" on his phone and proves his point by pulling up a Standard US Apparel Size Chart.

Craig goes on to talk about his small, fledgling company, and how they dare not expand into uncharted domain. Debbie points out that REIGN has done nothing *but* expand into new terrain since its inception. They started with vegan protein powder, conquered all forms of supplements, spawned into women's leggings, and went on to dominate all types of "standard-size" fitness apparel. Clearly, expanding is something they do well.

Craig thanks her and genially says that indeed they may expand into the plus-size market at some point in the future.

He's lying and I know it. REIGN will never expand into the plus-size market because they don't want their pricey clothes associated with fat people. It's one of the reasons people are willing to pay so much for their apparel. REIGN is exclusive because it excludes.

When the show is over, I pull a ten-second video clip of the interview. The one where Craig asks, "Is there the same demand for fitness apparel in larger size women as there is in standard-size women?" and post it to Instagram with the caption:

Hey REIGN, newsflash: Fat people exercise too. Increase your fucking sizes. #hater #fatphobic #effyourbeautystandards

I decide to leave the comments on for this post. I want to see what others have to say. Immediately the likes start rolling in. Some comments, too:

@queen_kylie: OMG, what a prick. Get a clue.

I like this comment and respond, Totally!

@FullBodyFiona: He doesn't want fatties like us sullying his brand.

I like and comment, Soooo transparent.

@living_my_best_life_94: It's his company. He can run it any way he wishes. If you don't like it, why don't you create your own company and, you know, do all the hard work and take on all the risk that comes with that?

I delete @living_my_best_life_94's comment.

@Lydia_Fed_Up: Stand up against oppression! Fight fat discrimination!

@living_my_best_life_94 responds to @Lydia_Fed_Up: This isn't oppression. A company can choose whom they wish to cater to. And this isn't discrimination. Fat is not an intrinsic characteristic, like skin color or sex. It's a result of life choices, like lung cancer can be a result of smoking.

I delete this comment and block @living_my_best_life_94 from my account.

@Lydia_Fed_Up: So @fat_and_fabulous, what are you going to do? Ball's in your court . . .

It's like an electric jolt. What *am* I going to do? Just complain and wring my hands? Or am I going to act?

As I'm mulling next steps, a post from Gemma, REIGN promotor, Diet Culture enabler, pops up on my feed. She's squawking about some Olympia contest she's going to be in.

' But wait. Her contest is at the Orange County Convention Center in Orlando? That's fifteen minutes from where I live. And isn't that the same contest that the douchey owner of REIGN is going to be at?

Ordinarily, I don't believe in fate, but this seems meant to be. I'll show Lydia exactly what I'm going to do about REIGN and their exclusionary sizes. Show her my leadership abilities. I post a photo of REIGN's iconic black Bad Bitch leggings, and scrawl "Fatties Unite" over it in bold red print. In the caption below, I write:

> Join me at the Olympia in the Orange County
> Convention Center in Orlando, Florida, this Saturday at
> 10 a.m. to protest REIGN's ignorance of fat women in
> America. Let's show them that we exist, we exercise,
> and we deserve decent fitness apparel. #takeupspace
> #fuckdietculture #fatactivism

I tag @Lydia_Fed_Up. Put up or shut up.

Chapter 33

ANDREW

Amari is so hot. And she's so into him. Andrew is certain.

His shift at Pizza Plaza started off slow, so he's hanging around the waitress station, carrying on a conversation with her each time she comes back. He's telling her his story about delivering pizzas to a possible drug house. As he tells it, he leans against the counter and crosses his arms, trying to look casual, while secretly flexing his biceps.

Amari comes rushing up. Her eyes fixed on the soda dispenser. Without tripping, she steps around his outstretched legs and begins scooping ice into three glasses.

Andrew picks up where he left off. "So this shirtless guy with long hair and bloodshot eyes opens the door, and an enormous cloud of pot smoke rolls out. Like, I'm practically getting high standing on the doorstep."

Amari jams the glasses, one by one, under the soda dispenser. She fills one with Diet Coke, one with plain Coke, and one with Sprite. She puts straws in the Coke and Sprite and leaves the Diet Coke strawless.

Andrew continues, "And I'm, like, 'Pizza delivery,' and the

guy looks at me like he has no idea where I came from or what
I'm doing at his door . . ."

Amari takes off, her ponytail swinging behind her, her ass
high and firm in the Pizza Plaza's black polyester uniform pants.
She's not on Instagram. Andrew's checked. Amari delivers the
drinks to a family of three. They ask her questions about the
menu, and she makes recommendations. Andrew's getting impatient and looks at them pointedly. He sighs loudly. Taps his
fingers on the countertop. They ignore him.

Finally, they place their order. Amari comes zipping back to
ring it. As she's punching their order in, Andrew continues, "So
he yells over his shoulder, 'Hey, somebody order pizza?' and this
girl appears." Andrew leaves out that the girl is a total babe. He
doesn't want to make Amari jealous. Andrew continues, "She
says, 'Yep!' and hands me fifty bucks and takes the pizza boxes.
While I'm handing them to her, some other guy comes up to
the door behind me. The shirtless guy pulls out a ziplock bag
of weed from his jeans and hands it to the guy, who gives him
some cash. And I'm, like, still standing there . . ." Amari walks
away again.

"Hey, Andrew, your order's ready," calls Andrew's manager
from the kitchen. Andrew can't believe what a cockblock the
guy is. How inconsiderate. Now Amari will have to wait to find
out how the story ends.

Andrew spends the rest of the evening delivering pizzas. By
the time he clocks out, he's exhausted. His plan had been to hang
around and wait for Amari to finish so he could tell her the rest
of his story, but lately her jagoff boyfriend has been showing up
at the end of her shift, throwing Andrew menacing looks (likely
sensing his competition). So Andrew heads home. He'll finish
the story the next time they work together.

In his basement apartment, Andrew peels off his work

clothes, which reek of pizza and sweat, and tosses them in the corner. He knows he should probably wash them before he works next, but he won't. After a quick shower to wash off the pizza smell (he now hates pizza), he crawls into bed.

Andrew hasn't checked Instagram since Gemma and @ fat_and_fabulous had dueling shaming posts. His absence was meant to send Gemma a message. He hopes that she's noticed and gone back to the business of sweating in spandex. He opens Instagram.

First, he checks his @calm_and_happy_111 account, the one he uses to keep tabs on that awful @fat_and_fabulous. There is a new post that reads "Fatties Unite" in bold red. How absolutely preposterous. He's about to close out, when his eyes snag on, **Join me at the Olympia in the Orange County Convention Center in Orlando, Florida, this Saturday at 10 a.m. to protest REIGN's ignorance of fat women in America.** So there it is. A place and time where she will be. Andrew doesn't have to work for the next few days, but he's not sure he wants to make a four-hour trip to have a talk with an ugly fat woman. He'll put this on the back burner to percolate.

He logs into his @hedgefundguy11 account and sees that Gemma's got two new posts for him. The first is a picture of her pulling a barbell up off the floor, her muscles flexed, her gaze fixed on him. Below it is a quote by John F. Kennedy, "Things do not happen. Things are made to happen." Now, this is more like it. Andrew very much likes this picture. He plans to come back to it. Her second post is a video of a hotel room. She says, "Hey there, Fit Fam! Guess what? I just arrived at the Hyatt Regency in Orlando, Florida, where I'm scheduled to compete in the Olympia this Saturday!" She goes on to invite Andrew to meet her on two specific occasions.

Andrew is stunned. It's like fate is tapping him on the

shoulder. Gemma and @fat_and_fabulous are both going to be in Orlando at the same time? And then it comes to him all at once. What he has to do. To quote JFK, "Things do not happen. Things are made to happen."

Chapter 34

ASHLEY

"The salads here are wonderful," my mom says.

I ignore her and tell the waitress, "I'll take the cheeseburger and fries."

My mother smiles primly. "I'll have the Summer Salad. No cheese or walnuts. And could you please bring the dressing on the side?" I know she thinks she's modeling good eating behavior, but what she's really doing is pissing me off. The waitress sighs and disappears.

My birthday lunch; I just need to get through it.

I cross my right leg over my left and admire my grape soda thigh-high boots. My gift to myself. My mother hasn't taken her eyes off them since I walked in.

She says, "Those are certainly a statement."

"They are, aren't they?" I extend a leg and turn it this way and that.

"Now, Ashley, how's everything going? I haven't heard from you as much lately." She leans in, conspiratorially. "Is it a man?"

"Nope. I've met a new group of friends and have been busy with them. I've also been working a ton."

She's disappointed but does her best to hide it. "Well, friends are nice. But don't work too hard, or life will pass you by." Translation: your eggs have a shelf life, and you better land a husband before they expire.

Somehow, we make it through our meal. We don't order any dessert because for my mom, watching me eat it would be akin to my putting a loaded gun to my head, and because for me, her watching me eat it would make me want to put a loaded gun to my head.

While we're waiting for the waitress to box up her leftover salad (yes), she slides an envelope, my birthday present, across the table.

I'd love for it to be cold, hard cash, but know it won't be. My mom would consider that tacky. At least it's not another too small piece of clothing.

I open the envelope, and my eyes swim. It's a gift certificate to A New You.

When I don't say anything, my mom pipes up. "Now, don't be mad. They have lots of options there. Everything from diet coaching to weight loss pills to surgery. Just think, you could be a whole new you by next summer!"

I sit quietly, the slip of paper quivering in my hands, and feel the anger build. It sloshes around and froths. Coalesces and fumes. Until the inside of me can no longer contain it. It rises up and up and suddenly escapes like a bubble. "Fuck you." It's even and measured. I stand.

My mother's eyebrows shoot to her hairline, which is impressive considering her face has been practically immobile since her facelift in 2018. "Ashley!" she says to my back, but I don't turn around. I stroll out the door, à la Nancy Sinatra.

These boots were made for walking.

Chapter 35

GEMMA

Four Days Out:
116.4 pounds | 130 g protein | 120 g carbs | 45 g fat

I stare at the empty grid of rooms on my laptop's surveillance app. Steve never came back to our apartment and I have no idea where he is. I could call him, but I don't want to tip him off that I'm spying on him.

Frustrated with sitting here, I decide to give FBI Agent Newman a call instead to see if there have been any new developments.

"Hey, Gemma. I'm glad you rang. I was about to call you, in fact. We've made some progress but could use your help. Because Bianca ran in the same circle as you, I was taking a look through your Instagram account and noticed a comment from a @queen_kylie the other day, indicating that you had recently coached her? I was wondering if that was the case, and what you could tell me about her? It appears that Bianca also coached her and that they had a falling-out shortly before she was murdered."

I didn't realize that Bianca and Kylie had a falling-out. Kylie

never mentioned it. As a matter of fact, Kylie was always telling me how much better of a coach Bianca was. And I don't
recall Kylie leaving Bianca any nasty comments, like the one
she left in response to my "How a Coach Can Help You" post
this morning:

> Maybe another coach, but not this coach. True
> testimonial: I recently finished Gemma's six-week
> program and was hungry all the time. This muddled my
> thoughts and caused me to slip into a dark place. My
> life fell apart. I lost my boyfriend, got in a car accident,
> and was put on a Performance Improvement Plan at
> work. Her program sets you up for failure. Gemma is a
> charlatan peddler of Diet Culture.

Upon reading it, my first thought was: @fat_and_fabulous.
The language. The tone. Could Kylie actually be @fat_and_fab-
ulous? Does the same person have two separate accounts and
has she used the @queen_kylie one to infiltrate my life? Was
she the one who hacked my email? The thought sent me into a
tailspin. That there was an enemy out there watching my every
move. I felt like a mouse swimming for my life in a tank while
a scientist with a stopwatch coolly observed how long until my
limbs gave out.

Of course, now that I think about it, I deleted Kylie's comment right after I read it. Bianca probably did the same thing.
Agent Newman must have seen Kylie's comment before I deleted it.

I give Newman a rundown of how batshit crazy Kylie is.
Her incessant phone calls. The ice cream episode. The boyfriend. The Adderall.

He asks, "Did she ever make you feel unsafe?"

"Well, considering that she lives in Tampa, not really. Although, I briefly got worried when I thought I saw her in a video at the Tampa FitExpo, where Bianca was murdered. But I asked her about it, and she says she wasn't there."

"That's what she told me, as well. But after reviewing GPS satellite and cell tower records, we can place her iPhone in the area at the time of Bianca's death. I'd like to see that video you're referring to, please. Can you tell me how I could find it?"

I can't speak. Kylie *was* at the FitExpo. She straight up lied to me. Why would she do that unless she had something to hide?

"Gemma? Are you there?"

"Oh, yes, sorry."

"Also, the last time we talked, you had mentioned a possible link between your teammate Anita Riddle and Rachel. I took a look into that. I'm wondering, did Anita ever mention that Rachel quit taking her calls?"

Nails screech across my brain. "What? No! I didn't know Rachel wouldn't take her calls. Anita posted about how tragic Rachel's death was."

"Yes, I saw that. But prior to Rachel's death, she was preparing to take out a restraining order against Anita."

"Why?"

"I was hoping you could tell me. Anita is denying it, but Rachel's photographer insists she was."

Somehow, I stumble through the rest of the call. I hear my voice coming from far away, answering more of Newman's questions. But, basically, I'm useless. Agent Newman knows more about the people in my life than I do.

Chapter 36

ASHLEY

The Cadillac Escalade cuts in front of me as I pull out of the salon parking lot. Something about its bumper sticker, "Keep Honking, I'm Reloading," niggles my brain. And then I have it: This is the same Escalade that almost ran me over outside my apartment. The one whose driver yelled, *Hurry up, you fat bitch*, and flipped me off. The one that made me trip and fall.

I remember that long-ago Ashley, who meekly got back up and carried on, as if nothing happened. Who never fought back. Who swallowed her pride.

She's long gone.

The Escalade travels through several lights, over a bridge, around a bend. Eventually, it turns into a strip mall parking lot.

So do I.

The man parks and heads into a real estate office.

I park in front of a darkened window with a faded Going Out of Business sign. Spindly limbs of naked mannequins haunt its depths. I sit in my car, deciding on a course of action.

The parking lot is deserted. The strip mall miserable, with

its costume shop, sketchy diner, and vacant storefronts. A veritable ghost town. It's two p.m. on a weekday.

A plan forms. I move my car to the front of a vacant party store, one spot over from the Escalade. I park with the nose pointing out, so that our driver doors face each other.

I march to the office and throw open its door. Something jangles. The air smells like tuna fish.

There are four women working, two of whom are also overweight. I see no men, other than Escalade man. He's eating a tuna fish sandwich and talking on the phone. He glances up at me, standing by the door, eyes boring down on him. "I'll call you back," he says and hangs up.

One of the overweight women, a middle-aged receptionist in a flowered dress, looks up and asks if she can help me.

I raise my hand and point at the man. My finger does not tremble. With a strong voice and level gaze, I declare, "He almost ran me over in the street a couple months ago. On purpose. He called me a fat bitch. As if my being fat somehow makes it okay for him to run me over and say cruel things."

All the office women's heads swivel in sync toward him.

The color drains out of his face. He clears his throat and replies indignantly, "You must have the wrong person." He starts to shuffle papers around his desk. The women look at one another, then back at him hatefully. They don't seem at all surprised.

"I don't," I say, and walk out.

I'm not done yet. The sizzle of vengeance coursing through my veins has not been quenched.

I start my car, leave it running, and get out, keeping the driver's door open. I pop the trunk and retrieve the tire iron. Look around to verify that no one is about. No one is. None of the stores appear to have cameras, and the Escalade is parked out of view of the real estate office.

I shut the trunk and walk to the driver's side of the Escalade, tire iron in hand. I stand there, like I'm standing on the edge of a canyon, deciding whether to jump. Teetering on the edge of before and after, feeling the stagnant air hang heavy around me. Slowly, I pull the tire iron back over my right shoulder like a baseball bat. I wait another moment. Then two. Finally, I take a deep breath.

Explosively, I swing the tire iron forward. Smash it through the driver's side window. I use my hips, just like Tony's taught me. There are millions of pieces of glass everywhere. Like diamonds. The car's alarm goes off.

I throw the iron in my car and am about to jump in when a hand grabs my arm. I smell tuna.

"Where do you think you're going?" says the Escalade man. "I'm calling 911." With his free hand, he retrieves his cell from his back pocket.

I remember Ruddy impeding my blow at the *Shrinking* campus. My humiliating defeat. Not this time.

Quick as lightning, I throw a left hook square to Escalade man's jaw. His face whips to the right. His body follows. His phone, airborne, travels in the same direction. All land on the pavement hard. The phone's screen shatters. Escalade man is out cold.

Everything is still. The only sound the blood whooshing in my ears. Then, slowly, my attention returns to my surroundings. The Escalade's alarm is still going off. There's a scruffy guy stopped in the doorway of the diner, carryout in hand, mouth hanging open.

Time to go. I jump in my car and peel out of the parking lot. Make a hard left and fishtail onto the main drive. My tires squeal. The smell of burning rubber curls through the air.

After a mile or so, I exit the main drag and park. My left

knuckles are red and puffy. A few are skinned. Both hands are reverberating from when the tire iron connected with the window. My whole body is reverberating with the thrill of it all. I look down and notice that my arms are sparkling amidst flecks of blood and realize that I have tiny bits of glass embedded in them.

That I am dazzling.

Chapter 37

KYLIE

Kylie throws her purse on the passenger seat and slams the car door shut. She places her hands on the steering wheel, mostly to keep them from shaking. Her manager sent her home for the evening, and she's afraid she's going to get fired. She can't get fired. She hasn't held a job longer than five months, ever, and she's twenty-three years old.

Tonight's shitshow was all because she screwed up the olives. To which her customer, apparently, was deathly allergic. Whatever. She's going to live. The paramedics said so. Right after they shot her full of epinephrine and wheeled her out of the restaurant.

In her shitty fifteen-year-old car, with its back fender held on by a bungee cord, she drives cautiously home. Back at Jim's apartment, she quietly lets herself in. She doesn't feel like talking, and he's been sort of moody lately. Tiptoeing to the bedroom, she overhears him having a one-sided conversation; he must be on his phone.

"I miss you," he says. Kylie stops in the hallway, afraid to move. Afraid to breathe. She places one hand gingerly against the wall, as much for balance as to touch something real and solid. Jim continues, "I know. I don't know what I was thinking." Kylie's breath is shallow and quiet. "She's just not you. No one's you." He must be talking to Shanna, who's at least ten pounds heavier than her. How could this happen? "I know. You're right." More silence. "Can I see you?" Silence. "When?" Silence. "Be right there."

Kylie hears him travel through the apartment. She ducks into the bedroom and listens as he scrapes his keys off the counter. The front door shuts definitively after him. She is all alone.

Jim's going to get back together with Shanna. He's going to kick her out. She will be jobless and homeless. Her credit cards are all maxed out, and she doesn't have any friends close enough to let her crash on their couch.

She briefly considers contacting her new follower, @fat_and_fabulous, who direct messaged her to see if she was coming to the REIGN protest in Orlando. Rather than tell her that she wouldn't be caught dead at a Fat Activism protest (it's seriously the stuff of nightmares), she simply wrote that it was a little early for her to make the drive from Tampa. Right away @fat_and_fabulous (call her Ashley) offered her a place to stay.

Should she take Ashley up on her offer? Feign sick on the day of the protest? Linger for a few extra days (or a week or a month)?

Almost immediately she comes to her senses. Of course not. Staying with Ashley would mean hanging out with her, and she might get fat as a result. Ashley's lifestyle being contagious, and all.

Kylie lays down on the bed, still in her work uniform, with its smear of disgusting sour cream above her left breast and smell of stale grease permeating the room. The smart thing would be to go to Indeed.com and apply for twenty different jobs, then to Craigslist to see if she can find a quick sublet or room share. But Kylie's never been a fan of the smart thing. Instead, she simply wants to zone out and pretend she's far away, living a different life.

She opens Instagram and sees all the girls who are prettier than she is, living lives that are more glamorous than hers. She no longer follows Gemma on general principle and tries not to look at her page, either. But she keeps getting sucked back.

Kylie remembers when she first stumbled on Gemma's account. It was like washing up on the shores of a warm, sandy beach after having been lost at sea. She had been adrift since Bianca fired her as a client. And Bianca didn't just fire her. Bianca told her to never contact her again. She went on to block Kylie's number, Instagram account, and email. Talk about poor customer service. Kylie left her a bad Yelp review.

But here was Gemma, shining the way like the northern star. It was one of Gemma's transformation posts that sucked her in. There was the Before picture, where Gemma was disgustingly fat. Kylie would never post a picture of herself if she looked that bad. Gemma had limp brown hair and was wearing a frumpy blouse and elastic waistband slacks (yes, "slacks" is the term one would use to describe such a hideous item). This regrettable picture was juxtaposed with an After, where Gemma now sported abs one could bounce quarters off of.

Kylie kept scrolling through Gemma's posts. Once she got to the first one, she read them through again, oldest to newest. The thing that struck her was that Gemma's life used to suck, but she changed it, post by post, and now it doesn't suck. She lost a bunch of weight and became beautiful and popular. Successful. She even scored a gorgeous husband in the process. It's like her posts are a trail of breadcrumbs, and if Kylie can only follow the trail, she, too, can be beautiful, popular, successful, and have a gorgeous guy.

Like a morphine addict craving a fix, Kylie navigates to Gemma's account, and can't believe her eyes. The bitch is in Orlando for the Olympia. What gall. Not that long ago, Gemma was telling Kylie that she shouldn't compete in a measly local bodybuilding contest because she wasn't "in a good space mentally." What-the-fuck-ever. Like Gemma is? What a hypocrite.

Kylie pulls a battered red notebook out from between the mattress and box spring. *GEMMA* is scratched in black ink on its cover. She's careful to only bring the notebook out when Jim's not around. Doesn't want to give him the wrong idea.

She turns to a fresh page, writes the date, and begins to detail this recent hypocrisy, along with any other grievances that come to mind. She writes and writes until her hand aches. Presses so hard that the pen occasionally tears through the page. Sometimes she doubles back and writes in the margins, or in the space between lines, to capture additional thoughts. Kylie knows it would be easier if she kept her notes in Word on her laptop, but there's something cathartic about scrawling her words down on paper. It's as if the pen is hooked up to her vein, and she's bleeding ink across the page.

She's been building this catalog for a while now. In addition to her journal-style entries, it includes pictures of Gemma, screenshots from Google Maps, and a table of details, such as Gemma's date of birth, address, license plate, and husband's name. The notebook's getting rather full. She may have to get a new one soon. That's what she had to do with Bianca.

Chapter 38

ASHLEY

Whenever I pummel the skull-size bag, I envision Gemma's head. Bouncing off my wraps, snapping back again. Speed bag is my favorite piece of equipment at Tony's.

In fact, for the last several training sessions, speed bag's been all I can talk about. Wanting to open with it like a long-lost friend. Close with it like a kiss goodbye. Then last night, as boxing was wrapping up, Tony handed me a box. "Hey, Ash, I ordered too many of these and thought you might like one." There was a picture of a speed bag on it.

Excitement surged inside me. "Oh, Tony, you're too nice! Here, let me pay you for it." I started to reach for my bag, but he waved me off.

"Nah, you keep it. I got no room in the back, anyway. You'd be doing me a favor."

"Really? You're sure?" Tears pricked at the corners of my eyes, and I blinked rapidly to keep them at bay. This was the sweetest gift anyone had ever given me.

"Yeah, I'm sure." His ears reddened. He looked at the floor, the wall, then finally back at me. "Hey, you want me to swing by and hang it up for you? You gotta anchor the supports to a couple studs."

I don't exactly know what studs are. Something behind the walls. "You'd do that?"

"Sure, I would."

"Well, let me at least make you dinner after to thank you."

"Yeah, I'd like that."

So here it is tonight. My hair is freshly highlighted, and there's veal cacciatore in the oven. Tony is standing on a step stool in the corner of my living room, hanging my new speed bag from a platform that he has expertly anchored to two studs—which it turns out are pieces of wood that run vertically behind the wall at sixteen inches on center. There is a screwdriver sticking out of his back pocket, a pencil tucked behind his ear, and a cordless power drill on the table nearby. I am mesmerized by his competence and find it wildly appealing.

Satisfied, he climbs down off the step stool and starts to lightly punch the bag. The bag swings freely and the platform doesn't budge. "Here, Ash, you try," he says, moving out of the way.

I step up to the bag and hit for a bit.

Tony watches from the side, then moves behind me. "Not bad. Here, step your feet a smidge closer to the bag," he says, placing his hands on my hips, guiding them forward. I can feel his breath on my neck. It's difficult to concentrate. "There you go. Perfect."

I hit for a few more minutes, then finally step away and turn toward him. "Thank you so much." His eyes lock on mine, then travel to the television where a blond-bobbed reporter announces, "Earlier today, a woman smashed an Escalade window with a tire iron. Then, when the owner tried to stop her, she assaulted him, leaving him unconscious on the pavement."

The camera cuts to a scruffy man being interviewed. "She

just punched him. Bam! And down he went." He pantomimes the hook; it's clear he has some boxing experience. "It was the craziest thing, man. A beautiful left hook."

A sketch appears of a fat woman with turbulent hair, dark like coiled snakes. The look on her face is menacing. The artist has clearly taken some liberties. I like it.

Tony looks from the sketch to me. Back to the sketch. Then at me again. He studies my face intently, then gently wraps a lock of my hair around his finger. "Have I told you how much I love your new look?"

I stand on my tiptoes, like I'm reaching for the sky. Tilt my face up and kiss him.

Chapter 39

GEMMA

Two Days Out:
116.7 pounds | 130 g protein | 135 g carbs | 45 g fat

Anita and I sit icily side by side, each arranging a stack of photos on the table in front of us. Meet the Olympians starts in fifteen minutes, and I can already see hundreds of people outside the glass doors of the auditorium. My photos show me squatting beneath the slogan, "Keep your squats low and your standards high."

It's almost embarrassing. I haven't heard from my husband in three days. Am I going to come home to some sort of "Dear Gemma" letter? End up pregnant and unwed? It's almost laughable, in a hysterical, maniacal, screaming sort of way.

Anita's photos have her bent over a red convertible with the slogan, "You've got to want it." What a pair we are.

As Anita's French manicured hands square her stack's corners, I imagine them pulling a waist trainer tight around Bianca's neck. So tight her eyes bulge, their blood vessels bursting like stars, and her face going eggplant. When Anita turns to ask if her eyeliner is smudged, I look into her pale blue eyes and can

only skim their surface. Could these eyes look on dispassion-
ately as Bianca scrambled to breathe, as Rachel banged on a
sauna door and screamed for help? Yes, I realize with a shudder. Yes, they could.

Anita rummages around in her bag. Without looking up,
she asks, "Did an FBI Agent Newman contact you recently?"

"Yes! After Rachel was murdered."

She pulls out a lipstick. Uncaps it and glides deep red gloss
across her lips. "He contacted me too. Knew an awful lot about
me. Like, not only about my history with Rachel, but about me
and Bianca. He'd also been fed some complete bullshit. I wonder
who he was talking to? Must have been someone close to all of
us. Someone trying to take the spotlight off themselves. Maybe
someone with a questionable alibi." She recaps the lipstick and
tosses it in her bag. Turns her cold gaze on me.

"He knew a lot about me too. Apparently, I was on Rachel's
Flop Girl list," I offer up. What does she mean "questionable
alibi"?

"Oh, yeah?" The corners of her mouth turn up. There's a
fleck of red on one tooth.

"Yep. I wonder how long that list was?"

"Bet it was miles and miles." She grins, seemingly buoyed
by the prospect of many murder suspects. Her eyes drift down
to the tattoo on my inner forearm. "That's a cool tattoo. What
type of flower is it?"

"It's a blue lotus."

"Why did you choose that tattoo?"

"Lotuses grow out of the muck and mud into beautiful flowers. And their seeds can withstand thousands of years without
water. They have this amazing will to live."

"That seems like something Craig would like."

"Maybe."

"Do you think he'll stop by tonight? He's so dreamy." Anita sighs. The spaghetti straps on her red sports bra strain as her cleavage heaves.

"I guess."

"Bianca was so lucky that she got to go to China with him. Now that she's gone, he's going to need a new travel companion," she says hopefully. My brain glitches. *Motive* flashes across its screen, followed quickly by *Bianca was with Craig in China?* "Wait. When did she go to China with Craig?"

"Right before she died."

"What were they doing in China?"

"No idea. They quit discussing it once they realized I was nearby. Totally sketch."

"But why—"

Anita cuts me off. "Quick, how's my lipstick?"

My mind is still stuck on Bianca and Craig in China. I respond distractedly, "It's fine."

"You think? Do I have anything in my teeth?" She bares them at me like a racehorse. The red fleck is now gone. They are gleaming, blinding white. Looking at them gives me a headache.

"They're good. Why, what's going on?"

"Shhh! Here he comes." Anita moistens her lips and tosses her hair over her shoulder. It catches me in the face.

I am pulling errant strands of her hair out of my lipstick when Craig walks up carrying a large box. "Hey, ladies, how's it going?"

"It's going great! I'm so looking forward to meeting all our fans," Anita gushes, leaning forward on the table, her biceps driving her breasts together and upward, like two melons proffered in a cornucopia.

"Wonderful. I've brought some REIGN samples that I thought you could hand out." He starts unloading individual packets of Vega, his vegan protein powder. "I'm not going to put them all out; I don't want to clutter up the table. I'll slide the box underneath in case you need to replenish."

Anita says, "Super, thanks so much! Vega is the best."

Craig says, "Say, I'd like it if you both could stick around until this event is completely over and give everyone a chance to meet you. Other years, we've had girls cut out early and that's disappointing."

"I will stay the entire time," Anita answers solemnly, nodding her head.

"Me too," I agree.

An Asian man, midforties, in a business suit approaches our table. Craig says, "Ladies, let me introduce you to a friend of mine. This is Feng."

Anitia and I both say hello. Feng gives us a polite nod, then turns to Craig. "You ready?"

"Ready as I'll ever be." Craig grins, and the two of them leave. Then the doors to the auditorium open and the crush is on. Fan after fan stops by our table. Men and women. Young and old. They want selfies with us. With each other. Autographed pictures. Advice on how to lose weight. Grow their glutes, their shoulders. The best hair extensions. Which flavor of Vega is our favorite? (My opinion: all vegan protein powder sucks, but I keep this to myself.) One relatively soft, thirtyish woman asks Anita, "How do I look like you?"

Anita gives her a once-over and answers, "Change your entire life."

After an hour, my hand is cramping from signing autographs, and I'm starting to feel like a petri dish from all the strangers hugging me. The line shows no signs of letting up, and I'm getting increasingly distracted with thoughts of Bianca and Craig's China trip.

I've just replenished the Vega samples on the table when Craig reappears. "Hey, Gemma, I know I asked you to stay here the whole time, but I need to amend that. Can you come with me, please? There's something I need a competitor's opinion on. Anita, you don't mind if we leave the fans in your very capable hands, do you?"

Oh, thank God. I can finally ask Craig my questions. My mind's been circling round them like a flock of blackbirds. And I can get away from Anita, who I'm starting to think is dangerous.

Anita's smile falters. While it seems she appreciates the compliment, she clearly wants to be the one to help Craig.

Anita answers, "More people have been asking for Gemma than me. Maybe I should be the one to help." She stands.

Craig arches an eyebrow and grins. "Oh, I very much doubt that." Then to me, "Come on, Gemma, let's go."

Chapter 40

ASHLEY

"Lose Five Pounds in a Week!" "Drop Two Dress Sizes in a Month!" "Get a Thigh Gap!"

The magazine headlines assault me as I wait in line at the grocery store. I'm doing my best to ignore them when one jumps out, "Megan Miller's Diet Pill Addiction!"

Everything inside me goes cold. Time slows as I pull the magazine from its rack. I fumble for the story, but the table of contents blurs in my shaking hands.

"Miss, are you going to buy that?" asks the cashier.

I cough an assent and break my women's magazine boycott.

Somehow, I make it home, *no, no, no* ringing in my head the whole way. *No, Lydia wouldn't have. No, this isn't happening. No, this isn't what it seems.* Yet, deep down, I know she did and that it is. I leave the grocery bags on the foyer floor and drop down at the kitchen table. Find the story and spread it open.

Inside sources report that celebrity trainer Megan Miller is a secret diet pill junkie! And she's been one for years. She's tried several times to kick the habit, but the pills keep pulling her back.

Our source states that Megan's partial to stimulants, such as phentermine, which not only suppress her appetite, but give her the energy boost she so desperately needs to get through her grueling days training contestants on the hit reality show, *Shrinking*. Apparently, the pills also give her heart palpitations and high blood pressure. When her last pusher, A New You, refused to prescribe any more pills, despite her pleading, she took her addiction elsewhere.

———

I slap the magazine down on the center table of Lydia's ostentatiously large foyer. "You fucked me over! I could go to jail for this."

Lydia, clad in billowing gold loungewear and matching turban, looks down at the magazine. She appears to skim the first several paragraphs, then looks back at me. Her hazel eyes are kaleidoscopes. "Well, I can certainly see why you might think that, but I had nothing to do with this article."

There's an enormous arrangement of dragon lilies on the table. Their fragrance heavy and sickly sweet. Lydia begins to lovingly finger one.

"But the timing," I protest. "It's too much of a coincidence. Is there someone else that has access to our Phoenix site?"

"No. The site is top secret. Just you and me. And your part in this project is almost done." Slowly, one by one, she pulls the stamens off the lily. Drops them on the table.

"What do you mean *almost*? I thought I *was* done?" Pollen drifts through the air. I suppress an urge to sneeze.

"No, I still need you to install ransomware on their site."
She moves on to another lily. Starts fiddling with it.

"No way. That's too dangerous. They're going to know they
were hacked."

"No, they won't. Look at the article again. It doesn't say
anything about a data breach. It says Megan's information was
provided by 'inside sources.' That could be anyone who worked
at the clinic. Or someone in Megan's inner circle. Her hair-
dresser, cleaning lady, a former friend. The timing just happens
to be coincidental.

"Now, Ashley, you're almost finished. I'd hate to see you fall
short at this juncture. In fact, I'm thinking of recommending
you for a captain position at next month's meeting. Usually, it
takes lieutenants at least a couple years to attain that position.
You're lucky this project came along when it did. I don't know
when another unique opportunity like this might present itself."

Lydia sweeps the discarded flower parts into her cupped
hand. Disposes of them as she walks me to the door. She wipes
her hands on her pants, leaving orange streaks across the gold
fabric. Then cups my cheek and kisses me goodbye. Juicy wet.
Sticky sweet.

Chapter 41

GEMMA

Everything changed between Craig and me the night that Bianca was murdered. The night that I found out my husband was a fucking liar.

After discovering Bianca was strangled, I returned to my room, wired. I needed to talk, needed comfort, needed to establish that indeed I had an alibi. But once I started asking Steve specifics about his evening, he clammed up.

So I left.

I went down to the bar for my own drink. And surprise, surprise, the place was a freezer. Seems the AC wasn't broken, after all. So if Steve wasn't in the bar, where was he? What was he doing? And most important, who was he doing it with?

I briefly shoved these unsettling thoughts aside to perform the mental algorithm necessary to accommodate one glass of chardonnay (125 calories, all carbs), and ordered. I hadn't had a drink since a lunch with Craig several months back. So let's just say my tolerance was negligible.

As I was finishing my glass, questions about my shitty

husband swirling through my brain, who should appear but Craig himself.

"My drinking buddy," I said.

"Oh my. What are you doing out so late? And on a bender, no less," he replied.

I told him how freaked out I was by Bianca's death. Craig had heard about her murder too. That's what brought him down to the bar.

Craig said, "I couldn't stay in my room by myself any longer. I didn't feel safe, you know?"

I did know. It was such a relief to talk to someone who felt the same way.

He bought me a second glass of chardonnay. I threw out the algorithm and told him about my lying husband. Before I knew it, it was last call. Then the lights came on.

Craig and I walked back to the elevator, me weaving slightly. Him holding me by the elbow. No sooner had the elevator doors shut, then we were kissing. Somehow, we made it to his room. And had the best sex I've had in years.

What makes good sex? Someone who desires you. Someone who wants to please you. Craig is both, and it's such a refreshing change. The mysterious La Perla lingerie that arrived at my apartment? Turns out, that was from Craig.

When I got home from the FitExpo, I put a flag on my calendar on October 9. I decided that if my relationship with Steve didn't change by the Olympia, I was filing for divorce.

Once my freedom flag was planted, something inside of me flipped. I no longer felt like I was trapped, like I had to stick this out. Craig and I started seeing each other whenever he was in town, which was suddenly a lot more. We had long calls where we discussed our hopes and dreams (a family, a home in the country). We texted each other good morning and good night. I started making an exit plan for my life with Steve.

I've bobbled a few times, briefly deciding to not give up so easily on my marriage, to make one last herculean effort, only to have my hopes dashed. At which point I doubled back down on the plan. The final dashing was the night I found out Steve wasn't at work, like he said he was.

So here it is, October 7, and I'm in Orlando. Craig and I have left Anita at Meet the Olympians and headed to his room. As soon as the door clicks shut behind us, Craig envelops me. "God, I've missed you," he says.

Chapter 42

ASHLEY

I sit with my finger poised over the Enter key.

Everything is wrong. I shouldn't be doing this. I know I shouldn't be doing this.

And yet . . . I take a deep breath, squint my eyes shut, and click.

Right about now, A New You is realizing that their systems are locked out and they cannot access anything. Ransomware messages are popping up with further instructions from The Phoenix demanding fifty thousand dollars to unlock them. Lydia's going to give me ten percent "for my services" and because I've lost two software programming accounts in the last week. Between my work for her and planning the REIGN protest, I haven't had much time for anything else.

Disgusted with myself, I leave the screen and take a shower. I scrub and scrub, but the dirty feeling won't leave. It's radiating from inside of me.

I towel off and return to my computer, check my inbox. There are several client emails with titles like, "Where are you?" "Urgent!" and "ACTION NEEDED!" I ignore them all.

With a heavy heart, I cancel today's boxing session with Tony. He texts me back a question mark, and I tell him that I have an important deadline for work. As a precaution, I add that I might not be free for dinner either. Tony had planned on taking me to Mariano's. Apparently, they have the best Bolognese sauce in town. I promise him that I'll let him know when my project is finished.

I need to stay available so that as soon as A New You pays, I can get their systems back online. Lydia insists it won't take long, but I'd rather be safe than sorry.

While I wait, I take a look around The Phoenix's site. I'm a hacker, after all.

I peruse org charts, projects, meeting minutes, and the like. I'm a few weeks back, when my eyes snag on a meeting titled "Fit Gurl" and stop. Wasn't *Fit Gurl's* editor the woman that Lydia had me surveil? I open the minutes. They're sparse, with lots of abbreviations and acronyms, but there's her name: Rachel Ballaster. It seems her magazine has waged a war against the Fat Activists, with articles like "Healthy At Any Size? Fat Chance" and "There's Nothing Positive About Body Positivity." Out of curiosity, I navigate to *Fit Gurl's* site to read some of these horrid creations.

My stomach drops like a brick. There's a hot pink banner across their home page with curling white letters, "In Loving Memory." Below it is a photo of Rachel, her breasts bursting over a hot pink sports bra. The dates of her birth and death.

The date of her death kicks me in the ribs. It's the same date that I'm to tell anyone who asks that Lydia and I spent the day binging *Downton Abbey.*

This has to be a coincidence. It just has to be. I google more about Rachel's death and learn that she died locked in a sauna. I breathe a sigh of relief. Whomever killed her would have had to know her well enough to have access to her home. That's none of Lydia's crew.

Nevertheless, I'm still rattled. As if to prove to myself that everything's fine, I return to The Phoenix's site and dig deeper. I paw through hidden and deleted files. Back and back I go, until I stumble across a folder named "Utilities."

Inside is all sorts of information about making bombs. Ingredients and where to buy them, how to assemble, blast radii, choosing a location, how to transport, and . . . practical tips. Practical tips? There is nothing practical about any of this. Thousands of imaginary spiders race across my skin.

Frantically I try to exit the system, to unsee what I saw, but spot the note. It starts out: *To the hacker who replaces me . . .*

Chapter 43

GEMMA

"What were you doing in China with Bianca?" I ask.

Craig's face tightens briefly, then relaxes into a good-natured smile. "Where'd you hear that?"

"Anita told me just now."

"Well, she certainly is a nosy one."

"So what were you doing in China with Bianca?"

Craig laughs at my persistence. "If you must know, I was looking at a factory, thinking of doing a small amount of business there. Turned out to be a no-go. Bianca wanted to tag along. Learn more about the garment business. She was thinking of manufacturing her waist trainers there, or something like that. She spent most of her time at the spa. You're not jealous, are you?"

He seems so genuine. The explanation fits. I guess. "No. I was just wondering. You never mentioned it."

"There wasn't much to mention. Now, what does a man have to do to get some attention around here," he says with a grin, slipping down the shoulder straps of my sports bra.

Ever since my positive pregnancy test, which seems like ages

ago, I've been practicing over and over how to tell him. My plan
had been to do it as soon as we were alone. But I keep losing my
nerve. Now after the Bianca/China discussion, this doesn't feel like
the right time either. Also, I don't know for sure that this baby is
his—although I sort of think it is (Steve and I have barely had sex
since my last period). But what if it's not? This conversation will
be pretty heavy. It might be nice to have sex first (and soften him
up?) before I share my news. My mind is racing with these thoughts
as Craig leads me to his suite's bedroom and strips off my clothes.

Before I realize it, Craig is on top of me. There doesn't seem
to be a good opening to say, *Hey, I've got something to tell you.* So
instead I keep my mouth shut—or rather, open but occupied.

Once we're done, Craig rolls off of me. He props himself
up on his elbow, traces a finger over my stomach, and asks, "Is
everything okay? You seem sort of distracted." God, am I that
transparent? As much as I hate that I must be, this is the perfect opening.

I take a deep breath. "Well, actually, something has come up."

"You're filing for divorce." He says it flatly, and my stomach
twinges. Although we never discussed me filing for divorce, I
thought he'd be excited to learn that I'm about to become single.

I work to keep the waver out of my voice. "Um, yeah, but
that's not what I wanted to discuss." At least not yet.

He looks relieved that he's not going to get sucked into
my drama, and I dread the blow that I'm about to deliver. "So
what is it?" he asks.

I look directly at him. His clear blue eyes search mine. "I'm
pregnant."

Craig's eyebrows shoot up. His bottom lip drops and he
retracts his torso a couple inches. He looks down at my stomach, where his hand is frozen, like he expects to see some sort
of answer there.

An overwhelming urge to explain (explain what?) bubbles up inside me—a desire to fill the silence with words. But I won't let myself speak. I will keep my mouth shut until he asks me to leave or walks out of this room, if that's what it takes. The next move is his.

The only sound is the rise and fall of his breath for several seconds. Then finally, he pulls his eyes from my stomach, back to mine, and asks, "Is it mine?"

The question stings. I was prepared for it—although I hadn't expected it to be the first question, I had expected a little more finesse—but nonetheless, it smarts. It's not the question you want to hear when you tell someone you're expecting their child. But considering I'm married to someone else, and this baby may very well not be Craig's, the question is warranted.

I swallow and hold his gaze. "I don't know. But I think it is."

Craig closes his eyes, takes a deep breath. Eyelashes, long and dark, dust his cheeks. They open and he exhales. "What are you going to do?" I note that he says "you," not "we."

"I'm going to have it." My voice is confident, but inside I'm reeling. Can I do this without Craig's help? Can I do this without Fat Gemma winning?

If I win the Olympia, I'm sure I can. The win will bring me more sponsors, better sponsors. There will be appearances on talk shows, spreads in magazines. People buying my fitness plans and products galore. Maybe I'll remarket myself as some sort of maternal fitness goddess. I could do a whole Fit Pregnancy series. Then a Fit Mom series. The opportunities are endless.

Now, I just need to win this Saturday. And stay alive.

Chapter 44

ANITA

Anita *does* mind that she's been left at the Meet the Olympians alone. In fact, she minds very much. But neither Craig nor Gemma really gave her an option, did they? And Gemma, who's married, knows Anita has the hots for Craig. Gemma should have graciously bowed out. But she didn't, because she's selfish that way.

Anita's been stuck at this table ever since they abandoned her. Fan after fan bombards her with questions, but one question in particular is really starting to piss her off: "Where's Gemma?"

Gemma's name card is still on the table next to her stupid stack of photos. All Anita can answer is that Gemma had to step away. Through the onslaught of questions, Anita comes to realize that, no, she doesn't know when Gemma will be back, where she went, or even *if* she will be back. Anita notes that Gemma took her purse with her.

One annoying scrawny teenager, Andrew, apparently decides to wait for Gemma. He constantly checks his phone and scans the crowd. Occasionally he peppers Anita, who is trying to interact with *her* fans, with the most inane questions: "Do you think she's okay?" "Should you try calling her?" "Should we alert someone?"

When Anita can take it no longer, she says, "Don't you need to go home? Isn't it, like, a school night?"

"I already graduated. I run a hedge fund now." The teenager puffs up his nonexistent chest.

Anita thrusts a fistful of Vega samples at him. "You need to start benching and eating more protein."

Andrew doesn't accept the samples. Instead, he stalks off fifteen feet and leans against the wall, glowering at her. Waiting for Gemma.

Finally, the whole debacle is over and the fans are gone. All except Andrew. A heap of a man in a tight Staff shirt has to ask him to leave. Andrew scowls at Anita on his way out, like it's her fault Gemma blew off her fans.

There's still half a box of Vega left. This is not a bad thing. She now has an excuse to stop by Craig's room. Someone needs to return these samples.

Anita places her extra photos inside the Vega box. Leaves Gemma's on the table for the staff to dispose of. The box is large and awkward, but she manages to pick it up. She carries it out of the auditorium, up the stairwell, and across the skyway. At one point, a couple of fans stop her for a picture. *Um, where were you during Meet the Olympians?* she wants to scream. But instead, she poses with each fan while the other snaps photos. She lets them drape their flabby, sticky arms around her, even lets them pick out a couple packets of Vega. And then they go on their merry fucking way, without even asking if she could use some help.

She picks the box back up and soldiers on. Has a dim recollection from high school mythology of someone rolling a stone up a hill for punishment.

Once she's in the hotel, she gets a bellboy to watch the box for a few minutes while she heads to the bathroom. First, she pees. Next, she washes her crotch in the sink. An older woman in elastic pants exits a stall while she's doing this and blanches. Anita ignores her. The woman quickly washes her hands and leaves, dripping water after her as Anita is patting herself dry with paper towels. Anita's shaved completely bare, so everything dries quickly. She fixes her lipstick, checks her teeth, and fluffs her hair.

Okay, she's ready.

She retrieves the box and heads up to Craig's room. She knocks, but there's no answer. She knocks again. "Craig! I have the extra Vega samples."

From inside, Craig answers, "Okay, hold on a minute."

It's longer than a minute. Possibly two, maybe three. Finally, Craig opens the door. "Thanks, Anita. You can leave them here," he says, indicating the foyer. But she's already carrying the box into the main room. He has to step out of the way to keep from being run over.

Once in, she drops the box. Craig stands there holding the hall door open. She ignores the open door, and says, "I tried texting both you and Gemma but neither of you responded. She never came back, you know. I stayed at Meet the Olympians all by myself."

"Wow, thanks so much. I really appreciate everything you do." Craig is still standing there holding the door open.

"Do you want me to take these to your room with the others?" She picks the box back up and starts walking down the hall toward the bedroom.

"No! Anita, seriously, no. I've got it. Please. I need a little privacy. I've had a long day."

She is already halfway to the bedroom when, through its

partially open door, she catches a glimpse of a woman's leg, paused while slipping into a pair of leggings. Like the woman doesn't want to be discovered. And then Anita spies it. The blue lotus tattoo on the woman's forearm.

Anita slowly turns back to Craig. For the first time, she notices that his T-shirt is inside out. His feet are bare. She drops the box.

What an idiot she's been, working slavishly away while Gemma and Craig fuck in bed. She wonders if they were laughing at her? Then realizes they weren't thinking of her at all.

"I've got to go," she says, and stumbles out the door.

That bitch. Gemma thinks she can have it all—a handsome husband, Craig, a flourishing business, and the Olympia crown. Bianca and Rachel thought the same thing. And look what happened to them.

Anita doesn't feel sorry about that. Not one bit.

Chapter 45

GEMMA

One Day Out:
117.0 pounds | 130 g protein | 150 g carbs | 45 g fat

The video grid of my apartment rooms starts to bend and bleed. I've been watching it at every opportunity since Steve left. I watch it while I eat. While I brush my teeth. While I talk on the phone. I watch it when I wake up in the middle of the night. First thing in the morning. All I see are empty rooms. When I shut my eyes, I see a grid-like pattern on the back of my eyelids.

As the video rooms blur, I consider how epically bad yesterday went with Craig. The tightness in his face when I told him I was having my baby said it all. It's clear he wants no part of this. His feigned concern and thinly concealed self-interest were insulting.

"I don't know, Gemma, have you really thought this through?"

"Yes."

"That's a lot to take on. I don't know how much I can be there right now for you. I'm really busy with work and just got divorced."

"Noted."

"Is that really fair to a child? To bring them into such uncertainty?"

It went on like this until I finally said, "I need to get going."

I was getting out of bed when there was a knock at the door. We both looked at each other, and then the clock on the nightstand. I don't think either of us had realized how late it was. The knock came again. "Craig! I have all the Vega samples from today."

"Fuck," Craig said, springing from bed and looking around for his clothes. "Wait here," he mouthed to me, pulling a T-shirt over his head and stepping into a pair of shorts as he hopped out of the room.

I had no intention of waiting. While Craig was dealing with Anita I got dressed. At one point, I could hear her walking toward the bedroom. I ducked away from the door and held my breath, but she turned and left.

Craig came back to the bedroom and wanted to talk, but I'd heard enough. However, I didn't want to walk into the hall yet. I couldn't risk ending up on the same elevator as Anita, reeking of sex. Not only would she view me as a romantic obstacle to be done away with, she'd consider my dalliance with him a personal affront. In fact, I wouldn't put it past her to follow me to my room, smash my head into the door, and drag me inside by my armpits. Then fix her lipstick in the vanity while I bled out in the background.

So I locked myself in Craig's bathroom for three long minutes, ignoring his incessant attempts to talk, then walked out. And kept walking. Out of Craig's room, out of his life. Craig trailed after me. "Gemma, I really think you're making a mistake."

I pressed the down button and prayed for the elevator, just this once, to be there. "No, Craig, I *made* a mistake. I'm not making another." And like an answered prayer, the elevator doors slid open. I stepped into it and was saved from further conversation by an audience of passengers. Craig's eyes bored into me as the doors shut.

What a mess I've made of my life. And of my baby's, before it's even born.

Because I never knew my father, I always promised myself that if I ever had a baby, they would get to have a real dad. Someone to lift them high in the sky. To read them bedtime stories. To chase away the monsters. All the things I never had.

Growing up, I badgered my mom for any information about my mysterious father. She would always reply that she didn't know who he was, or claim she couldn't remember, or ask why the hell I kept asking the same damn question.

But I had a hazy memory of a man, big as a giant, carrying me on his shoulders. His hair was soft and brown and wispy on top. Where it was thin, his sunburned scalp peeked through. He smelled like the forest. Out of all my mother's boyfriends that had come and gone, this one stood out. I asked her about him repeatedly, but she stubbornly maintained that she didn't know whom I was talking about.

I knew she was lying.

A couple of years ago, she was hit by an SUV while crossing the street in the middle of the block between two parked cars. She had been leaving a bar and died on impact. It was a twenty-year-old boy that hit her on his way home from his shift at a 7-Eleven. He has since apologized profusely. Told me he thinks about it every day.

Her death was so typical—fucking up someone else's life with her dumb, selfish choices. I told that boy that I don't blame him at all. That it was her fault.

After she was gone, I realized I was never going to get any

more information about my father unless I sought it out myself. So I hired a genealogist. It cost me almost a thousand dollars. I had to put it on my credit card, but it was worth it. Because the genealogist delivered.

Once I had my father's name, I looked him up on Linke-dIn. It was the shoulder-ride man, mostly bald now. We had the same dark brown eyes. The same nose.

But I hesitated to contact him. The genealogist's report included a note that he was married and had a daughter. Imagine that. He already had a daughter. A legitimate one. Why would he want one who's illegitimate (not recognized as lawful off-spring, not sanctioned, illegal, irregular, not in good usage)? I was the daughter he actively chose to walk away from. The one he knowingly rejected. I wasn't even a second-class citizen. I was exiled. How do you reach out to that?

Eventually, I convinced myself that just because he knew he had a daughter, that didn't necessarily mean that he walked away from me. My mother could have spirited me away in the night. Or threatened him to never contact us again or she would tell his wife. Maybe he thought about me every day?

Thanks to LinkedIn, I had his place of employment. I booked his last appointment on a Wednesday. I had hopes of him hugging me and taking me out for dinner.

Hope, it should be noted, is a four-letter word.

Although I had rehearsed this moment a zillion times, I was unprepared for the real-life experience. As soon as I walked in, I could feel that he was my father. Feel a magnetized pull from him at a cellular level, like all my atoms lined up with his and hummed. I forgot everything that I had planned to say. Instead, I stood there staring at him. Finally, I realized that he had asked me a question. "I'm sorry, what did you say?" I asked, my tongue too big for my mouth.

He looked perplexed. "I said, what can I do for you?"

And without further ado, out tumbled, "I'm your daughter."

He sat forward in his chair. Put his palms flat on his desk, as if to steady himself. He seemed embarrassed. Like he'd been caught cheating. I suppose, in a way, he had.

The genealogist had suggested I bring documentation to show him. Since I didn't know what else to do, and it was suddenly so quiet, I began showing him the documents. He accepted them one by one as I walked him through them. I don't think he'd have noticed if they were in Greek.

After the last document, he sat back in his chair, removed his glasses, and sized me up. He looked ten years older than when I walked in. Gone was the mask of affable professional. Rubbing a hand across his face, he asked, "What do you want?"

I recoiled like he slapped me. After considering all the possible scenarios of how this could go, never once had I imagined that question. "I just wanted to see you again. I remember you from when I was little. I remember you carrying me on your shoulders."

His face crumpled. He looked at his desk, blinked a few times, and swallowed. "I remember you too. I'm sorry I wasn't around for you."

The air hung still and silent. He looked back up. "But as you're probably aware, I'm married; I already have a family. As a matter of fact, I have plans with my wife this evening, so I'm afraid I need to get going." He began stacking the papers I gave him. Once the stack was assembled, he placed it neatly in a desk drawer. His desk was now clear and empty. Free of my mess.

I must have looked crestfallen, because his face softened. "Look, Gemma, this is a lot for me to take in. Give me some time to work through it, okay?"

This was my cue to leave. I stood. "Well, it was nice to see you again," I said, and held out my hand. We shook awkwardly and I left. Never in my wildest dreams did I imagine it ending with a handshake.

That was in Orlando last year, three days before the Olympia. The evening before the *Fit Bodies* anniversary cake debacle. Before Fat Gemma's resurgence.

My father never contacted me again. In fact, he died of a massive coronary three weeks later. A part of me wonders if seeing me again somehow triggered it. I never contacted my half sister. What if she blames me? There's only so much rejection one can take.

So here I am now, back in Orlando. Pregnant and alone. Bringing a baby into this world to potentially the same fate. I am so ashamed.

Order a chocolate sundae, whispers Fat Gemma. *After this day, you deserve it.*

It's like a siren's song. I'm so lonely and so tired. What I wouldn't give for the comfort of heavy cream and sugar. But I have to win this competition. Now that I'm having a baby, this may be my last chance.

"No, Fat Gemma, I'm going to win the Bikini Olympia and do away with you forever."

She laughs like an evil witch. "Honey, I'm not going anywhere."

My phone starts buzzing. Several messages *bing* through in rapid succession, part of a group text between the Bikini competitors on Rick's team:

"OMG! Did you see? Rick's ex Megan Miller is dead!"

"Are we all fucked? We're all fucked. Who is killing all these fitness girls?"

"Hey, don't overreact. No one is saying she was murdered. Who knows why that shed blew up? I heard Shrinking kept a lot of shit in it, including gasoline and a generator."

"Bet you dollars to donuts it was murder, and by the same person who killed Bianca and Rachel. I mean, Megan was blown up. 'Blow up your metabolism' anyone?"

"Rick is going to freak! He couldn't have done it, could he? I wouldn't put it past him, but he's been here, like, all day. How far is Daytona Beach from Orlando?"

"About an hour."

The phone slips from my hand and lands on the bed next to me. Megan makes three. Three is a trend. I know in my bones that someone's picking us off one by one. Whomever it is, they're on their way to Orlando now. By nightfall, they'll be in this hotel. Come tomorrow, they'll be at the Olympia. Sunday, another one of us will be dead.

I silently get up and shut the drapes. Slide the deadbolt across my door.

The *Jaws* ringtone sounds. Kylie.

Chapter 46

ASHLEY

Pounding. Pounding on my brain.

I burrow deeper under the covers and will it to go away.

"Ashley, open up," Lydia yells.

I drag myself awake, blinking at the midday sun squeezing around my bedroom drapes. More pounding.

"Ashley, open the fucking door!"

It was four in the morning by the time A New You paid. I was on my second pot of coffee and totally strung out. I couldn't believe it took them so long to cough up a measly fifty grand.

Despite trembling fingers and a frazzled brain, I managed to get their systems back online. It feels like I've barely slept.

"Ashley!"

I rub the sleep from my eyes and roll out of bed. Plod to the door. I open it and am hit by the smell of smoke. Lydia's hair is singed at the ends. Her eyebrows are charred. "Oh my God! What happened to you?"

"I was lighting the pilot light in my friend's oven and having trouble, when all of a sudden it exploded."

"Wow—"

"I wasn't far from here and have a meeting shortly. I can't go like this." She gestures to her dress, which is frayed in places. "Then I remembered that you live nearby. Can I use your shower and borrow some clothes?"

I want to ask her about Rachel but don't dare. Not only is it ridiculous to think Lydia had anything to do with Rachel's demise, but to even suggest it will make me sound like I don't trust her. *Do* I trust her? I remember the ominous note from Lydia's former hacker and hesitate.

"Ashley! Are you going to let me in or what?"

I jump aside. "Oh, yes, sure. Sorry, I'm just tired."

I remind myself that I don't know anything about that hacker. Maybe she's just disgruntled? Unreliable? Malicious? I get Lydia a pair of pants and one of my favorite tops. Wordlessly, she takes them into the bathroom.

She emerges fifteen minutes later in a cloud of steam, shaking water from her hair. Wearing my clothes, she carries her old ones out into the hall and tosses them down the garbage chute. I trail her, peppering her with questions that she largely ignores.

Finally, she declares, "I need you to cut my hair."

"What?" I've never done anything like that in my life. "Um, I don't know how to cut hair."

"Oh, come on, it can't be that hard. Just take about a half-inch off everywhere. *Believe* in yourself."

I try. I use my good scissors, the ones I use for wrapping presents, and follow the cut. Actually, it isn't that hard once I get the hang of it.

When I'm finished, snips of hair litter the floor around Lydia's chair. She gets up and goes to the mirror over the bathroom sink.

"What do you think?" I ask, holding my breath.

"It's perfect! See, I told you that you could do it. You can do anything."

She has no idea. "You clean up well," I quip.

Lydia looks at me in the mirror, as if seeing me for the first time. "I do, don't I? And it's a good thing, because sometimes we need to get a little dirty."

I swallow. "I'm starting to realize that."

"Well, I need to run. See you at tomorrow's protest. And, Ashley, it's game on." With that, she gives me a fist bump and sweeps out the front door, leaving a trail of debris in her wake.

Chapter 47

GEMMA

Bianca, Rachel, Megan. Three fitness girls, all dead. All somehow connected to me. Could I be next? I try to convince myself that I'm overreacting but can't. Someone is killing us.

And they're accelerating. Two months ago, it was Bianca. One week ago, Rachel. Today, Megan. Tomorrow is the Olympia. Who will go home in a body bag?

Could the killer be Kylie? She called me three times, back-to-back, after Megan was blown up. The *Jaws* ringtone filling my room. When I finally picked up, simply to stop that infernal tune, she hung up. Just like high school. Just like a scary movie.

If only I can make it until Sunday. Then I can get on a plane and fly out of this death trap.

Fat Gemma keeps picking up the room service menu and perusing the options. I finally shove it under the door, out into the hall, and call housekeeping to take it away.

A text from Craig comes through. "Hey, I'm sorry about yesterday. I've had some time to reflect, and I don't think I handled it as well as I could have."

A new thought slaps me. Craig knew all three. Bianca.

Rachel. Megan. But that's ridiculous. Yes, Craig was angry with Bianca for abandoning REIGN to hawk her waist trainers, but surely not enough to kill her over it. And he had a great working relationship with Rachel and, as far as I know, got along fine with Megan.

I read his text again, and my jaw reflexively clenches at "handled." What an infuriating word. What am I supposed to say? *Oh, that's okay.* It's not how he "handled" it that's the problem, it's the sentiment. When our future was hanging in the balance, he only thought about himself. He didn't offer a whiff of support. Not a single word of encouragement. Not even a hug. I received more support from that mom on the flight the other day, when I was puking into a paper bag.

As much as I don't want to, I need to leave this room. I'm due down at the REIGN booth in twenty minutes. Even though Bikini doesn't compete until tomorrow, lots of other divisions have their Prejudging today. While the Prejudging is going on, an enormous fitness expo takes place around it. To break through the noise and help draw customers, vendors expect their sponsored athletes to make guest appearances at their booths.

I change into the Red Flame leggings and sports bra and head down to the expo, periodically looking over my shoulder and scanning my surroundings. When I reach the REIGN booth, the first thing I notice is the Bombshells Only banner, decorated with exploding fireworks. Apprehension tingles the back of my neck as I recall Megan and her "Blow up your metabolism" tagline.

Anita is wrapping up her own guest appearance, and I look away, not wanting to bother with fake pleasantries. I doubt she could have killed Megan—Anita had her own REIGN booth appearance to worry about—but she sure could have killed Bianca and Rachel. And maybe Megan being killed in that shed's explosion wasn't murder, but just an unfortunate coincidence?

While I wait for Anita to finish, I pull out my phone and check my messages. There are no new security texts from my home. I'm about to slip my phone in my bag when a text comes through from Steve. My heart jumps to my throat. I click on it.

Steve: "Hey, how's it going?"

Not well at all, considering that you packed a bag and left without so much as a giving me a heads-up. It's got me seriously wondering how well I know you. Me: "It's going great! How's everything at home?"

Steve: "Same old, same old. Miss you!"

That lying snake. Me: "Miss you too!"

Steve: "Gotta run to work."

I'm giving him a thumbs-up—all I can muster—when I feel hot breath on my ear. I whirl around, and there's Anita. Close enough to stab me in the back.

"Steve is your husband? You're married, right?" She's got an evil smirk on her face. She knows Steve is my husband. She met him at the FitExpo in Tampa. Where she was, in my opinion, a touch too friendly with him. She asked for his phone number, for crying out loud, under the guise of having an emergency contact for me.

"Yes." I quickly tuck my phone in my purse.

"God, you're no better than Bianca." She rolls her eyes.

All thoughts drop out of my head, and I'm left standing there empty. I don't know what she's talking about. I don't *want* to know what she's talking about. However, I can't stop myself from squeaking, "What do you mean?"

Anita's eyes light up. She leans in close, like we're best friends. Or like she's going to bite me. "Didn't you know? Bianca was getting it on with Craig at practically every show. I mean, why do you think he took her to China? You weren't stupid enough to think it was business related, were you? He must like his women married. That way they can't expect any-thing from him."

It all clicks into place. Bianca, though polite, was always reserved at shows. I invited her out numerous times for drinks after Finals, only to be turned down again and again. She always said she wanted to go to bed early. Well, I guess in a way, that was true. And the La Perla lingerie I saw her wearing? I bet he bought the same set for both of us.

I feel my cheeks flush and just want Anita to go away. So with more bravado than I feel, I say, "Well, looks like you're all done here. Why don't you split?"

Anita picks up a sample protein bar. "Ooooh, look, Gemma! A REIGN protein bar." She holds it up for effect, peels the wrapper halfway down. "Of course, you're already swallowing *loads* of REIGN protein, courtesy of Craig." She suggestively slides the thick bar into her mouth, wraps her lips around it. She bites off a large chunk and winks at me. Turns and saunters away.

Several people are filming the exchange. One mimics the sound of a cat hissing. I want to crawl under a rock.

Instead, I stay and meet the fans. Force a smile. Say the right things. Shelf the thoughts racing through my head.

A young man with peach fuzz on his face says, "It's so great to finally meet you! I'm Andrew, but you know me as @hedge-fundguy1."

"*You're* @hedgefundguy1?" I realize that my eyes are pop-ping, and work to rein them back in, to smooth out my face. "Sorry, you're just younger than I expected. You're in hedge funds?" There's no way this kid is in hedge funds. He's just one more person pretending to be someone online that he's not. This shouldn't surprise me anymore.

"I'm older than I look," Andrew says, straightening up.

"What can I say. I hit success early. There was some luck involved, but it was mostly hard work."

"Well, that's great to hear." I look beyond him, to the increasing line.

"Anyway," Andrew continues, "I was thinking we could
grab a bite after this."

"I'm sorry, I already have plans." This isn't true, but a white
lie never hurts.

A large man, possibly a power lifter, behind Andrew seems
to grow impatient with him. Pushes his way past and says,
"Gemma, my wife's a huge fan of yours. Could you please au-
tograph a picture for her? Her name is Katie."

Andrew appears dumbstruck, but eventually drifts away,
scowling.

When my guest appearance is over, I return to my room,
constantly checking that no one is following me. Once safe, I
sit in front of my laptop with its grid of my apartment's empty
rooms and ponder the two bombs Anita dropped this morning.
First, that she knows Craig and I are sleeping together. She must
have seen me in Craig's room yesterday when she brought the
supplies up. I remember how her footsteps stopped halfway to
the bedroom, when I was only partially dressed, then abruptly
retreated. If indeed she is a serial killer, could I now be next?
And the second, that Craig was seeing Bianca before she died.
Craig never mentioned it.

With shaking fingers, I go to @bianca_summers_xo and
reread her last post, sent from the FitExpo. She's standing in
front of her bubblegum pink Bianca Summers Fitness booth,
decorated with cartoonish figures with exaggerated waists.
There is a tower of Cinch Me! waist trainers to her right. In
the background is the REIGN booth, where Anita looks on
disapprovingly.

There are dark circles under Bianca's eyes. The post beneath reads, "Sorry I've been MIA for the last week. A lot has been going on—the revelations have been never-ending. Suffice to say, things are about to change. Anyway, one of the things I've been working on behind the scenes is my new line of Cinch Me! waist trainers. They're made with industrial strength, American-made fabric. Unlike some other companies. Many thanks to FitExpo for letting me debut them here. If you can't make it to Tampa, you can order them on my website bianca_summers.com. #bossgirl #dreambig #makeawish #thetruthhurts."

There are over a thousand comments below her post. After the first hundred or so, which say things like, That's awesome! and I soooo need one of these, the comments change to RIP, Just heard the news, will miss you terribly, and Heaven got a new angel. I read every single one. From Rick, Bianca, my love, the world will miss your warm heart and smiling face. #devastated. I don't see a comment from Craig.

I read some of her older posts, trying to get a better feel for who Bianca was. Most of them revolve around weight loss or her white Pomeranian, Sam. She hadn't mentioned her husband in the last six months. I stop on a photo of her peeling a neoprene "fat-loss" wrap off her waist. In the post below, she claims that wearing this wrap ($49.95, available on her website) will increase your core body temperature, enabling you to lose inches, drop weight, and tone up loose skin. One of the comments below jumps out, "The world would be better if people like you didn't exist." It's from @Lydia_Fed_Up. Something about that handle looks familiar. I scroll through more of Bianca's posts and find additional comments from @Lydia_Fed_Up, similar to the ones @fat_and_fabulous has left on my account. Lydia has commented on just about every post Bianca made in the last few months before she died, except for the very last one.

I go back to my account, scroll through the history, until I find why @Lydia_Fed_Up looks familiar. This account has liked almost every nasty comment @fat_and_fabulous has left on my account. A cold chill forms in my belly.

It dawns on me that @fat_and_fabulous hasn't commented on my last couple of posts, either. Did she finally get sick of me? Find a more interesting account to harass? Or is she getting ready to take things offline?

I glance at my laptop, expecting empty rectangles, and instead see that Steve is back. And he's with Todd.

They're in the living room. Todd is gesticulating wildly. Even without sound, I can tell he's yelling at Steve.

I leave the grid and zoom in to the living-room-only view. Todd starts pacing around the perimeter with his hands in his hair. After a few laps, he stops abruptly, whirls around, and faces Steve. Says more angry words.

Steve is pleading with him.

Todd throws his hands in the air. Sits down on the sofa and rakes them through his hair.

Steve sits next to him and says something.

Todd pulls his hair down around his ears. Looks at Steve, blinks back tears. More words.

Steve replies and shrugs.

Todd pushes his hair back up, then abandons it and folds his hands tightly in his lap. His hair is sticking up every which way, like waves on a stormy sea.

Steve looks down at his hands. Then up at Todd. He wipes his eyes. Reaches for Todd's hand.

Todd rips it away. More words get said.

Todd abruptly stands. Grabs Steve's bong off the table—the bong I threw away, its crack now duct-taped—and hurls it at the wall. It explodes. Amber glass scatters everywhere.

Steve gets up and goes to Todd, who is now collecting his things. Steve gestures plaintively.

Todd looks at him, as if seeing him for the first time and realizing he's a fraud. I read Todd's lips: *Fuck you*. He turns and walks out. Yanks the front door shut behind him so hard its window cracks.

Chapter 48

ANITA

With Bianca gone, Anita finally thinks she has a chance with Craig. In fact, just the other morning, she had been trying to decide if they should have two or three kids. What would they name them? Private schools or public?

Anita can't believe that Craig ever wasted his time with Bianca. First, she had an ugly horse face. This was amplified when she laughed and made a neighing sound. Second, she was a thief. Stealing people's hard-earned pay with her bullshit fat-loss wraps and worthless waist trainers. And finally, she was a cheating slut. Anita made sure her husband knew, but then he blocked her. *He* blocked *her*! Anita thought it would never end. But then righteousness prevailed, and Bianca was gone.

Since discovering that Gemma and Craig are fucking, the indignation of the whole thing has been on an endless loop in her head. It's not enough that Gemma has over ten times the Instagram followers that Anita has, gets paid (Anita suspects) ten times the amount for her REIGN posts as Anita, and is married to a totally hot guy while Anita is single.

No, Gemma's got to go after the one guy that Anita's been crushing on.

It's so incredibly unfair. And not only to Anita, but to Craig, who deserves to be with someone who's free. In fact, it's unfair to all women everywhere. Gemma's hogging more than her share of hot men. And then there's Gemma's poor, unsuspecting husband, Steve. Anita remembers meeting Steve—she remembers more than just meeting him, in fact—and he's perfect. He looks like a Canadian hockey player. She's seen Gemma's stupid posts where he goes for picnics, and even apple picking, with her. How did she ever coerce him into that? Someone should alert him that his wife is a cheating slut.

Anita decides to be this person. Fortunately, she still has his number from the FitExpo. But will he pick up? He hasn't answered her last few calls. Well, she'll have to try.

She spends a few minutes rehearsing what she'll say and how she'll say it. She'll use a compassionate tone of voice. Though she wants to, she won't call Gemma a slut or say anything that might make him jump to her defense or hang up. She suspects this is where she screwed up with Bianca's husband. This time, she'll stick to the facts. *Hey, I saw your wife getting dressed in another man's bedroom, and his shirt was on inside out.* She'll give him a chance to ask questions.

When she's ready, she dials Steve's number. The phone rings several times and goes to voicemail. A deep tenor answers, "Steve-o here. Leave a message." She doesn't want to leave a message. There's too much to say, so she hangs up. She inhales a great gale of air and realizes she's been holding her breath. After taking a few minutes to collect herself, she repeats this entire process a couple more times, getting the same results.

When it becomes apparent that he's not going to pick up, she decides to text him. She keeps it brief, so he'll have to call her back for details, "Hi Steve. Please call me when you have a chance. You deserve to know what your wife has been up to." Before she hits send, she reviews what she wrote. She asks herself if she really wants to do this. Yes. Yes, she does. Her phone makes a whooshing sound as her text goes out into the ether.

Chapter 49

ASHLEY

"I'm telling you, she looked like she escaped a burning building. Her hair was singed and her clothing tattered. She smelled like a campfire," I say to Tony, next to me on my couch.

"Lydia's an odd duck." He places a slice of meat lovers pizza on a plate and passes it to me.

My stomach rumbles, and I realize that I've barely eaten since yesterday. "This looks amazing. Thank you."

"Babe, I've been worried about you." He opens my sweating Corona.

I take a swig. It's yeasty and delicious, and my head starts to swim. "I've been worried about me too. But I'm finally finished with that horrid project." It's such a relief to see him again. I feel like a storm-throttled ship easing into the harbor.

Tony insisted on coming over tonight and bringing me dinner. He thinks I've been working too hard. And that it's imperative I watch the movie *Rocky*. He can't understand how I've never seen it. Um, maybe because it was released over a decade before I was born?

I'm about to change the TV station when a blond newscaster

says, "And now we have some tragic news. Megan Miller, celebrity trainer of the hit reality TV show *Shrinking,* and ex-wife of renowned bodybuilding coach Rick Schwann, was killed today in an explosion at the *Shrinking* campus."

The screen flashes to a photo of Megan, clad in turquoise shorts so tiny I can see the contours of her vulva. She's filming an episode of *Shrinking,* holding her bullhorn, and apparently shouting at the contestants in front of her doing burpees. The newscaster continues, "Megan joined *Shrinking* in 2016 as an associate trainer and swiftly rose to the position of lead trainer. She was known for her tagline, 'Blow up your metabolism,' tough love, and for pushing contestants to their limits. In recent years, *Shrinking* has come under fire for its extreme diet methods and for encouraging excessive exercise—sometimes for as much as eight hours a day. In 2018, the show was briefly halted after one of its contestants suffered a heart attack while running sprints.

"Megan is the third fitness girl in less than two months to meet an untimely death. First, Bianca Summers was strangled by her own Cinch Me! waist trainer. Next Rachel Ballaster, editor of *Fit Gurl*'s Sweat It Out series, met her demise in a sauna that was locked from the outside. And now, 'Blow up your metabolism' Megan has been, aptly enough, blown up. We're going live to the scene with Eileen Brachman. Eileen, what do you have for us?"

Eileen and a man who looks like an army sergeant appear. Behind them are the blackened remains of a small warehouse next to a running track. The same area I was spying on last week. Inside the track, several monster truck tires lay flat on the grass. Eileen says, "I'm here with FBI Agent Sean Newman. Agent Newman, is Megan's death simply a coincidence, or could it be due to something more sinister?"

Newman answers, "We have not yet been able to determine that. Here's what we do know: While the *Shrinking* contestants were performing tire flips, the batteries on Megan's bullhorn died. She went into the fitness shed to retrieve a fresh set and the shed exploded. No one else was injured. As to the cause of the explosion, we currently have a team at work on that."

Eileen says, "There's been talk of a possible Fit Girl Killer. Could this be the case?"

"We have not yet ruled that out."

"The Olympia is taking place in Orlando tomorrow. Should female contestants be worried?"

"I would encourage all contestants to be mindful of their surroundings. Of anything that doesn't look right. If you see something suspicious, please don't hesitate to notify law enforcement."

"Thank you, Agent Newman. Back to you, Julie."

Tony and I sit perfectly still. Our mouths agape.

Tony runs a hand across the back of his neck and turns to me. "When did you say Lydia showed up here with singed hair and smelling like smoke?"

"Earlier today."

He swallows. "Ash, I don't know about this protest you've got going with Lydia tomorrow. In fact, I think it might be good if you spent a little less time with her."

I stand up, march to the kitchen, and dump my crusts in the trash with a thwack. Start rinsing off my plate. "Tony, it's way too late to back out now."

Tony follows me. "It's not too late. Nothing's ever too late. Take it from me." He puts his plate in the dishwasher.

"Yes, it is! I've already promoted it and have people coming." Not to mention Lydia's whole team.

"So what? Lydia can handle a protest without you. Trust me."

"You think this is just some frivolity?" I slam the dishwasher shut. Start it churning.

"Babe, that's not what I'm saying."

I spin to face him, "Quit calling me 'babe'!"

Tony jerks back like I've slapped him. His face gets red, his voice quiet. "I'm sorry. I didn't know you didn't like that. Maybe I should go." He turns and walks to his jacket.

I hurry after him. "Wait! Tony, wait. I *do* like it when you call me 'babe.' I'm sorry. I've just been under so much pressure lately. With work, the protest. Just everything." My shoulders start to shake.

Tony lets out a sigh. Comes back and puts his arms around me. "Shh. It's okay. But, Ash, I gotta say, I'm worried. I feel like you're getting sucked into Lydia's vortex. That's a risky place to be."

"Don't worry, I'm not. It's just been a busy week with her, that's all. After tomorrow, things will slow down."

He brushes the hair from my face. Looks me in the eyes. "Just promise me that you'll be careful. You don't know Lydia as well as I do. She can be dangerous."

"Don't worry, I'll be fine." At least I hope I will. "Anyway, let's watch this *Rocky* movie you keep raving about."

And so we do, me snuggled into the crook of his arm. Somewhere near the bottom of my second beer, it hits me that the actual fight is almost an afterthought. That the movie is really about a David type of guy who takes on a Goliath, not unlike me taking on the seventy-billion-dollar diet industry. How the hopes of others hang on Rocky because of it. I watch the scene where Rocky runs through the streets of Philly, with the shopkeepers and everyday Joes cheering him on, the kids running after him, and something inside me stirs. I blink back tears as I realize that tomorrow isn't just about me. Tomorrow is about all of us.

Tony has nothing to worry about. Tomorrow, Lydia and I are doing something good.

Show Day

Chapter 50

GEMMA

Show Day:
117.0 pounds, 130 g protein, 150 g carbs, 45 g fat

I wake up all at once. There are no cobwebs to shake off. No moment is needed to identify my surroundings. It's show day.

Nervous energy rattles through me, but not the good kind, typical of a show day. No, this is the energy of Wendy in *The Shining*, hiding from Jack as he calls, "Come out, come out, wherever you are."

My apartment's video feed shows Steve tucked in bed, sleeping. It looks so cozy and safe.

Suddenly, I want to go home. To my warm snuggly bed, with my big strong husband. To my souped-up security system. But I can't just yet. I'm pregnant. And if I'm going to win the Olympia, it's now or never.

Resignedly, I get up. Strip off the oversized shirt I slept in, its insides stained brown from last night's base coat of spray tan, and make my way to the full-length mirror. My tan has darkened into a deep, coffee brown. I look for creases or streaks and don't find too many. Nothing that can't be buffed out at touch-ups. I assess my conditioning and it's spot on: There is some separation between my muscles, but no visible muscle striations. My muscles are full, particularly my shoulders and glutes. So at least I look good, even if inside I'm a wreck.

My mind on the day ahead, I rotely post a photo of my breakfast (raspberries, Greek yogurt, and coffee). I add the hashtag #eatforyourgoals and call it good, then set my phone aside and dig in. The simple meal is divine, and I close my eyes and savor every bite.

Once I'm finished, I pick my phone back up. My lame breakfast post already has hundreds of likes and many comments. I read the first one, and it's all I can do to keep from hurling out my breakfast.

@bikini_wanna_be_me: "Aren't you worried about the dairy causing bloating?"

Shit! What was I thinking? Rick will flip if he sees this. I immediately delete the post. How could I be so careless? Dairy during Peak Week is a big no for Rick. Could he have already seen it? Doubtful, it was only up maybe ten minutes. Nevertheless, acid curls through my stomach.

As if I'm not already rattled enough, a text comes through from Craig, "Please call me."

Not a chance.

On its heels comes a text from Steve. It's simply a screenshot from his phone of a text message, "Hi Steve. Please call me when you have a chance. You deserve to know what your wife has been up to." There is no phone number visible in the screenshot, so I can't see who sent it. Steve provides no more context. I don't know if he called the sender to find out what

I've supposedly been up to. If it's about my affair with Craig or something else.

Who would send this? The obvious candidate is Anita. But she's got enough on her plate with today's contest. What about Craig? Could he be trying to get Steve to drag me (and my baby) home, caveman style? As my employer, he's got Steve's number. And of course, there's Todd, who's always trying to stir up drama between Steve and me.

I should probably just call Steve and ask if he called the sender, if he knows whom it is and what I've supposedly done, but I can't bring myself to. I consider texting him back a question mark, but that could lead to a back and forth exchange, eventually resulting in a phone call anyway. I don't want to talk to him until I can better get my mind around this pregnancy, the fact that he disappeared for four days, and the future of our marriage. I know it's over; I just don't yet know how to unravel it.

Feeling off balance, I head down to tanning touch-ups. The room is abuzz with energy. I check in, strip off my robe and flip-flops and leave them in a corner with my bag. A tanner with a terry-cloth mitt on her hand waves me over. I go and stand completely naked as she assesses me critically, looking for any wrinkle marks left by my bedding, or streaks that have appeared. Then she squirts a dollop of tanner on her mitt and gets to work buffing me out.

While she moves around my body, periodically asking me to extend a leg or arm, to bend over slightly so that she can get the crease where my butt meets my thighs, I survey the room. There are naked women everywhere, all the exact same shade of brown. I see Anita over at the drying station and hope she's almost done. Touch-ups move pretty quickly, and I don't want to get stuck there with her.

Unfortunately, I do. I position myself in front of the open fan next to hers and bury my nose in my phone. I refuse to give her the satisfaction of looking rattled, or of asking her about the text. Anita doesn't look up from her phone, either, but I know she sees me, because she stiffens. We stand there awkward and naked, studiously ignoring each other, while giant fans whir.

A petite brunette joins us at the drying station. "You're Gemma, right? I follow you on Instagram. In fact, that's how I got into bodybuilding in the first place. I can't believe I'm actually standing next to you now. This is my first Olympia. I'm really nervous, you know? Do you have any tips?"

I give her a reassuring smile. "Just be yourself and soak up every minute. It's the journey." To my right, Anita makes a gagging sound.

The brunette turns to Anita. "And you're Anita. I follow you, too. Any tips?"

Without looking up, Anita says, "Not really."

"I'm Crystal from Kentucky, @Kentucky_Girl_Crystal. I was barely able to sleep last night, and then I had makeup at four o'clock this morning with Marissa. It's the only time I could get. I've been up ever since, sitting in my room sort of freaking out. What do you think? I'm wearing a purple bikini. Do you think the purple eyeshadow is too much?" The nerves are rolling off her in waves.

"Not at all! You look fabulous!" I reply. Even if her makeup didn't look good, I wouldn't tell her unless I somehow thought I could fix it. Half of stage presence is confidence. The morning of a show is not the time for anything that could jeopardize that.

Crystal looks to Anita, waiting for a response, but doesn't get one, so I say, "Marissa's the best. In fact, I have an appointment with her in fifteen minutes. I hope I'm not late."

Anita sighs, like our mere presence is annoying her, and walks away. I inwardly breathe a sigh of relief.

———

After tanning, I head to Marissa's room and emerge an hour later a different person. Makeup so thick it could have been applied with a palette knife. Hair dense as a rain forest.

I'm about to head back to my room when I realize my key card is missing from my pocket. It's not in my bag, either. I head to the front desk, and the nice manager, Dale, gets me a new one.

I'm walking through the lobby when one of the girls working the REIGN booth flags me down. "Gemma! Gemma."

"What's up?"

"We're almost out of small Banging Blacks and medium White Hots. Craig's not there, and he's not answering his phone. I left Lacy at the booth by herself and need to get back. Can you swing up to his room and get some more, please? Get, like, twenty each."

"Sure." She hands me Craig's room key that we keep in the booth for emergencies such as this.

As I make my way to his room, I assure myself that he won't be there. That I'll zip in and out without seeing him. Nevertheless, when I arrive at his door, I lean in and listen. The last thing I want is to walk in on him and another woman. Or on him alone. Hearing nothing, I knock on the door loudly. "Craig, we need more leggings."

There's no answer. I knock and call out one more time, then open the door. I walk through the living area and head to the bedroom, where the apparel is kept.

The door to the bedroom is open, and I can see that the

bed has been made up. I breathe a sigh of relief that indeed Craig is not here.

I get to work collecting the needed leggings, piling them into my arms. They stack up to my nose, so I can barely see over them. I am getting ready to head out when I hear voices from the hall. The front door opens.

Not wanting to startle Craig, I'm about to call out that I'm in the bedroom, when I hear him say, "I keep trying to talk to her, but she won't return any of my calls or texts." I take a step closer to the wall, so that I'm not visible from the main room.

A familiar male voice answers, "Women. What you gonna do?" I realize that it's Feng, Craig's friend from Meet the Olympians.

Craig continues, "I need her to end it. Just end it. I don't want to have a kid right now. Especially with a *fitness influencer.*" I can hear the eye roll in his voice. "Besides, I'm having fun playing the field."

"Indeed, you are, my friend. Now, regarding REIGN's apparel, what do you think about letting our factories double our production for you? We have the capacity. And you know our price is unbeatable."

"I've been thinking about it. The only thing that worries me, is our relationship becoming public. It's one thing to hide how forty percent of REIGN's garments are produced, but if we had you produce eighty percent, we would have to considerably reduce the amount our fair-trade factories produce, and that might raise eyebrows."

So after all his woke global citizen bullshit, Craig's been producing his fancy hundred-dollar leggings in sweatshops? My brain bends and twists trying to absorb this revelation. How many times have I listened (and listened) to him wax poetic over ethical fashion? Over unsafe factories, hazardous chemicals, and forced labor? Often with tears in his eyes. At his behest, I slogged through *Wear No Evil: How to Change the World with Your Wardrobe* and jotted down talking points.

How did I ever fall for such a fraud? For such a liar. For such an asshole. I start to get hot with anger, and from the stack of leggings pressed up against my chest. My hands start to sweat.

Craig continues, "Even at forty percent, it managed to catch the eye of Bianca, a fucking 'Fitpreneur,' of all people. If she can figure it out, anyone can. I never should have brought her to China with me. I thought she'd hang out in the spa. Not turn into Nancy Fucking Drew. The shit was set to hit the fan when she died. We got lucky there. I don't know that we can contain it again.

"I mean, I was just on a talk show the other day where I went into the whole ethically sourced, small eco-footprint thing. I'll be strung up if the public realizes that's not necessarily one hundred percent the case. On top of that, there have recently been a few people snooping around, asking questions about the ingredients in our protein powders not aligning with the labels. A sweatshop controversy would throw gasoline on the potential protein powder fire. In fact, I've been thinking of moving out of the United States because of all this. I don't want to end up in jail."

The leggings are getting excruciatingly heavy, and my arms start to shake. My hands are slippery with sweat.

Feng answers, "Okay, okay. Maybe you keep the current volume of business with your fair-trade factories, and send any new growth our way?"

The top pair of White Hots starts to slide off the stack. I press my chin down to hold it still.

"Yes, I think that makes the most sense," Craig replies.

The pair of leggings under the top pair now starts to slide

out. I dig my chin deeper into the stack, but it's no use. The pair clatters to the floor, tag facing up. Near the bottom, it says, "WH – L – m," for White Hot – Leggings – medium. And then it clicks. The rows on Bianca's spreadsheet were abbreviations for REIGN apparel. I stand perfectly still. No one says a thing.

Craig asks, "Who's there?" Footsteps approach the bedroom.

I adjust the leggings in my arms and hide my face behind them. Make for the hallway and answer brightly, "It's just me. The booth is running low on leggings and sent me up for a refresh." I barrel past Craig and Feng and keep moving, the leggings acting as a barrier.

"Gemma, hold on a sec," Craig says, catching up to me as I reach for the door. I jerk the door open and spin sideways. The tower of leggings sways precariously toward him.

I see housekeeping down at the end of the hall and yell, "Hey, housekeeping." The housekeeper turns around to look as I exit Craig's room. "Could you please send a few more towels down here?" I continue to the elevator. Presumably not wanting to create a scene, Craig ducks back into his room.

Chapter 51

ANITA

Decisive. That's what she is. As soon as Anita heard Gemma was getting her hair and makeup done in fifteen minutes, she was out of the drying station. Her tan was dry anyway. The only reason she was still there was because Kentucky Crystal was a Chatty Cathy. Anita figured if she kept her own mouth shut, it might lead to opportunity.

Opportunity is where Anita excels. She sees it where others don't, isn't afraid to reach out and grab it where others won't. Take this morning, for instance. In addition to finding out that Gemma wasn't going back to her room after touch-ups, Anita was able to steal Gemma's key. Silly Gemma had left it in the pocket of her robe, tossed mere inches from Anita's own. While Kentucky Crystal was talking Gemma's ear off, all Anita had to do was reach out and nab it.

Ten minutes later, Anita was on her way to Gemma's room, knowing that she'd have to be quick—she had her own hair and makeup appointment to get to—but when she stepped off the elevator, she stopped short. A housekeeping cart was outside Gemma's room. This was a setback, sure, but not game over. A master adjusts to curveballs. Adapts. Anita took it as a challenge.

Now here she is, hair and makeup complete, back outside Gemma's door. Gemma's likely in her room by now, but fate favors the bold. Anita knocks. "Gemma?"

There's no answer. Is Gemma just ignoring her, or is she really gone? There's only one way to find out.

Anita looks left and right, determines the hall is clear, and lets herself in. "Gemma?" Barely breathing, she tiptoes into the space. It's empty. What luck! Of course, Anita firmly believes that we make our own luck.

She's come for Gemma's suit. Anita hopes it's not in the room safe. That's where she keeps her own. But then, she's smart like that. Gemma, not so much. Gemma has left her ruby red suit, with its scarlet, sapphire, and rainbow crystals, out on the dresser. Anita knows this suit is her favorite. What a nitwit.

Anita retrieves a nail scissors from her pocket and uses it to carefully pluck out over half the stitches on the left side of the bottoms. Her hope is that the suit breaks just prior to, or during, Prejudging. She had considered simply stealing the suit, but figured that then Gemma would have time to find another, whether by purchasing one at the expo, or borrowing one from another competitor. Gemma would need to, because her backup bottoms, which all top-level competitors have, are about to disappear.

Once the red suit bottoms are compromised, Anita digs through Gemma's bag looking for her backup suit. At the bottom, she finds a small carrying case and opens it. Inside is an aqua blue bikini bedazzled with multicolored crystals.

Anita doesn't take the whole suit. That would be too obvious. She only takes the bottoms. Slips the sparkling, beaded fabric into her robe pocket, then puts the carrying case, with the bikini top inside, back in the bottom of Gemma's bag.

She's about to leave, when she spies Gemma's heels in the corner and inspiration strikes. Why not a multi-pronged approach? She picks up the right shoe and works the heel back and forth until it's slightly loose. Maybe it will break while Gemma's onstage, maybe it won't. The uncertainty is thrilling.

She returns to Gemma's bag and finds her backup heels. Breaks the right heel clean off. It makes a popping sound, like a bottle of champagne. Like the sound of success.

Realizing the clock is ticking, Anita swiftly makes her way to the door and peeks out in the hall. It's still clear.

She has barely left the room, when the elevator chimes and Gemma exits, full force, whooshing down the hall at her. The door behind Anita hasn't even shut yet, and she fears she will be caught red-handed. But just in time, it quietly clicks shut.

"Excuse me," Gemma says, elbowing her way past, vanishing into her room in a flurry of blond hair extensions.

Oxygen floods Anita's lungs. On shaky legs, she begins the walk back to her own room at the other end of the hall. She's about halfway there, when the elevator chimes once more. This time, it spits out Detectives Cooper and Stark. These two again?

She remembers the night they met. She was on her way back to her hotel room with a bucket of ice, when a man groomed like an ape and dressed like an accountant came out of Bianca's room. What was a man like that doing with Bianca? Anita took a closer look and saw Bianca in the background—waist trainer around her neck—and promptly dropped the ice bucket on her toe. It really fucking hurt. In fact, her toenail ended up turning black and falling off because of this guy.

"Hi, Anita. We meet again," Cooper says. He eyes her shrewdly, and she knows he doesn't like her. That's okay. She doesn't like him, either. Nor his tight-ass sidekick, Stark, whose eyes are too big. Gemma's suit burns in her pocket.

Anita says nothing.

Cooper continues, "After Megan Miller's death in Daytona Beach yesterday, we thought it might be a good idea to swing by today's Olympia and keep an eye on things. If there is indeed a Fit Girl Killer, they're likely here right now." He gives her a pointed look.

Anita shrugs. "Well, good luck." She turns toward her room.

Detective Stark steps in her path. "See anything unusual?"

Anita considers the question. If she wants these two off her back, she needs to come up with something. "Actually, now that you mention it, there was this weird guy hanging around Meet the Olympians on Thursday night. He was waiting for Gemma. Seemed totally obsessed with her. Security had to ask him to leave. And then yesterday, he stopped by the REIGN booth to see her. Total stalker-like." She makes her eyes go big for emphasis.

Anita goes on to describe Gemma's superfan, who was in desperate need of protein powder and a lifting regimen. Detective Cooper takes notes in a small green notebook. She wonders if there is a page in that notebook on her.

There are several.

When she has nothing more to say, Cooper flips his notebook shut. "Well, thanks Anita. Let's stay in touch."

"Sure." Anita continues on her way. She has no intention of ever talking to these two again.

Chapter 52

GEMMA

The knock is polite and firm. A single double rap on my room's door. No "Housekeeping," no "Hey, Gemma," no nothing.

Still reeling from Craig's *We got lucky there* about Bianca dying, from learning about REIGN's use of sweatshops, I creep to the door and peer through its fish-eye lens. It's Feng, his face bland and placid. Scarily serene. The hallway bends and flexes around him.

Why would he be outside my door? And why wouldn't he announce himself?

On shaky legs I back away. Clutch my phone in my sweaty hand. Has Craig sent Feng here to shut me up? The spreadsheet on Bianca's USB drive must have been product that Craig was having Feng manufacture in China. She must have downloaded it from his laptop. Did Craig realize she copied it? Is that what got her murdered? Could Craig or Feng be the Fit Girl Killer? But if so, I don't understand how Rachel, and possibly Megan, factor in.

I stand motionless, barely breathing. Waiting for him to go away.

Voices approach, a man and a woman. There's another knock. This one is louder. "Gemma? It's Detectives Cooper and Stark."

What are they doing here? I open the door, relieved to find that Feng is gone. But unsettled that I'm on a first-name basis with so many members of law enforcement. I invite the detectives in.

Cooper gets down to business. "We're working with the FBI and thought you should be aware: Megan Miller's death has now been ruled a homicide. That shed didn't explode by accident. Someone planted a homemade bomb inside it and remotely triggered its explosion."

I stagger to the bed and take a seat. The patterned carpet starts to swirl, pinwheels of blue, gold, and sand giving me motion sickness.

Cooper continues, "So if you see anything suspicious— anything at all—or if something doesn't feel right, please call us immediately."

I hesitate, keep my eyes on the spinning carpet, then push out, "Actually, there's a lot that doesn't seem right."

I tell them about the data on Bianca's USB drive. What I heard Craig say this morning about producing REIGN's leggings in Feng's sweatshop. Once I start talking it's hard to stop. It's such a relief to finally get it all out there.

Cooper scribbles in his green notebook while Stark appears to clock my every nuance. When I have nothing left to say, Cooper tucks his notebook away.

He says, "Gemma, we need to run now. But please be careful. And call us if you see anything else suspicious. Anything at all."

Once they're gone, I collapse on my bed and stare at the popcorn ceiling. It looks like a blizzard in a whiteout.

I don't feel safe here. I wish Steve had come to Orlando with me. I could sure use a bodyguard right about now. It sucks that we've grown so far apart, right when I need him most.

There's a pounding on my door. "Gemma, open up. We need to talk." Craig.

I don't answer. My phone starts to ring. Craig's number comes up.

"Gemma, I know you're there. I can hear your phone. Open the damn door."

I silence my ringer and don't budge. My back starts to sweat under all this hair. My breath gets rapid and light. I remember that he's paying for my room and can get a key from the hotel anytime he wishes. I start to scroll through my phone looking for Detective Cooper's number.

Craig pounds a few more times, calls me once more, then appears to give up. Or is he heading down to the lobby for a key?

I've found Cooper's number, but who knows how long it will take him to get here. And Craig's already gone. The best course of action seems to be to flee the room.

I force myself up and prepare to head down to Prejudging early. My hands shake so badly that I can't get one of my earrings in. Finally, I jam it through the hole, and my earlobe starts to bleed.

I toss items in my bag and am about to throw in the case with my backup suit, when out of habit, I open it to verify the suit is inside. Then do a double take. Something is wrong. There is not enough fabric in the case. I pull out the bikini top, and the rest of the case is empty.

This can't be. How could I lose the bottoms? Could they have fallen out and be loose in my carry-on? I dump out the carry-on and repack it, item by item, moving as quickly as I can. The bottoms aren't there. And one of my backup heels is broken!

Why is this happening to me? One problem at a time, I tell myself. I'm not going to worry about the broken heel right now. The pair I'm wearing is new and unlikely to break. And I won't lose them because I won't take them off. Focus on the suit bottoms.

Maybe they're under the bed or between the bed and night-stand? They're not. I check the dresser drawers and bathroom. Time drips through my fingers. Any moment, I expect to hear the room's doorknob turn.

How could the bottoms just disappear? I remember think-ing that someone was in my closet back in Chicago. Did they take my suit bottoms? That seems unlikely.

Then it dawns on me: someone has been in my hotel room. Ice spreads through me. What if they come back? I must get out of here. I grab my bag and bolt.

Once in the lobby, on the off chance my suit bottoms simply fell out of their case and were picked up by housekeeping, I head to the front desk.

People buzz past me in every direction, talking into their phones, talking to each other. Taking selfies and laughing. The fear that was coursing through me five minutes ago starts to dissipate. Maybe I simply needed to get out of my room? Maybe all those people knocking on my door made me paranoid?

The hotel manager, Dale, is finishing up with a guest. As soon as she walks away, I rush up. "You've got to help me! My bikini bottoms disappeared from my hotel room!"

Dale looks baffled. He eyes at my hips, and replies, "You're wearing them." In my haste, the belt on my robe has come open, and indeed, I am wearing bikini bottoms.

"Not *these*. My backup bikini bottoms. I'm wondering if they somehow got mixed up in housekeeping's linens or dropped in the hall? Maybe someone turned them in to the lost and found?"

"Hold on one second." He walks down a few feet and reaches under the counter, produces a wire bin. He brings it back to where I'm standing, and starts pulling items out of it. There are a few cell phones, a makeup bag, and a lightweight jacket. No bikini bottoms. "What did they look like?" he asks.

"They were aqua blue with turquoise, topaz, and peridot Swarovski crystals."

Dale looks momentarily perplexed, then nods. He picks up a phone and dials what must be housekeeping. He asks them if they have found a pair of blue bikini bottoms with beads. They have not. I blink back tears as he asks me for my room number again. I give it to him, along with my cell. He promises that he will let me know the second he hears anything.

I thank him and head backstage. As I'm walking through the lobby, out of the corner of my eye, I see a blond woman in a gold lamé Gucci baseball cap looking at me. I turn to get a better look, just as she turns and walks away. She isn't cut-up enough to be a competitor, but something about her catches my attention. I feel I know her from somewhere. That's not uncommon at competitions, where I see many of the same competitors, their friends and family, makeup artists, coaches, and the like. But I don't feel like I know this woman from a previous competition. Seeing her stirred a wariness in my gut.

The blood drains from my head and pools in my feet. I pull up Anita's Instagram post from the Tampa FitExpo, the one where I thought I saw Kylie in the background. And indeed, both women are wearing the same gold lamé Gucci baseball cap. Kylie has arrived.

Chapter 53

ASHLEY

"Let's Get Ready to Rumble! (club mix)" blares through my speakers. A little pump-up music. I shadowbox in front of the full-length mirror bolted to my bedroom wall. I like what I see: a fierce warrior. My eyes are determined. My skin glistens. Muscles I didn't know I had are starting to emerge.

Since my "Fatties Unite" post, I've had about a dozen people, including Lydia's Florida group, message me that they will be attending today's protest. The plan is to meet in the lobby of the convention center at 10 a.m. We're all dressing in workout clothes and sneakers.

The day feels finely balanced on a wire. Like a breeze could send it toppling in either direction. Every now and then, Tony's warning about Lydia niggles at me, but I swipe it away.

After a quick shower, I drive my Toyota down to the convention center. Make my way to the lobby and behold the scene. There are competitors, coaches, and guests everywhere. Coming and going. Draped over sofas. Scrolling through their phones. Making videos.

The competitors are immediately apparent. They all have

makeup like drag queens and are unnaturally brown. Their hair is so artificial looking, they look like Barbie and friends come to life. I'm a bit early, so I sit down on a nice wide sofa, next to a woman talking animatedly on her phone.

She looks at me in annoyance, stands up, and starts to pace. "They fucked it up. My hair's all fucked-up," she says to whomever is on the other end. I look at her hair, and aside from the garish blond color, it looks fine. "No, it is," she continues. "It's too straight. It looks like a sheet." Well, indeed her hair is straight. I still think it looks fine, though. I consider telling her this, but due to the look on her face, decide it's best not to interfere. "Okay, you can't miss me. I'm right in the middle of the lobby. I'm the one with the fucked-up hair," she says and hangs up.

She sits back down on the sofa next to me. Out of the corner of my eye, I can see veins running down her arms. She looks like she could use a sandwich.

A man in a tracksuit, who could pass as a mafia hit man, appears in the lobby. He's consulting an iPad and talking on a cell phone. He nods at my seatmate, hangs up the phone, and walks over. "Anita, your hair's perfect! It's exactly how we discussed."

"Are you sure, Rick? You don't think it's too straight?"

"Darling, it's supposed to be straight. Now let's get you backstage."

"You don't think I should have them fix it?"

"Not at all, love, let's go." His phone rings, he looks down at it, sighs, and tells Anita he will meet her backstage. He answers his phone, listens for a moment, and says, "Darling, I'm sure you look marvelous," and walks off.

Anita remains on the sofa next to me for a beat, then spins in my direction. "What?" she says accusingly.

Startled, I look to the other side of me. The person there is facing away, talking to someone else. I turn back to Anita and realize that she is talking to me. "Nothing," I say.

"Quit looking at me. And you breathe too loud. Quit breathing so loud."

I try not to breathe so loud. Trying not to breathe loudly just makes me need to breathe more loudly. After a few shallow breaths, it becomes hopeless, and I need to take deep breaths to compensate.

"Ugh, you're disgusting," she says, getting up.

As she rises, her robe starts to slip off her shoulders. There is a ripping sound, as we both realize that the edge of her robe is caught under my enormous ass.

"Get off my robe!" she screams at me. "You're wrecking it!" Everyone in the lobby turns to look at the shrieking woman and the person wrecking her robe. I hastily adjust my heft, releasing the fabric. "Ugh! Why are you even here?" she asks and stomps off.

Chapter 54

ANDREW

Once Andrew discovered that both @fat_and_fabulous and Gemma would be at the Olympia, Gemma's post, "Things do not happen. Things are made to happen," clicked. He understood, on a deep, gut level, what Gemma was trying to tell him: we create our own destinies. In short, it was time for Andrew to man up. To quit dreaming about life, living vicariously through Instagram and *Grand Theft Auto*, and make his dreams a reality.

Upon this realization, Andrew packed a bag, hopped in his car, and drove straight through to Orlando. Then something auspicious happened. The desk attendant at the Hyatt Regency informed him that, although they had been completely sold out ten minutes ago, they had a last-minute cancellation. However, the available room was part of a package that had been booked by the Olympia, and the entire floor would likely be all Bikini competitors. Was Andrew okay with that? Yes, he most certainly was. In fact, Andrew viewed it as further confirmation that he was on the right path.

Today, when Andrew wakes up in the king-size hotel room bed, it takes him a moment to get his bearings. No, he's not dreaming. He's actually in the same hotel as Gemma. She may even be down the hall. He stretches out in the clean linens and imagines the possibilities the day offers. Will he bump into her waiting for the elevator? Will she need help adjusting her bikini? Will he take her to dinner? For a postshow drink?

So far, he's struck out at Meet the Olympians and at the REIGN booth meet-and-greet. But Andrew is undeterred. He is certain that today is going to be momentous. At least about this he's correct.

Andrew takes a shower but doesn't shave. He read an article in *Maxim* that women are attracted to men with scruffy facial hair. That it makes them look more virile. He's unaware that on him, it makes him look like a pubescent teen with patchy peach fuzz.

He generously applies cologne and deodorant and slips on a button-down Ralph Lauren shirt that his mom bought him over a year ago. It's been hanging, laundered and ironed, in his closet ever since, along with the "just in case" khakis and loafers he's now wearing. Finally, in the mirror, he practices saying "May I buy you a drink?" while raising an eyebrow ironically. Once he's convinced himself that he's got game, he heads downstairs to check out the scene.

In the elevator, a housekeeper coughs from the cloud of cologne surrounding him, but he doesn't notice. He exits at the lobby and it's like entering the Promised Land. There are scantily clad fitness girls everywhere. They are videoing themselves, videoing each other, taking selfies, posting selfies, liking posts, and scrolling through their phones. No one so much as glances in his direction.

He crosses the sky bridge to the convention center and sees an angry blond yelling at a fat woman. It's the blond from Meet the Olympians that didn't seem at all concerned when Gemma disappeared. The one that told him to start benching and eating more protein. He really doesn't like her, but at least she's hot. The fat woman, on the other hand, he totally despises on sight.

Why would she let herself get so fat? Doesn't she realize how unattractive she is?

Andrew doesn't consider that she doesn't give a shit if he finds her attractive.

The fat woman's eyes leave the blond and fix on something across the lobby. Andrew follows them, and there is Gemma. Gemma and the fat woman lock eyes. Then Gemma breaks away and rushes off. Andrew follows her, but she has gone backstage. That's okay. She's got a busy morning. He will catch up with her after Prejudging. Maybe they'll grab lunch?

He walks back to the lobby and glowers at the fat woman, now sitting by herself on the sofa. He notices her T-shirt's slogan, Riots Not Diets! It's how @fat_and_fabulous suggested people identify her at today's protest.

So this is the disgusting woman who has been terrorizing Gemma. She's here to ruin her day. Andrew will not allow it. He will keep an eye on her.

Chapter 55

GEMMA

A woman is screaming. "Get off my robe! You're wrecking it!"

I would know that whiny, nasal pitch anywhere. I look, and sure enough, there is Anita yanking her robe out from underneath an enormous woman sitting on a sofa.

My stomach plummets like an elevator cut loose. I stop in my tracks and blink a few times in case I'm imagining it. I'm not. Fat Gemma is sitting on the sofa.

I've finally gone full-tilt loony tunes.

She's wearing a short-sleeved shirt and stretchy pants. Her arms are like segmented sausages.

I don't breathe. Don't make a sound. Maybe I can sneak away.

She looks up and our eyes meet. Dark brown pools filled with hate. Pools to drown me. To swallow me whole. To obliterate my insubstantial life.

I turn and flee. (As quickly as one can in five-inch heels.) I look over my shoulder, sure that she's chasing me, but she's not. She just sits, heavy on the sofa, watching.

By the time I arrive backstage, I'm out of breath. I stumble to my team, camped in a corner, and practically collapse. There are seven of us who will be competing in Bikini today, but no one whom I can talk to about what I just saw. Most of my teammates are wearing headphones and scrolling through their phones. Anita inches away from where I sit trembling.

What is wrong with me? Is it the stress of my pregnancy? Of Peak Week? Of a killer on the loose? I sigh with the realization that it's likely all of the above.

In an effort to calm down, I pull out my phone. There's a text from Craig, "We need to talk." Nothing from Steve since the "You deserve to know what your wife has been up to" screenshot he sent earlier. None of this is helping me unwind, so I navigate to @bretcontreras1 (a.k.a. The Glute Guy) and am finally soothed by the sight of a jacked woman hip thrusting.

Coach Rick arrives, whips out his iPad, and starts checking off our team. Once we are all accounted for, he says, "Gemma, a word, please." He prissily leads me about fifteen feet away. "Anita sent me a screenshot of your post this morning. Specifically, your breakfast. Raspberries and yogurt? Was that just for Instagram, or did you really eat that?" He looks like he's having a hard time wrapping his head around my potential disobedience.

Here it goes. I swallow hard. "Yes, I really ate that." Looks like Plan A, breaking up with Rick from the safety of another state, is no longer an option. Breaking up with him from the safety of a crowd will have to do.

"But why? Why would you do that after we've worked so hard?"

"Because it's raspberries and yogurt. Don't worry, Rick, it's fine. I've never had a problem with dairy before. In fact, I've been eating like this all week, and I've never felt or looked better. You said so yourself the other day. I felt like it was time to try something new."

"Try something new?" Rick's face is eggplant. "You try something new when I tell you to." A vein pops out of his forehead.

I steel my nerves and plunge ahead. "Look, Rick, I know you run a tight ship. And that's great, but it's not for me anymore. After today's show, I think it's best if we part ways. You're a great coach, and I so appreciate everything you've done for me." I could simply tell him I'm pregnant. But that's not what's driving this conversation. And though I won't be on prep for at least a year, if I plan to coach other girls, it's best to get this out in the open.

His eyes harden. "Pack up your things and find another spot backstage." He turns on his heel and stomps off.

Rick owns no real estate backstage. But in the interest of peace, and because it gets me farther away from both him and dangerous Anita, I return to where my now former team is camped on the floor and start to pack. They awkwardly look away and whisper amongst themselves. I know they saw Rick yelling at me, and I'm sure Anita filled them in on my crime. I don't blame them for not making eye contact with me. If they show me any compassion, they, too, risk Rick's wrath.

Chapter 56

KYLIE

Kylie walks around the Olympia expo soaking up the environment. Different vendors have tables set up and are selling all manner of protein concoctions—powders, shakes, cookies, chips, and nut butters. There are vendors hawking competition bikinis, posing-practice bikinis, plastic heels, sparkly jewelry, and all types of workout clothing.

She knows Ashley has her REIGN protest here today but wants no part of it. She doesn't want to be associated with fat women, period. They lower your brand.

Out of the corner of her eye, she spies FBI Agent Newman, with his tough-guy buzz cut, watching her. He's not exactly discreet about it. In fact, he gives her a wave. She pretends not to notice. After their previous encounter, in a concrete room with a two-way mirror, where he basically called her a liar when she said she wasn't at the Tampa FitExpo—and okay, so she was—he probably finds it suspicious that she's here. Whatever. It's a free country.

Like a moth to the flame, Kylie makes her way to the REIGN booth, where two women sit behind a table. They look so similar they could be sisters. Or clones. Both have long, straight blond hair, wear matching white REIGN sports bras and leggings, and have the same sculpted shoulders, arms, and midriffs. They have identical firm, upturned breasts and look eerily like they are made out of plastic, reinforced by the fact that they sit perfectly still.

Kylie approaches them shyly. "Hi. I'm interested in repping for REIGN. Do you know how I could go about that, please?"

The women give Kylie a once-over and, without moving more than their eyes, exchange a look. Clone One says, "The owner, Craig, makes all of those decisions. He's not here right now."

"Do you know when he will be here?" Kylie asks.

Again, the clones glance at each other. Clone Two says, "Not really. Why don't you leave your name and Insta handle here and we'll pass it along for you." With delicate, French manicured fingers, she hands Kylie a pad of lavender Post-it notes and a sparkly pink pen with a white feathery poof on top.

Kylie dutifully writes down the requested information and wishes she could hide her stumpy fingers, with their chipped purple nail polish. She returns the pad and pen and watches as Clone Two peels off Kylie's Post-it and sticks it inside the front cover of a notebook, where there are several other Post-its. Some look quite old, with faded ink, curled edges, and bent corners. This doesn't strike Kylie as very promising. She's about to leave when a tall man who looks like a Pilates instructor walks up and says, "Hey, ladies, how's it going?"

The clones snap to attention: breasts out, shoulders back, gleaming white smiles on megawattage. Clone One says, "We've sold half the Red Flames in small, and we're nearly out of the two-pound Vega protein powder."

Kylie guesses that this must be Craig. She notes that neither clone introduces her, mentions her interest in repping, or even hands Craig her Post-it. Fucking cunts. As usual, it's up to her to advocate for herself. She takes a deep breath, turns toward Craig, and flashes her own megawattage smile. "Are you Craig, the fabled owner of REIGN?"

"Why yes, I am," Craig says with polite reserve.

"It's so great to meet you! I love your entire line. I was just telling the girls here that I would love to be a rep for REIGN."

Craig's smile falters slightly, but he recovers well. "I'm so happy to hear that. We put so much pride into everything we produce. Unfortunately, we're not looking for new reps right now." He turns back to the table and opens the notebook with her Post-it on the inside cover. He flips to a page in the middle with a bunch of rows and numbers and appears to start reviewing them.

Kylie notices that he doesn't ask for her contact information, or even tell her when in the future they may want reps. It stings. He's not interested. Why is no one ever interested in her? In the last two months, Bianca dumped her, Miles kicked her out, Gemma didn't renew her contract, her manager fired her, and Jim wants her gone. This losing streak started with Bianca. She briefly wonders if this is some sort of cosmic payback.

Chapter 57

ASHLEY

I splash cold water on my face. After that awful woman yelled at me for sitting on her robe, I needed to get up and regroup.

In the ladies room, I blot my face with paper towels. Comb out my hair. Put on fresh lipstick. I remind myself that I'm a warrior. That I am strong. Feeling better, I square my shoulders and stride back out to the lobby.

I don't get far.

There's a young man with peach fuzz on his face just outside the bathroom. He's leaning against the wall. Our eyes meet, and he pushes himself off. Stalks over to me. Doesn't stop until he's a foot from my face. He leans in. His cologne is overwhelming.

"Let me guess: @fat_and_fabulous?" he sneers.

I'm taken aback. Is he here for the protest? He doesn't seem to be. But if he knows who I am, and he's not here for the protest, then why is he here?

It dawns on me: he's a hater. I get those on Instagram from time to time. It's why I never post any pictures of my face. Why I limit who can comment on my posts. Why I block certain people. My mouth goes dry, and I consider denying it.

Then I remember why I'm here and decide to own it. I look him level in the eyes. "Yes. That's me."

"You know, it's bad enough that you hate yourself. I mean, look at what you've done to yourself. But then you have to hate on the fitness scene. On people who are trying to help others get healthy. You hide behind your comments on their posts, spreading your malice, but you turn off the comments on your own posts. You're a coward."

"Not tolerating people calling me names doesn't make me a coward. It means I have boundaries."

He scoffs. "But you don't respect other people's boundaries. What fucking business is it of yours what Gemma does with her body? If you don't like it, quit following her. Quit coming inside the *bounds* of her account. You know why you hate her? Her health makes you feel bad. It makes you feel like a failure. But the world doesn't exist to cater to you. To pussyfoot around your fragile feelings. The world exists for all of us. If you don't want to live out here in the big, wide world, go hide in your safe, little corner, so you don't have to be offended."

His voice is escalating, his gestures becoming more dramatic. A couple of competitors look up from their phones. A man shaped like a gorilla asks, "Everything okay here?"

The hater gives me a once-over and says, "Yep. Nothing to see here." He walks away in disgust.

I'm left standing outside the bathroom, feeling unsteady. For the second time today, I want to hide. But I can't. I have a protest to run.

I start to reflect on what the hater said but stop myself. He was cruel and awful; it's best not to consider it. Good vibes only!

Chapter 58

GEMMA

"How do you do it?" Anita asks without looking up from her phone.

We're standing backstage, waiting for a final tanning buff-out. I keep my eyes trained on my phone, where I'm scrolling through @Cats_of_Instagram. I contemplate ignoring Anita, but curiosity gets the best of me. With bored nonchalance, I answer, "Do what?"

"Look your husband in the eyes when you're fucking another man."

I don't glance up. I like a video of a cat playing with a glitterball. Anita's breath is hot on my cheek. She's waiting for an answer.

My mind races back to the screenshot Steve sent me, "You deserve to know what your wife has been up to," and now I'm certain that Anita sent it. Are they closer than I realized? I recall the FitExpo, where Steve mysteriously disappeared in the middle of the night. Could he have been with Anita?

Or could Anita be the person killing all of us? She surely had a motive to murder Bianca (knock out a rival for Craig, win the Olympia) and Rachel (stop her from taking out a restraining order), but what about Megan? Then again, just because I'm not aware of a motive doesn't mean she didn't have one. I recall a rumor that Anita and Rick were fucking back when Rick and Megan were married. What if Anita was trying to get a job at *Shrinking* and Megan was blocking her? Would Anita kill her for that? Sure she would. But more pressing, what if Anita's now targeting me?

I make a split-second decision. Even though I'm a pretty private person, in the interest of staying alive, I blurt out, "You know, Craig and I aren't seeing each other anymore. He's completely free."

"You're still a slut," she says, and saunters off to the next available touch-up lady.

Chapter 59

ASHLEY

Lydia shows up early, rocking leopard print leggings, a bright red tank top, and metallic gold sneakers. "Let's get this show on the road," she says, rubbing her hands together.

Behind her, a slim cat-eyed woman appears, wearing overalls and carrying a toolbox. She glances our way, then straight ahead. She keeps walking. Something red glitters from her right ring finger. It's another phoenix ring.

"Lydia, look. It's one of ours."

"Where?" she says, looking everywhere but where I'm pointing.

"Right there. The woman with the toolbox."

"I don't see anyone with a toolbox."

"Right there!" I point again.

"Put your hand down," she hisses, and slaps it out of the air. "There *is* no woman with a toolbox. Never was one." Lydia's eyes are monoliths. She holds my gaze, brooking no room for argument.

I look at her and wonder, not for the first time, if she is insane. Finally, I answer, "Okay," and look down at the floor, the chastised student.

Just then, Heather arrives, her crossed-pistols tattoo bursting from cleavage barely contained by a teal tank. She takes a seat across from me.

Over the next ten minutes, the rest of the protesters arrive. Lydia has alerted a local news station about our event and is expecting them to show up shortly, so we need to get rolling. I pull the homemade picket signs out of my bag and divvy them up. They say things like REIGN = SHAME!, Take Up Space!, We are the 68%!, Fat People Exercise, and Fight Fat Discrimination! As we make our way to the REIGN booth, all heads in the expo follow our path, like sunflowers tracking the sun.

Then I see the sign. A giant banner above the REIGN booth declaring Bombshells Only! Red and orange explosions pop against its smoky gray background. I'm so startled that I stop in my tracks, causing Lydia to run into me. My stomach goes cold. I remember the bomb-making instructions on The Phoenix's site. How Lydia smelled like smoke the very day that "Blow up your metabolism" Megan was literally blown up. Could an explosion happen here today?

"Come on, Ashley, no turning back now. It's showtime!" Lydia gives me a push, but my feet stay frozen to the floor. So she simply steps around me and strides up to the REIGN booth. After a beat, I numbly follow.

Craig is busy explaining something to a pair of blond twins seated at a table when our dark shadow falls upon him. He looks up and widens his eyes, like he's about to be run over by a Mack truck.

"We are the sixty-eight percent of American women. And we exercise," Lydia announces. That was supposed to be my line.

Craig recovers. "Well, it's nice to meet you. I'm Craig, but I suspect you already know that." He smiles, showing his teeth. His pointy canines unsettle me. On television, he just seemed like a douche. In person, despite his clear pores and dewy skin, there's an ugliness leaking out of him.

Nevertheless, I stick to the plan. I jostle to the front of our group and lead the march, hold my sign high above my head. Craig sits down and watches us, like a fox eyeing chickens in a coop.

Off to the side is that FBI agent from the news the night Megan was blown up. He doesn't interfere with our protest, just watches us with icy blue eyes. At one point, he takes a few photos. Is he here because Megan's death was in fact a murder? Does he think another murder could happen? The Bombshells Only banner screams at me. I do my best to ignore it.

After several minutes, I realize that this was as far as we took the plan. Our chant, "Fat people exercise," is becoming choppy. Picket signs rest on shoulders. Thanks to my boxing, I'm doing okay, but I'm not sure how much longer the group can keep this up. Yet we can't quit now, not with everyone watching us.

So onward we trudge. Our voices raspy. Our hair droopy.

Eventually, our audience loses interest and drifts back to whatever it was doing. The REIGN Barbies get bored, although it's hard to tell with their bland Botoxed faces. Right when I'm thinking we may need to change strategy, Eileen Brachman, from *Orlando's Nightly News*, and a camera guy show up. With renewed vigor, we march on.

Eileen is trim and elegant, her head capped with a sleek brunette bob. She approaches me and says, "This is Eileen Brachman with *Orlando's Nightly News*. What's your name and can you tell me what you're doing here?"

"My name is Ashley Shermer. We're here today to protest REIGN's discrimination against the fat community."

Eileen asks, "How is REIGN discriminating against them?"

"REIGN refuses to produce plus-size attire. Did you know that sixty-eight percent of American women are plus-size?"

"No, I didn't." She turns to Craig, who has stood up and come around from behind the table. "And who are you, please?" she asks.

"I'm Craig Higgins, the owner of REIGN. And while it's true that we don't produce plus-size attire at this time—we're a small company, and that's not our market—it has nothing to do with discrimination. We can't be all things to all people. We produce high-end workout attire for fashion-forward, fitness-minded people."

I pipe up, "Who says you can't be fat, fashion-forward, and fitness-minded?" My teammates whoop in agreement.

Craig answers, "You certainly can be. But you will have to do it in someone else's clothes, because ours do not go into plus-sizes."

"Exactly! You don't want fat people wearing your brand," I charge.

Craig replies calmly, "It's not that we don't want 'fat' people wearing our clothes." He makes actual air quotes around "fat." "It's that we are a young company and not in the position to expand into that space right now. We need to be very judicious because of our high overhead. None of our garments are produced in sweatshops and all of our factories are solar powered to reduce our eco-footprint. We strive to be a good global contributor. That's expensive."

"But you would make so much more money if you made plus-size clothes. The market is so large." My face reddens as I inwardly acknowledge the pun.

"And one day we may expand into that market. We are certainly evaluating it."

He's lying. I know he is. He knows he is. He knows that I know he is. It's like some totally messed up game of trying to outwit each other with words that are simply window dressing.

He's good at this and he knows it. In fact, the smirk on his face tells me that he is enjoying it, which has the effect of pissing me off and making it harder for me to think of what to say next.

As it turns out, I don't have to say anything. A couple of cops walk up. The burly redhaired one says, "I'm afraid I'm going to have to ask you ladies to leave."

I reply, "You can't make us leave. We have every right to be here."

"Actually, no you don't. This is private property. Now, what's it going to be? Are you going to leave, or are we going to have to arrest you?"

The camera man takes a few steps back to ensure he captures both of us in the frame.

Chapter 60

GEMMA

"Competitor eleven, Gemma Jorgenson, from Chicago, Illinois!" says the announcer. While the event may be called "Prejudging," make no mistake about it, this is where the decisions are made. The next minutes will make or break my placing.

I take a deep breath, smile like my life depends on it, and walk out to the center of the stage. The lights are blinding. I maintain eye contact with the center judge, Sandy. She looks right back at me, scrutinizing. I smile so hard my lips tremble.

I hit my front pose, right hand on my hip, left hip popped out. Briefly, I scan the entire panel of judges. I hear a man in the audience screaming, "Number eleven! Let's go, eleven!" I can't imagine whom it could be. It's certainly not Craig's voice. I peer out into the darkness to see my fan, but the stage lights make it impossible.

I continue my presentation, my brain buzzing, my body on autopilot. I pivot this way and that, toss my hair, and keep eye contact with the panel of judges whenever possible. When I face the back, I arch my spine and pop my glutes as high in the air as I can, pressing my palms into my thighs. This is the most crucial pose, and I hold it for an extra beat, feeling my knees quiver. Finally, I spin back to the front, strike my last pose, and give a high wave to signal that my presentation is finished. I maintain eye contact with Sandy as I exit the stage. It's over in less than a minute, but I'm exhausted. The whole thing's a blur.

I make my way around the back of the stage and get in line again. This thing isn't even close to over.

Once all forty of us have completed our individual presentations, we file back out onto the stage, half lining up on either side. This is the moment of truth. No one speaks. It's possible no one breathes. Then Sandy starts rattling off numbers, "Thirty-six, twenty-two, eleven . . ." She continues to call numbers, but I don't hear anything past eleven. My number. It's rolling through my ears, crashing about my head.

I step onto the front line, dead center, with five other girls around me. I don't get too excited, there's still lots of shuffling to take place. Once we are lined up, Sandy asks numbers twenty-two and thirty-six to switch places. It turns out that Anita is twenty-two. She is now standing right next to me. I can feel a wall of coolness coming off of her, like I'm standing next to a glacier.

I hear the same man who was cheering for me during my individual presentation call out, "Eleven! You've got this!"

Now a woman starts screaming, "Twenty-two! Twenty-two is the best!" My stomach flips. I know that voice. Kylie. I'd be willing to bet she doesn't even know Anita and is simply rooting for her because she's in direct competition with me. Has she come all the way from Tampa to torment me? To seek some sort of vengeance? Is she the one who's been killing all these fitness girls? I feel exposed, out in the open under all these lights while she watches me from the dark.

Sandy continues to move competitors around me while I

stay put, smile plastered to my face. She has us all turn toward the back. As we are turning, Anita steps slightly closer to me. I don't move out of her way. With Anita encroaching from the side, and Kylie shooting daggers at my back, I feel my knees tremble. My right heel briefly wobbles.

Sandy has us turn back toward the front, and Anita steps even closer. She tosses her hair and it whips me in the arm as I bring my right hand to my hip. My bracelet snags a few strands, which get yanked out and now dangle against my leg. Anita takes a step away from me.

Kylie continues to cheer for Anita with such vigor that her voice becomes hoarse. My admirer keeps yelling for me, as well. They're like two competing bidders at an auction, or two crazy fans at the Super Bowl. I try to tune them out, keep my eyes pinned to Sandy and the panel of judges. Sandy shuffles a few more competitors again. Finally, she seems satisfied and dismisses us.

We go back to our respective diagonal lines and another group of six is called. It's not over yet. I continue to smile at the judges and hold various uncomfortable poses, should they glance my way. Once Sandy has worked through all forty of us, she calls me, and the rest of first callouts, back to center stage for a confirmation round. She twirls us around, has us walk forward and back, shuffles us some more, but keeps me in the top spot the whole time. My right calf starts to cramp, and I fear I may get a charley horse. Just in time, Sandy dismisses us back to our diagonals, then all of Bikini from the stage.

Only after I am safely backstage do I relax my lips. My face is numb, exhausted from all the smiling.

Kentucky Crystal rushes up. "Oh my God, you held center stage the whole time!"

"Well, let's not get too excited yet. Finals still have to

happen. Hey, looks like you might be third. That's amazing! Especially for your first Olympia."

More people stop by to congratulate me while Anita glowers in my direction. I can't believe she's so sour about a potential second place. Hell, if I don't play my cards right, she could still take first.

I have seen competitors who were presumed to be first place at the end of Prejudging get second at Finals, which take place later in the evening. But in those instances, the head judge had shuffled first and second around a few times, or even the top three placings, and was waiting for Finals to make her decision. I have never seen anyone hold center stage the whole time and then lose it at Finals, but I have heard of it. It's been known to happen when the competitor shows up at Finals with a distended stomach from a large meal, or some other unusual event taking place, like a tanning mishap, or being hit in the back of the head with a threaded pipe. Something that either changes how the competitor looks at Finals compared to Prejudging, or that removes them from the equation. As long as I don't do anything stupid, like let Fat Gemma out of her cage or a serial killer into my room, tonight is looking promising.

Coach Rick's face is red. He stalks up to Anita with a forced smile. "Hey there, doll."

"Gemma ripped out my hair. That's it hanging from her bracelet." Anita points to several long blond strands dangling from my wrist.

I ignore her. Or at least pretend to. I need to get out of here before she can follow me. Or Rick or Kylie follows me. Or someone else I haven't even thought of yet. Whoever the killer is, they are likely either backstage with me now or out in the audience. I need to get back to the safety of my room. Barricade myself in until Finals.

I shrug on my robe and slip away.

Up ahead in the lobby is a commotion. There are a couple of police officers, a news reporter, a cameraman, and a bunch of fat women holding signs. Fat Gemma's in the middle of it all, leering at me.

Now is not the time to have a mental breakdown. I tear my eyes away from her and focus on the exit. On getting back to my room. I pick up my pace, hoping to go unnoticed.

Turns out, someone notices.

Chapter 61

ANDREW

Andrew follows her. Out of the convention center and into the skyway bridge to the hotel. There is no one else in the skyway. She is twenty paces ahead of him. Then ten. Five.

"Gemma! Hey, Gemma!" Andrew calls out, running to catch up as she exits the skyway.

Gemma turns. "Yes?"

"Hey, you did great out there! Do you think you won?"

Gemma smiles shyly and looks at the floor. She's so hot when she's demure. Andrew wants to reach out and tip her chin up with his finger, but he knows it's too early for that. She looks tentatively back up, her eyes on his, and he feels his cock twitch. "Well, I won't know for sure until Finals. Was that you cheering for me?"

"Yes, that was me." Andrew feels his cheeks flush and digs his hands deep into his pockets.

"Thank you so much." Gemma's eyes slide to her phone, where the message "We need to talk" has popped up. Her face registers annoyance. She ignores the message and drops the phone in her bag.

She looks back up and seems surprised to find Andrew still

standing there. She says, "Okay, well cool. It was nice seeing you again," and resumes walking.

Andrew hurries after her. "So what time are Finals?" Andrew knows they are at 7 p.m.

"Seven o'clock," she answers, stopping in front of the elevator. She presses the up button.

Andrew stands next to her, waiting for the elevator to arrive. He frantically tries to think of something to say.

She saves him the trouble. "So what brings you to the Olympia?" Obviously, Andrew's not a bodybuilder.

"One of my friends is competing. I came to support her." This is supposed to give him cred. He read an article in *Swagger* that women are more interested in guys if they think other women find them attractive, whether it's as a mate or as friends. It somehow signals that he's passed other women's sniff tests.

The elevator dings and its doors slide open, purging yet another load of fitness girls. Andrew is amazed at the never-ending supply of hot babes in this place. He respectfully ignores them, not wanting to make Gemma jealous.

Gallantly, he holds the elevator door with his hand. "After you," he says, and motions for Gemma to step inside. Only once Gemma is safely inside does Andrew release the door and step in, as well.

Gemma presses 7. "What floor?" she asks.

"I'm going to seven too," he says. Andrew can't believe his good fortune, that she's staying on the same floor as he is. That it's just the two of them on the elevator. It's fate.

The elevator doors are shutting when a hairy arm thrusts itself between them. A shaggy man with sweat stains at his armpits enters. He doesn't press any buttons. Gives Andrew a solid once-over, nods at Gemma, then ignores them both.

The elevator begins its slow ascent. Andrew fantasizes that it will get stuck between floors. That they will be trapped in here for hours. Gemma will panic and cry. The hairy guy will be a pussy, or maybe have a heart attack and die. But Andrew will be strong. He will selflessly give her the lone breakfast bar in his pocket, refusing even a nibble. The elevator will start to get warm and she'll remove her robe. Andrew will remove his shirt.

The elevator jolts to a stop at seven, snapping Andrew back to reality. It's now or never. "Hey, would you like to grab a bite to eat before Finals?" Andrew asks.

Gemma steps out into the hall. "I'm sorry. I really can't eat much before Finals or it could ruin everything."

Andrew follows her out. "What about after?"

"I'm sorry. Finals get done so late. By then I'll be exhausted and just want to take a shower and go to bed." She stops to fiddle with her robe's tie, which has come loose.

"How about breakfast tomorrow?" Andrew feels opportunity slipping through his fingers.

Gemma drops the tie and looks up, like he's starting to freak her out. Like maybe she thinks he's a serial killer. "I'm sorry. My husband probably wouldn't like that." She gives him a tight smile. Her robe is undone, her taut tummy so close.

Suddenly, there's a snapping sound. Gemma's bejeweled bikini bottoms spontaneously break apart on one side, flop open, and Andrew is staring at her tanned, hairless crotch. He forgets to breathe.

She makes the most amazing squeak and frantically pulls the bottoms back together, but Andrew can't stop staring at the place where she was momentarily bare. Right on the other side of that red fabric.

She spins away and flees into her room.

Andrew is still standing there. Still staring at where she was. He is rock hard.

Chapter 62

ASHLEY

We are large cargo. While the burly policeman calls for extra squad cars to transport us to the station, his lanky partner stands by, supposedly guarding us.

An Asian Bikini contestant in a tangerine suit approaches the lanky cop. "Officer, can you please help? My top's tie is loose and all tangled up in the back of my hair. Can you help me fix it, please?" Beneath sparkly tangerine eye shadow, she bats her false eyelashes.

I wait for the policeman to tell her to buzz off, to say that he's working. That tying bikini tops is not in his job description. Instead, I watch in amazement as he agrees. The contestant turns around, scoots within six inches of his chest, and drapes her hair over one shoulder, exposing the misbehaving tie at the back of her neck. And just like that, he gets to work.

My eyes slide to Lydia. We are standing right next to the skyway bridge. The perfect escape. *Let's go*, I mouth.

While the officer is retying the bikini, Lydia and I silently slip away from the group. Across the skyway we go and out into the hotel. We break into a run. Through the lobby, down a hallway we race, our hearts thumping. We hang a left into another hall, skidding around the corner like the gang in *Scooby-Doo*.

Halfway down, I duck inside what looks like an empty conference room. Except it's not. Down on her knees is the overalled woman from earlier, toolbox at her side. There's a large, wooden zero, painted white, on the floor in front of her. She's attaching something to it with a cordless power drill. She looks up, startled.

Behind me, Lydia stops abruptly, her breath wet on my neck.

The woman shoots a questioning look over my shoulder.

Lydia says, "Come on, Ashley. Let's go." She grabs my arm and pulls me from the room. I keep my eyes on the toolbox woman until the door swings shut.

"What was that about?" I ask.

Under the fluorescent lights, Lydia's face is greenish gray. The lines around her mouth grim. "It's not important. Now, let's find another room to regroup in."

I want to ask more, but know it'll get me nowhere. We find an empty room down a different hall and collapse into a couple of chairs. My arms are limp by my sides. My legs tired from all the marching and our recent run. "What an afternoon," I say. "Can you believe that policeman agreed to retie her bikini while he was guarding us?"

"With those tits? You bet."

"Do you think they'll even notice we're gone?"

"Yes, because there will be two less fatties. That's all they'll know."

"True."

Lydia looks around the room and notices a table of office supplies. She gets up and starts sorting through them. "You know, as long as we're 'at large,' we should have a little fun," she says with a smirk.

"What do you mean?"

"All these bitches. They're part of the problem. The fake breasts and hair. The emaciated bodies. They inspire eating disorders. They are the very fuel on which the seventy-billion-dollar diet industry runs."

"So what are you thinking?" I try not to sound nervous.

She picks up a couple black Sharpies and a pair of scissors. Hands me one of the Sharpies, then walks to the door. "Follow me," she says, and strides out into the hall.

I follow with a heady mixture of apprehension and excitement. Adrenaline clouds my mind, making it difficult to think.

We round the corner and see two women up ahead. One is a competitor. She's in a robe and has blond hair so enormous that one could smuggle drugs across the Mexican border in it. It spills over her shoulders and reaches down to her ass. The other woman is clearly not a competitor. She has limp, dishwater-brown hair, a chubby body, and is wearing sweatpants. The blond is crying big, shoulder-heaving sobs. Eye makeup runs down her face in streaks. "I don't understand," she weeps to her friend. "Last time I placed third. My feedback was to come in tighter. I came in tighter. And now it looks like I'm placing somewhere in the mid-fucking-twenties? What is this shit? I can't keep doing this. I can't afford to keep doing these shows. I have kids. I have a life. What the fuck am I doing here?"

Her friend is rubbing her back. "I don't know what those judges were thinking. I really thought you were the best one out there," she soothes.

"Do you think I'm fat?" the blond asks her fat friend.

"No! No! You're absolutely perfect! Beautiful!" She reaches out and hugs her, just as we're about even with them.

The blond's back is to us and her friend is shorter, so she can't see over the blond's shoulder. Lydia deftly brings the scissors up, reaches out, and grabs a hunk of the blond's hair and slices it off. We keep walking, Lydia with about twelve inches of hair in her hand. We round another corner and slip into a bathroom with an Out of Service sign on the door.

"Oh my God! I can't believe you did that," I say as the door shuts behind us.

Lydia throws the hair in the garbage. "I'm just getting started. We should split up. We can cover more ground that way. Here's what I'm thinking. We'll use the markers to write 'Fuck Diet Culture' on the walls, I'll use the scissors to cut hair and bikinis. Unless you want the scissors?"

"No! That's okay. I'll stick with the marker."

"You can always use the marker to write on these bitches too. You could scrawl 'Diet Culture Whore' or 'Feminism Traitor' across their foreheads," Lydia says, her eyes ablaze.

"That might be tricky. And we'll probably get thrown out of here faster that way."

"Who cares?" Lydia shrugs. "If we're getting thrown out, let's make it worth our while. Listen, if I don't see you again today, you need to get out of here before Finals, understand? And whatever you do, stay away from the stage."

"Why?" Electricity shoots up my spine.

"It's better you don't know. Just do it. Repeat after me: Out before Finals, stay away from the stage."

I repeat it numbly.

She gives me a fist bump and strides out of the bathroom.

Chapter 63

GEMMA

Thank God Dale had a sewing kit. That YouTube has sewing videos. And that my bottoms broke when they did and not onstage.

I sit on the bed and stitch them up. Reinforce the other side and the top, as well.

Once my bikini is as strong as medieval chain mail, I check my phone. Bizarrely, there is a voicemail from Steve's friend Todd. "Gemma, call me when you get a chance. It's about Steve. There's something that you should be aware of."

I remember their fight the other night. Todd's anger with him. Steve's pleading.

Then jump to the night of Bianca's murder. Steve's unaccounted hours. His bizarre late-night shower.

I realize how close Rachel's murder was to our home.

My mind leaps to earlier this week, when Steve packed his carry-on and vanished for days. During the same time that Megan was murdered.

Oh my God. What has Steve done?

This feels like the edge of before, like one step from my life toppling off a cliff. I don't want to talk to Todd. I want to stay right here, swaying in the breeze.

Dread creeping up my throat, I go to my apartment's video feed, bracing to find Steve strung out, being arrested, or gone.

Instead, I find him lolling in bed in his boxers, chuckling at a video on his phone, a bowl of cereal precariously near his elbow.

Common sense smacks me. There's no way that Steve is the Fit Girl Killer. Megan was offed by a homemade bomb, for goodness' sake. The notion of Steve creating a bomb is laughable. And as for covering up the other murders, he's unlikely to even hide that he was eating in bed (not allowed) by washing the spilled cereal and sloshed milk from the sheets before my return.

Maybe Todd's voicemail is about Steve's weird text, "You deserve to know what your wife has been up to." This makes much more sense, and I feel my shoulders relax. Todd is, after all, a total drama queen. Either way, I don't feel like talking to him right now.

Frankly, I don't feel like talking to self-important Todd ever. Whenever he's at our place, he gives off this vibe like *I'm* intruding—in my own home. I ignore his voicemail. Instead, I post to Instagram that Prejudging went well and that I will be making a big announcement tonight after Finals.

The announcement will likely be that I've won the Bikini Olympia and am moving in a different direction with contest prep. That I disagree with all the craziness of Peak Week. The cutting of carbs, the vile asparagus, the dehydration and water pills. That I eschewed all of that nonsense during this prep and look how it worked out. I'm going to announce that if other competitors are interested in a sane way to prep, I am taking clients.

This should excite me more than it does. I chalk it up to

stress—being pregnant, a crumbling marriage, not to mention a serial killer stalking fitness girls. I just need to chill out in my room and decompress.

I'm having a snack of rice cakes and peanut butter, and have taken exactly one bite when the phone on my nightstand rings. Like, the actual hardwired phone. This baffles me. Who would be calling me on the landline? I'm about to ignore it, when I realize that it could be Dale, calling to say he's found my backup suit bottoms.

"Yes?" I pick up.

"Gemma, it's Todd." On the landline? I don't know what to say and consider hanging up. But because this is so unusual, I don't. I don't respond, either. I'm actually speechless.

After a few seconds, Todd continues, "I'm in the lobby. It's really important that I talk to you about Steve."

"What are you doing in the lobby?" My voice sounds like it's coming from far away.

"I had to come to Orlando for business, and I thought this might be a good opportunity to talk." Rubbish. Why is he really here? It can't be just to discuss me cheating on Steve. Does Steve have a gambling problem? Cancer?

"Okay. I'll come down."

"No, don't worry. I'll come up," he says. It's only after I've given him my room number and hung up that I wonder how he was able to call my room. I checked in under the alias Jane Doe.

Two minutes later, there's a knock at the door and I let Todd in. He looks terrible. His face is sickly white under a thin sheen of stale sweat. His hair unwashed and disheveled. It doesn't look like he's shaved since yesterday. There's no way that he's here on business. Todd is usually impeccably groomed and emotionally collected. My anxiety rachets up even further.

I step out of his way as he strides past me and plunks down

on the bed. I sit across from him in a chair. "How were you able to call me? I checked in under an alias."

"When I couldn't find you under Gemma Jorgenson, I tried Jane Doe. Bingo." He smirks smugly, and I'm slightly reassured. Surely, he wouldn't smirk if Steve had cancer.

"So what's going on?" I ask, crossing my arms over my chest.

"Have you talked to Steve at all in the last couple of days?"

"Todd, that's none of your business. Just tell me why you're here."

Todd takes a deep breath and sits forward. He opens his mouth. Lets his jaw hang for a moment. Then exhales, closes his mouth, and slumps backward.

I let out an impatient sigh and pointedly look at the clock on the bedside table.

He tries again, taking a deeper breath, leaning forward and opening his jaw, as if to speak. After a beat, he appears to change his mind. He exhales and sits back, closing his mouth.

"Jesus Christ, Todd. What is it?"

Todd levels his gaze at me, clearly relishing the power of the bomb he is about to drop. "Steve knows you're pregnant." His eyes take me in. Waiting.

Fuck. I remember hiding the pregnancy test in the bottom of my underwear drawer. What was Steve doing digging through my things? Oh yes, the text, "You deserve to know what your wife has been up to."

I didn't see this coming. Still, I remain expressionless. Considering that I was braced to find out that Steve was thousands of dollars in debt or about to start chemotherapy, this is small potatoes. Plus, I refuse to give Todd the satisfaction of a reaction. Instead, I respond with annoyed nonchalance. "So what? Why are you telling me this?"

"Because there is something *else* that you should know."

This guy is so fucking annoying. I never should have let him up. I should have insisted on meeting him in the lobby where I could walk away from him whenever I wanted. "And?"

"Steve and I are in love. We've been seeing each other for over a year. In fact, I flew to the Tampa FitExpo to be with him, he missed me so much. He was planning on leaving you after the Olympia. Before he found out that you're pregnant."

I absorb the blow well, taking it to the gut like a strongman taking a cannonball. I hold my face neutral. Feel the knowledge wash over me. Through me. Change my very DNA.

Todd's news certainly squares with the distance I've felt between Steve and me over the last year. I need to talk to Steve. Todd doesn't belong in the middle of this.

The annoyance I feel for Todd shifts. Like a tectonic plate sliding beneath the surface. Something inside of me cracks open.

How dare this guy barge into my room? Into my marriage? Into my life?

Anger that has been roiling around inside me ignites and bursts forth. It comes out as hot, ugly laughter. I lean forward, my voice dripping with condescension. "He was *not* planning on leaving me." My eyes are level with his. "Don't you know? People never leave their spouse for the affair partner. It's the oldest rule in the book."

Todd's face darkens. "Gemma, he's been lying to you the whole time."

"What makes you so sure it hasn't been *you* that he's been lying to? Steve's not going anywhere. We both want this baby. You may have been some side piece of strange, but I'm his wife and the mother of his child."

Todd's face is only inches from mine. His bottom teeth are crooked. His lips ragged and chapped. His breath coffee sour.

"Gemma, he doesn't love you. He can't love you. You will be chaining him to you if you have this baby."

"Todd, there's no 'if.' I'm having this baby. And Steve isn't chained. If he wanted to be with you, he'd be with you right now."

Todd rocks back like I've punched him. Then sits still on the bed, his hands on his thighs, his gaze at the floor.

I'm about to ask him to leave when he abruptly slaps his legs and stands. He picks up the plate with my rice cakes and hurls it at the wall, where it smashes. A glob of peanut butter sticks to the wallpaper. Ceramic and rice cake fragments litter the floor. "Gemma, do not do this." He pounds his fist on the bed with each syllable.

He lifts a heel of his pretentious Golden Goose sneakers while he does this, and my eyes snag on the tread. It's got a distinctive, a finely spaced zigzag pattern. There's something about it.

Then it clicks. It's the same pattern as the wet footprints in my dining room after the break-in.

Everything goes cold. Slows down.

Todd was in Tampa when Bianca was strangled. He lives near where Rachel was murdered. Was he in Daytona Beach when Megan was blown up? I'm not sticking around to find out.

"I'm going to the bathroom," I say, and stand.

I wade through the seconds. Feel Todd's eyes bore into the back of my skull. Once I reach the bathroom doorway, I turn toward it, as if about to go in. I register Todd out of the corner of my left eye, watching.

I take a step toward the opening and simultaneously shoot my right hand for the hall door. In one fluid movement I spin the knob, yank it open, and run out into the light.

The carpet is soft, muffling the sound of my feet. I race to the elevator and frantically hammer both the up and down buttons. I'm getting in whichever one shows up first.

Todd emerges from my room, out into the hall, advancing toward me with his long legs. "Gemma, get back here. Where are you going?"

I continue to bang buttons. He is almost upon me when the elevator dings and the doors sweep open.

I hurl myself inside. A middle-aged couple in shorts and T-shirts look surprised by my abrupt arrival. "What floor, dear?" asks the woman, eyeing my skimpy robe.

I look at the panel and see they are headed to the lobby. "The lobby, please. Hurry!"

The doors are about to shut when Todd jams his arm between them and gets on too. "Lobby," he says tightly. I feel his eyes on me as we ride down, but don't acknowledge him. As the doors open, I start to step out, but he grabs my wrist. "Gemma, stay here. We need to talk."

"Ouch! You're hurting me! Get away from me!" I scream, going for broke. I frantically try to twist out of his grasp. The couple's eyes are wide.

The man speaks up. "I think you ought to let her go."

"Press the alarm button!" I yell. "He's hurting me."

Todd drops my wrist like it's on fire. "That won't be necessary. God, Gemma, get a grip." He says it to my back.

I'm already out the door.

Chapter 64

ANDREW

Andrew needs a drink. He heads down to the bar, the reel of Gemma's bikini snapping open playing over and over in his mind.

The bartender takes one look at Andrew, and says, "I'm going to need to see some ID, son." Andrew smoothly pulls the fake ID out of his pocket. He got it from a connection he made while performing community service for that whole Sara Fucking Conley mess at the community college. The bartender studies Andrew's ID, smiles wryly, and says, "What can I get for you, Sven?"

"I'll take a twenty-year Macallan." Andrew has always wanted to say that. It's a total hedge fund guy drink. The bartender raises an eyebrow in just the manner that Andrew's been practicing and cracks a grin. He sets Andrew up with a heavy pour.

While Andrew is sipping his scotch—holy shit it's strong— and planning his next move, a somewhat attractive blond, in a trying-too-hard sort of way, sits down next to him. "Hi there," she says, looking up at him from beneath globs of mascara.

Andrew looks around. Women never spontaneously talk to him. He assumes she must be addressing someone else. But all the seats around him are empty. "Hi," he replies, at which point he runs out of conversation. The bartender is watching from the other end of the bar.

"So what brings you to Orlando?" she asks, a smile curling the corners of her lips.

"I have a friend competing. I came to support her." Again, he tests the social credibility theory.

"Oh, really. Who's your friend?" Kylie saw Andrew cheering for Gemma during Prejudging. Saw them ride up the elevator together. Andrew doesn't know it, but that social credibility theory is bang on, a 100 percent hardwired truth.

"Gemma Jorgenson. She's a Bikini competitor."

"Is she your girlfriend?" Kylie asks playfully and kicks him with her foot.

Andrew swallows and looks down at his drink. "No. Not really. We just hang out sometimes." Kylie sees his cheeks color and suspects that Gemma and Andrew are carrying on a torrid affair when Gemma is at shows, otherwise she would bring Steve. Kylie reasons that Andrew must be loaded, a really great lay, or both. She notes his freshly pressed button-down, the linen twill of his khakis, the even stitching and rich grain of his loafers. Andrew's mom has great taste.

Kylie leans into Andrew. She rests her hand on his thigh. The khakis feel expensive. "Well, she's sure missing out," she breathes.

Andrew's eyes drift down to where her hand rests, a mere six inches from his cock, which is engorged. Throbbing. In fact, he can see it bulging beneath his khakis. He's pretty sure Kylie can too. And that hairy guy from the elevator, sitting at a table near the window.

Nothing like this has ever happened to Andrew before. Unsure what to do next, he slips into *Grand Theft Auto* mode.

His eyes travel back up to Kylie's. "May I buy you a drink?" he asks, raising his eyebrow ironically.

———

All it took was one glass of cabernet, and Kylie suggested they move somewhere more comfortable. They are now traveling up the elevator. Kylie has her hand on Andrew's cock, which is so hard it hurts. She's breathing all over his neck, and he's not sure if he can make it to the seventh floor.

Mercifully, the doors finally open, and they stumble down the hall to his room. For one panicked moment, he is sure he won't be able to find his key, but here it is in his pocket. Like the golden ticket. He waves it in front of the door and in they go.

No sooner has the door shut, then Kylie drops to her knees and unzips his fly. His cock bobs out, pointing skyward. So hard you could hang a wet corduroy jacket off it. Right there in the entryway, Kylie starts sucking him off. She takes it all the way down her throat to the base of the shaft. Andrew is impressed. He happens to have a rather large cock. He knows this from all the porn he's watched. It's oddly surreal having a real live woman go down on him. It's wet.

With one hand pressed against the wall, the other on Kylie's bobbing head, it occurs to him that he should take the lead right about now. He pulls her up by the armpits, and they make it to the bed. Andrew's a virgin, but due to extensive porn use, he manages to get the right thing in the right place and then nature takes over. He finds a rhythm, and within four minutes of entry comes copious amounts of semen. His orgasm lasts an epic twelve seconds and occurs in multiple waves.

When it's over, he collapses on Kylie. "Wow," he utters.

"That was amazing," she breathes. It really wasn't. It was

four minutes. And there was no foreplay directed her way. "Hey, let's get a picture."

Andrew thinks this is a strange request, but due to his recent orgasm, is rather pliable. Kylie retrieves her phone from her purse, which she dropped in the entryway, and climbs back in bed. She snuggles up against him and says, "Say cheese."

Before Andrew can say cheese, she's snapped a picture of the two of them from their bare shoulders up. A pillow and hotel nightstand in the background. Andrew watches, growing increasingly alarmed, as she uploads it to Instagram with the hashtag #newfriends.

"Why did you upload it to Instagram?" he asks.

"I just think we look cute together."

Chapter 65

COACH RICK

Coach Rick is pissed. He's back in his room, going over this morning's fallout. His Wellness and Physique competitors did respectably, but Bikini was a fucking disaster. He had six total Bikini competitors. And just one, Anita, made the top five. One more, Kat, made the top ten. Only the top ten are called back for Finals. After that, no one gives a shit.

This is not typical. Not at all. Rick is used to having at least two or three girls place in the top five for Bikini, and usually one of those takes first. Normally, his girls clog the top ten, leaving little room for others. Frequently, following the Olympia, he receives calls from girls on other teams looking to defect. That won't be happening this time. It's been years since something like this morning's debacle happened.

Rick blames Gemma. Prior to their breakup, he had seven Bikini competitors. Her departure brought that down to six, and everyone knows that seven is a lucky number. Secondly, after she packed up and moved her things away from his team, morale seemed to plummet for his girls. All except Anita. Women are so goddamn moody.

Although Rick no longer competes in bodybuilding, he's on a cycle of Dianabol, a popular anabolic steroid he sells. He's been on it in the past and knows it has a tendency to make him more aggressive and hostile. In fact, he swore it off after Megan left him. But the stuff works so damn well that he recently decided to give it another go.

As he ruminates over today's poor showing, anger courses through his veins and he feels the need to move. He stalks around his room like a caged tiger. Periodically he checks his phone for incoming messages.

The condolences for Megan are relentless. He deletes them all. Suppresses the urge to respond with streams of bomb, flame, and laughing emojis.

He receives an alert that Gemma just posted to Instagram. Because he subscribes to the principle "know thy enemy," he clicks on it.

> Hey, Fit Fam! Prejudging went well! I have a SUPER exciting announcement planned for after Finals. Hint: I will be embarking on a new path. Massive changes are on the horizon. Tune in later this evening to find out more!
> #newdirection #change #beginnings #takeachance

That fucking bitch. She's going to announce to the world that she quit following his program, quit his team, and won the Olympia in the process. She's going to start coaching Bikini competitors, he knows it. This will kill his business. So much of what his clients are buying is the belief that they, too, can look like his girls, if only they hire him. Get all the accolades, business contracts, fitness magazine spreads, and hot guys that come with that.

They fail to realize that his girls have these things because they bust their asses, day in and day out. They are able to endure hours of training when they are exhausted. Forgo eating when they are famished. Get back up on the stage after humiliating losses. Frankly, they are insane. Most people aren't. That's why most people don't win.

Breaking his concentration is a text from Anita, who can't be left alone for more than an hour. She's like a gaping, never-ending hole of need. Figuratively and literally. The rumors are true. Rick has fucked her. She wants to discuss strategy for this evening.

Strategy? How about brace yourself for second place?

Rick recognizes that he's getting worked up and knows from experience that nothing good ever comes from that. Prior to the end of his marriage, he took an anger management course (court mandated), where he built a "Calm Down Tool Kit." He reaches into it now and pulls out the mantra, *This, too, shall pass.* He lets his mind go blank and repeats it over and over.

While he's repeating it, Anita texts a question mark, unable to wait even a fucking minute for him to answer. The buzzing of her text makes him want to hurl his phone at the wall.

He pulls out another tool and visualizes a beautiful blue ocean. Then realizes that once his business is in the shitter, he won't be able to afford to visit the ocean any time soon. His blood pressure spikes.

He tries a third tool: Reframe the situation. Maybe Gemma dumping him isn't such a bad thing; maybe there is opportunity here. As he mulls this over, it occurs to him that Anita has a point. Rather than accepting defeat, maybe he should be thinking strategy.

What if there was some way to prevent Gemma from placing first tonight? That would solve everything. His girl Anita takes first, Gemma announces that she's split with him, and no one gives a shit. Maybe in another year, Gemma will win the Olympia. But by that time, it will be a blip on the radar, and not a repudiation of his coaching.

Rick doesn't plan on hitting Gemma in the back of the head with a pipe like he did with Russel. He understands now that that was a bad way to handle the situation. Unfortunate, really. He's also learned that you can't force a woman to be loyal. She might pretend to be for a while, but then the lying, conniving bitch will betray you the moment you turn your back. He's got Megan to thank for that nugget. And Bianca. Fucking Bianca.

But what if, say, Gemma's tan got messed up. If she somehow fell into the shower while the water was running? That would knock her out of first place, maybe even out of the top five. But how could he orchestrate something like that?

Either way, Rick is not involving Anita. She's too unreliable.

He texts her back, "Steer the course. Relax and stick with the plan."

Then Rick gets to work strategizing.

Chapter 66

ASHLEY

Suddenly, I'm not sure that I'm up for this. It's one thing to punch a guy who almost ran me over and called me a fat bitch, but it's quite another to harm these women, who haven't directly done anything to me. I think of the woman with the toolbox, down on her knees working on something. The reams of bomb information on The Phoenix's site. How Lydia turned up at my place with singed hair on the same day that Megan was blown up. How Rachel, who Lydia sent me to spy on, is now dead. A cold sickness roils in my stomach.

Alone in the bathroom, I look at myself in the mirror. How did I get here? I think back to what inspired me to ditch Diet Culture. I simply wanted to accept myself the way that I am. To be happy, despite what others may think or say. How did that morph into a hatred for those who are living their lives differently than I am? All this hatred is making me tired. Is this really the way that I want to live my life?

A news alert comes through my phone. "Young Mom Almost Dies Due to Cyberattack." I click it open and the print swims.

Amanda Lovelace, mom to five-year-old Holden and three-year-old Jessica, almost lost her life recently when she suffered a medical emergency while A New You's systems were down due to a ransomware attack. The criminals demanded half a million dollars, which took A New You fourteen hours to come up with. As a result, Amanda's doctor was not able to access her MRI records. Says Dr. Berlin, "If the systems had been down for five more minutes, Amanda's children would be motherless."

There's a family photo of Amanda with a big toothy smile, her husband, and the adorable towheaded Holden and Jessica. Jessica is holding a stuffed rabbit by the ears.

My heart squeezes so tight it weeps. Weeps with shame and weeps with grace. Thank God Amanda is still alive. I could never live with myself if she wasn't.

And a half-million-dollar ransom? Lydia told me it was fifty thousand.

I splash cold water on my face, but it's still splotchy and red. I'm in the middle of drying it off when my email chimes. It's one of my old clients, Barry, who I did some website work for last year. I miss my old clients, my old life, the time before I got sucked into all this craziness with Lydia and my business tanked.

I scan the email. Pretty standard stuff, he wants me to revamp his site and update his cybersecurity. Until I get to the end:

Hey, I hope you don't mind. I gave your name to a business associate a couple months ago. I keep forgetting to tell you. She was looking for someone with your special skill set. Her name is Lydia in case she contacts you.

I reread it three more times, parsing each word. Could he be talking about another Lydia? It seems unlikely. Lydia's not a very common name, and the timing certainly lines up. But if he gave her my name, why didn't she just say so? And what was she doing at the clinic the day we met? I thought she was there because of her mom.

My brain jerks like a two-by-four smacked it.

With slippery fingers, I dial Tony's number. He picks up on the first ring, "Hey, Ash, everything okay?" In the background are the sounds of his boxing club.

"Tony, did Lydia ever say anything to you about her mom?" My voice is a couple octaves too high. It bounces off the bathroom tiles.

"Babe, what's going on? You don't sound too good." I hear a door close on Tony's end, like he's gone into his office. The background noise falls away. Only Tony's breathing remains.

"Tony, for the love of God! Did Lydia ever mention her mom?"

"I mean, nothing specific. I met her once. Reminded me of a witch. Sort of like Lydia, come to think of it. Why? What's wrong?"

"When? When did you meet her mom?"

"I don't know. Maybe three, four years ago?"

Lydia's thirty. She told me her mom died the week of her high school graduation.

"I gotta go," I say, and hang up.

———

I'm sitting on the bathroom floor, legs akimbo, mind twirling, when the door creaks open.

A shadow falls over me. "I knew I'd find you here."

Chapter 67

ANDREW

Kylie and Andrew are lying in bed. She's tucked into the crook of his arm, scrolling through her phone, liking and commenting on various posts while simultaneously telling him that she dumped her boyfriend and quit her job, both this week, and that she's looking for a new adventure.

Abruptly, she climbs out of bed. Andrew wonders if she's embarking on a new adventure right this minute. Instead, she starts rummaging through her purse, explaining that she has ADHD. Andrew is not surprised. She retrieves a vial of Adderall and heads to the minibar, where she pulls out a bottle of cabernet. "You don't mind?" she asks, holding up the bottle as she unscrews the top.

"No, help yourself," Andrew answers, though she is already washing down a postcoital Adderall with great gulps. She tosses the empty bottle in the garbage, grabs another, and climbs back into bed. Resumes scrolling through her phone.

Andrew is pretty sure you're not supposed to mix alcohol with Adderall, but hesitates to point this out. Instead, he asks, "So this guy you dumped, he's back in Tampa?" Andrew doesn't want him showing up at the door.

"Yep. Oh my God!" she exclaims, thrusting her phone in his face.

Andrew's heart leaps to his throat. He's certain there's a text that her ex is on the way up. Instead, it's a picture of a green bikini.

"Don't you just love this suit?" Kylie asks.

"Yeah, I guess," Andrew answers. His stomach is starting to feel wobbly.

Kylie has already scrolled past the bikini and is liking a post from a fitness girl Andrew happens to follow. So at least they have that in common.

"I'm planning on being a Bikini competitor. That's why I'm here. To check out an actual competition and get the lay of the land. I thought I might interview that Bikini coach Rick Schwann. That's the same coach Gemma uses." Kylie slides her eyes over to him, as if to gauge his reaction.

"You know Gemma?" He involuntarily jerks away. Kylie appears encouraged by this.

"Yeah, just in passing, you know?" Andrew doesn't know. "Anyway, I should pee or I'm going to get a UTI." Andrew makes a mental note to google "UTI."

He studies her naked body as she walks to the bathroom. She's got some work to do to be a Bikini competitor, he thinks, but he likes her like this. She looks real. Real is actually quite nice.

The toilet flushes. From the bathroom, she says, "Did you hear about the Bikini competitor who fell in the toilet?"

Andrew sits up. "No. Who was it?"

She emerges. "Just another girl who had a shitty day." Her lips curl up expectantly.

He doesn't understand.

Her smile spreads. There's a slight, rather charming gap

between her front two teeth. "Get it?" she asks. "Fell in the toilet? Shitty day?"

And then he does. He laughs, maybe a little too hard. But it's funny, in a cute, corny sort of way.

Kylie says, "Finals are going to start soon. Do you want to go together?" Her eyes, ringed in smudged eyeliner, are hopeful, bright, and blue.

Andrew hesitates. His plan had been to try to catch Gemma again after Finals and see if she'd changed her mind about a drink. He realizes now that this was a fantasy. That there's a real girl in front of him, a fun girl, and she wants to hang out. "Yes, I'd like that very much," he says.

The Adderall seems to kick in and her confidence soars. "Awesome!" She jumps back into bed and rests a hand on his moist cock. As if reading his mind, she says, "We've only got about fifteen minutes before I need to start getting ready."

"I can rise to the challenge," he says.

He already has.

Chapter 68

GEMMA

Up ahead, Detective Stark appears in the lobby, like a beacon in a storm. I run to her. "That man"—I ostentatiously point to Todd—"I think he's the man that broke into my apartment. Maybe even the Fit Girl Killer!" Todd sees me pointing at him and hastily makes for the exit.

Stark takes off after him.

I'm left standing in the lobby. Dale is looking at me, his mouth hanging open. I'm about to return to my room, when I realize that I left without the key and am locked out, once again. Dale simply nods and gets me another. I think he secretly suspects I'm a mess.

As I'm heading back to the elevators, I notice Craig talking up one of the REIGN girls in the lobby. He's making eye contact with her, doing his best to be charming. He reaches out and touches her arm, the way he used to touch mine. Suddenly, I feel so very alone.

And then it hits me: *There is no one coming to save me.*

I think all little girls, at some point, fantasize about a man saving them. It's a cornerstone of all fairy tales: Snow White is awakened with a kiss. So is Sleeping Beauty. Cinderella is saved from poverty by a prince. Why are they all saved? Because they are beautiful and kind and demure, and apparently can't save themselves. We are steeped in this lie that if we just look pretty (in none of the fairy tales is there any mention of the damsels being clever or industrious) and are patient (some of them wait for one hundred years), then a wealthy man (preferably a prince) will rescue us.

That someone was coming to save me was especially appealing to me when I was young. Through my whole shitty childhood, my savior in my head was my missing biological father. Sometimes I would imagine that he was watching over me, waiting for the right time to appear. I strove for good grades to make him proud. Other times, I would imagine that he didn't know what had become of me and was frantically searching.

His lifelong absence left me with this profound desire for a man to come in and save me.

I thought Steve might be that man. How very wrong I was. I pay the majority of the bills, keep our home clean, food in the fridge, our clothes laundered. Steve smokes pot and fucks other people.

For a while, I thought my savior might be Craig. He runs a successful business, is responsible, and genuinely wanted to fuck me. But he's an unethical liar. Possibly even a murderer. And now, when I need him most, he isn't here. For me, for us, for our child. I'm realizing that there is no greater time of need than when you are pregnant.

So there is no one I can count on. I am an orphan. I am also soon to be an unwed mother. But strangely, as I consider this, instead of feeling fear, a calmness washes over me. I can finally quit worrying about who is going to show up and just get on with the business of taking care of myself. As it turns out, I've been doing it the whole time.

Reeling from this heady realization, I want a quiet place to process it. Not my room, which no longer feels safe. I remember seeing the hotel chapel the other day on my way back from the gym and head there.

Chapter 69

ASHLEY

"I know your mom's not dead," I say, pushing myself up off the bathroom floor.

"Yes, she is." Lydia looks me straight in the eyes. It dawns on me that she is a sociopath.

"Lydia, I just talked to Tony. He *met* your mom. Like, three years ago."

"That was my biological mom. My stepmom is the one A New You killed."

"Jesus, Lydia, enough already! Barry emailed me that he gave you my name. I know you were at A New You to meet me." This last sentence is a bluff. I don't so much know as feel it.

Neither of us says a word. Water drips in the sink to my left. Behind me, a toilet runs.

Finally, Lydia throws up her hands. "Okay, fine. I went there to meet you."

"How did you know I'd be there?"

"I followed you when you left your apartment, then improvised." She shrugs, like it's no big deal.

"Why didn't you just email me? I'd have met you for coffee."

"Because I wanted to check you out first. Make sure you were someone I could trust. Someone who'd be sympathetic to the cause. Then when I saw you outside A New You, I thought maybe you wouldn't be the right fit, despite how highly recommended you came. So I had to probe that. And it turned out you were perfect. You were exactly what I needed."

I don't say anything. I notice that for once, my heart doesn't warm to her praise. That it's closed tight like a fist.

Lydia continues, "And I think I was what you needed, as well. Even if you don't realize it right now. I gave you life. A purpose. Before you met me, you never left your home. I tried for almost two weeks to run into you before finally following you to A New You."

A dry laugh escapes my throat. I shake my head. "Lydia, you were the last thing I needed. Since meeting you, my business is in tatters. I'm barely sleeping. I've somehow entered the criminal underworld. And I almost killed a woman. Did you see the news?"

"Yes, I saw it. And it's unfortunate. But, Ashley, you simply must think big picture. We're talking about one woman versus lord knows how many dying from weight loss surgery complications, anorexia, and bulimia. And how many others suffering from mental health issues as a result of Diet Culture. The low self-esteem, depression, and anxiety. The subversive message it sends to all of us. How it keeps us down. Shrinks and diminishes us!"

Lydia is gesturing grandly, as she so often does when she gets going on this topic. Usually, I'm sucked into her gravitational pull. Not today.

I say, "The article also said the ransom was half a mil. You told me it was fifty grand and that I could have ten percent."

"Fifty was my take for closing the deal. Your ten percent

was coming out of my own pocket. The other four hundred and fifty goes to the cause. Look, if you want fifty grand, you can have it, but you'll be taking it away from women everywhere."

"Lydia, this isn't about the money! This is about you lying to me."

"But I haven't been lying to you." She takes a step closer. Her eyes wide and beseeching.

I sigh. There's no point in arguing.

Lydia places her hands, like hooks, on my shoulders. "Now, it's time to get out there and take action. Ashley, I'm recommending you for captain at our next meeting. And I expect my captains to rally."

I don't budge.

She leans closer, her rancid breath sears my face. "I'd hate for you to no longer be part of The Phoenix. Bad things tend to happen to our castoffs."

With that, she releases me. Turns and struts out the door.

I look at myself in the mirror. *What have I become?*

Fearing Lydia's return, I exit the bathroom and blindly stumble down the hall. I need somewhere to think. Somewhere quiet. My eyes land on the door to the hotel chapel. I push it open.

Inside is a small room with a couple pews. I take a seat. Warm afternoon sun streams through a nondenominational stained glass window. It illuminates my body in geometric reds, blues, and greens. I'm not a terribly religious person, but suddenly I don't feel so alone.

Chapter 70

ANITA

Anita stands silent in the entry, listening. For the second time today, she's used Gemma's stolen key to access her room. Motionless, she tries to determine if Gemma is actually gone, or was simply ignoring her knock. Hearing only the hiss of the air conditioner, she creeps into the main room. It's empty. She breathes a sigh of relief.

So far, her efforts to thwart Gemma haven't produced. Though she still has high hopes that the heel she loosened or bikini stitching she pulled will give, she isn't content to hang her dreams on hope. She needs to up her game.

Anita slides a small vial from her robe. It's filled with an itching powder she made by pulling old hair from her brush and cutting it into tiny pieces. A long-ago trick from her youth. This will surely mess up Gemma's tan. Anita scatters it on the bed and both room chairs.

She's about to leave, when her eyes catch on a blob of peanut butter on the wall. They travel down to a shattered plate and broken bits of rice cakes on the floor. The hairs on the back of her neck stand up. An ancient part of her registers fear and sweat in the air.

There is a knock at the door. "Gemma?" It's Craig.

Anita stands motionless.

Again, a knock. "Gemma, we really need to talk."

Anita doesn't breathe. For the first time ever, she wills Craig to go away. Instead, she hears the click of the lock and watches as the doorknob slowly turns.

Anita crouches behind the bed. She hopes—prays—Craig will simply poke his head in the room, verify it's empty, and leave. Instead, she hears the door creak open. His footsteps, muffled against the carpet, travel inward. The door clicks shut. "Hello?" he calls.

She curls in upon herself, chin to chest, inhaling fake tanner and fear. Sweat trickles down her back. The hinges of the bathroom door squeak. Footsteps clack on tile. Shower rings clatter down a rod, its curtain rustles. The footsteps pivot and become thuds on carpet.

Again, Craig calls, "Gemma?"

The closet door slides open. Hangers chime. Fabric whispers. The closet door slides shut.

The footsteps come closer. A sheet is whisked off the bed. Its edge slaps her cheek. The footsteps continue, then stop behind her. Tucked in her ball, she can see the silver laces of Craig's Golden Goose Italian sneakers. She is about to stand, turn around, and explain (just stopping by to borrow a pair of earrings, found Gemma's door open, came inside to check on her), when she notices something disturbing. From her angle, she can see the tips of Craig's fingers. They are clad in purple latex gloves.

All her thoughts—the earring story, Finals, the heels she just put on her credit card—topple out of her head. Only one thought remains: *Why is Craig wearing latex gloves?*

Anita is yanked up and backward by the neck. Something is

around it, tightening, tightening. She can't breathe. Her head is going to explode. Her hands scramble at what feels like a belt. The edges of her vision darken and bright stars appear.

She shoots a desperate hand backward. It flails against Craig's legs, finds his balls, and latches on like a deranged octopus. She squeezes so hard she expects them to burst. Craig squeals. The belt around her neck slackens.

Gasping for breath, she finds her footing, keeping her vise-like grip on Craig's gelatinous sac. He howls and howls, then twists out of her clutches. His eyes pop open. "Anita?"

She realizes that from behind, he must have thought she was Gemma. She's in Gemma's room, has the same blond hair extensions, and is wearing the same *Rick's Girl* robe. Her thoughts race. Maybe she can salvage this. "Craig, I don't know what's up with you and Gemma, but it's none of my business. I never liked her anyway. My loyalty is with you." She attempts deep, meaningful eye contact. Tries to convey that if Craig is planning on killing Gemma, she won't tell anyone. Won't even stop him. And it's true.

Craig's eyes dart around the room like a trapped animal.

Anita continues, "Look, I've just stopped by to borrow a pair of earrings. No big deal. I'll see you downstairs at Finals."

She turns toward the door. Out of the corner of her eye, she can see his purple fingers twitching. She is almost there when he lunges at her. She races ahead, manages to get her hand on the knob and twist, but Craig's long arm shoots out overhead and holds the door shut. With his other hand, he yanks her away from the knob. He is careful this time to angle his sac away from her.

His hand is firm around her wrist. Anita abandons any illusions of a future with this guy. She leans down and bites his forearm, sinking her teeth deep into the flesh. Tissues crunch.

Capillaries burst. Blood fills her mouth and runs down her throat. Drips from her chin.

He screams and drops her wrist but is still blocking the exit, so she makes for the bathroom. He grasps for her as she slams the door. It ricochets off his fingers, vibrating like a violin string. He roars and forces the door in.

She grabs the porcelain back of the toilet and swings at his torso. It connects with his ribs with a wonderful thwack. He lands in the tub and appears momentarily dazed. Somehow the shower has come on.

Anita makes for the exit. Behind her she hears Craig scramble to stand. Slipping shoes. Sloshing water. She is almost to the door when he snatches her back by the hair. Several extensions rip out. One falls to the floor, a bloody chunk of her scalp dangling from its cheap plastic comb.

Craig bear-hugs her from behind. She twists and turns and kicks him in the shins, but he holds tight. He drags her backward toward the tub. She can hear him close the drain with his foot.

She takes advantage of his precarious state and kicks him sideways in the standing leg. His knee buckles and she's free. Suspended in the air.

The sudden freedom causes her to stumble backward. Her arms flail. She reaches for the shower curtain. Tries to hold on. But it slips through her fingers. The curtain's beautiful, really. Ethereal and pure white.

There is a sickening crack as the back of her head connects with the tub. That didn't sound good, she thinks. Then everything goes dark.

Chapter 71

GEMMA

I open the chapel door and freeze. It's Fat Gemma. She turns toward me. Her face awash in stained glass. Half green, half yellow.

"What are you doing here?" she asks.

This is it. I've finally lost it. Because I'm no longer sane, I decide to wade right into the crazy. "I don't know. Why are you here?"

"I thought it was to make the world a better place. But now I think I'm just making it worse. I'm Ashley, by the way."

She shifts, her face now blue. My racing thoughts hit the wall, full speed, and obliterate. Maybe I've got this all wrong.

Could it really be her? I know she lives in Orlando. Is she here to meet me? She looks a lot like the Ashley in the website security article I managed to dig up a couple years ago, but her hair is different. I look closer, and I'm sure it's her. I recognize her eyes. The same ones I see every morning in the mirror.

"I've wanted to meet you for so long," I say, stepping forward. "I thought about contacting you, but didn't know if you knew about me, or would even want to meet me. When did you find out?"

She seems confused and shrinks back into green. "Find out what?" She looks toward the door, like I'm possibly nuts and she might have to make a break for it.

Suddenly, I get the feeling that we're not on the same page and hesitate.

"Find out what?" she asks again.

"That you're my half sister."

Ashley's eyes open wide. "What are you talking about?"

"Our dad. Nicholas Shermer. I only found out his name a couple years ago. I hired a genealogist and she helped me find him. And by extension, you."

Ashley grips the pew in front of her like she's hanging on to the edge of a cliff. Her face is now orange. "Did he know you found him?"

"Yes, I went to his office and introduced myself. He seemed very keen that his family not find out about me. I'm four years younger than you. So, obviously conceived while he was married to your mom. I'm sorry about that."

"I can't believe he never told me." Her eyes are distant, like she's sifting through her memories, looking for an answer.

"Well, maybe he would have, once he recovered from the shock. But he died three weeks later. I was just happy I got to connect with him first."

"Why didn't you contact me?"

"I thought about it, but didn't know how it would go over. My meeting with him didn't exactly go as planned."

"I'm sorry."

"Don't be. It's not your fault. You haven't done anything wrong."

She laughs wryly and shakes her head. "Oh, I wouldn't say that."

"Why not?"

Ashley looks at her hands, red and yellow, clinging to the pew. Slowly, she unpeels them. Stands and walks toward me. All the colors fall away and it's just her. "Well, for starters, I'm @fat_and_ fabulous. The person who sort of beats you up on Instagram."

Her answer hangs there while I digest it. So this is the person who was hiding behind all those comments? Who caused me so much angst? The crux of our disagreement, what we do with our bodies, suddenly seems so unbelievably trivial.

I start to laugh. It begins as little bubbles, then wells up into great big, belly-heaving waves. "Oh my God," I say, striving to catch my breath. "I always wanted a sister."

"I always wanted a sister too." She seems dazed.

Chimes startle us. It's the timer on my phone. "Wow, I didn't realize it was so late. I need to get ready for Finals. Do you want to come up and hang out in my room with me? Maybe we can grab something to eat after?" I silence the timer and keep my eyes trained on my phone. I hold my breath.

What if she says no?

I was always so lonely growing up. In fact, I used to fantasize that I had a sister who was somehow lost to me. Perhaps I was secretly adopted? Or there was a mistake at the hospital? I would imagine her turning up on my playset, or at the edge of the woods behind my apartment building.

And now my real sister is here. What if she rejects me like my father did?

"Yes, that would be great," she says, and relief floods through me. She picks up her phone. "Give me a few more minutes here, though. There's something that I need to do. I'll meet you upstairs. What room are you in?"

"Room 751." I leave while I'm ahead.

Chapter 72

ASHLEY

I have a sister. A little sister.

Could she now be in danger because of me and what I started? I never meant for anyone to get hurt.

Deep down, a little voice calls me out. If I didn't anticipate that someone could get hurt through my work with Lydia, I wasn't paying attention. Multiple people have warned me she's dangerous. I saw evidence of making bombs on The Phoenix's site. She showed up at my place with charred eyebrows and smelling like smoke. Amanda from A New You almost died because of us. Willful ignorance won't buy me absolution.

I plug 911 into my phone but waffle. There is no way that someone from Lydia's group has planted a bomb in the building. None. This is crazy. The Phoenix might not be responsible for any of the Fit Girl deaths, either. It's all speculation on my part.

So what? the voice inside me says. *Better safe than sorry.* But there will be a record of my call. And when this all turns out to be a false alarm, which it will, I'll have some explaining to do. Lydia will hate me forever. Our alliance will be over. I'll no longer be a part of something bigger than me, fighting for large bodies everywhere. Instead, I will just be fat and part of nothing.

That's not true. I will be part of Gemma's family.

Tony will still believe in me.

And what if it's true? What if there really is a bomb? I brought Lydia's group to this protest. If Gemma, or anyone else here, dies today at Lydia's hands, it's on me.

Before I can talk myself out of it, I press the red button and make the call. I tell the dispatcher that I'm likely wrong. That I know I'm wrong. That I'm simply calling out of an abundance of caution.

As I talk, I look down at my phoenix ring, with its sparkling rubies and shiny black onyx. I remember how proud I was when Lydia gave it to me. How happy I was to belong. Today, its glittering eye is menacing. Its open beak mocking.

I finish the call and start to pull the ring off, but it sticks. I twist and twist. My hands start to sweat. Finally, it releases me. It leaves a rash behind.

I exit the chapel and drop the ring in the trash. Good riddance.

Chapter 73

GEMMA

I'm stepping off the elevator when I see Coach Rick knocking on my door. "Gemma? Please can I come in? I've given this some thought, and I'd like to bury the hatchet."

My stomach cramps, and I reach for the side of the elevator door for stability. It's his subliminal word choice of "hatchet"—I know he means me harm. I feel it deep in my gut. Images flood my brain: Rick smacking Russel Marks in the back of the head with a pipe, dragging Megan through their home by her hair, Megan exploding on the set of *Shrinking*.

Barely breathing, I tiptoe back into the elevator. It's not safe here. I will just have to get ready backstage, without any of my things. I hit the down button and head to the lobby. Shoot Ashley a quick text, "Hey, I decided not to go back to my room (long story, total nutcase outside it) and instead went backstage. It's almost showtime. Let's connect after Finals."

I'm hustling my way through the auditorium—all the vendor booths are gone, replaced with seating for Finals—when my right heel snaps. I crash to the floor, skinning my palms, getting dirt all over my tan. Strangers help me up, but I don't see their faces. All I see is my broken heel, the same side as my broken backup pair. Without heels, I'm done.

With shaking hands, I dial Alexa's number. She owns the Shoe Fairy and is in town for the Olympia.

"Hey, babe," she answers. "I saw Prejudging. Looks like tonight's your night."

"Alexa, I just broke a heel! Do you have any size sevens?"

"Oh no! I don't. Anita came by earlier and cleaned me out of all the size sevens and eights. Bought a total of eight pairs."

"What?"

"I know. So weird, right? Anita's, like, a size ten. I asked her what she was doing with all the shoes, and she said"—Alexa raises her pitch, adds a nasal effect—"'Alexa, if it was any of your business, you wouldn't have to ask.'"

Fucking Anita. I hang up and text my ex-teammates. Ask if any of them have a pair of sevens—hell, even eights—that I can borrow. No one returns my text. They've all circled the wagons. Afraid if they help me, then Rick will drop them and blacklist them in the world of bodybuilding.

With nothing else left to do, I head backstage anyway, hoping for a miracle.

Chapter 74

COACH RICK

That goddamn bitch, Rick thinks, his knuckles starting to bruise. He's been banging on Gemma's door for a good five minutes. At first, he figured she was just ignoring him. But he said all the right things, and she still hasn't responded, either by letting him in, or by telling him to get lost. He's finally starting to think that maybe she's not in her room.

Rick leans close to the door and listens. Unbelievably, he thinks he hears a shower running. What possible reason could Gemma have for running the shower? Water is the nemesis of spray tan. He decides he must be hearing water running from an adjoining room.

Finally, he gives up. Better to focus on the girls he has.

Since Anita and Kat are also on the seventh floor, he goes to their rooms to check in. To make sure they're ready for Finals and that there are no last-minute issues. While making his rounds, he keeps an eye on Gemma's door. If she returns, he'll revert to Plan A, which involves him ostensibly extending an olive branch, checking her shower pressure, and accidently-on-purpose knocking her into the tub. It's a stretch, but to quote Wayne Gretzky, *You miss one hundred percent of the shots you don't take.*

Kat is accounted for and set to go. But where the hell is Anita? She's not answering her door. Nor her cell. Could she already be downstairs? The plan had been that they would all head down together. And Anita always follows the plan.

Some of Rick's other girls, though not in the top ten, are coming down to Finals to watch. They now mill around in the hall with him and Kat, waiting for Anita. Making him look weak and inefficient. To set the record straight, he orders everyone downstairs. Tells them he'll join them shortly.

Once they're gone, he sets his iPad down and pummels Anita's door for a solid minute. His hands are going to be purple tomorrow. Finally, he gives up and calls her cell. It rings several times and goes to voicemail. This is odd. Anita is always reachable. He tries calling again and thinks he hears a faint echo of the same ring coming from inside her hotel room.

It's strange enough that she's not in her room, even stranger that she's not answering her phone, but off the charts strange that she would go somewhere without it. To confirm that the phone he hears ringing is indeed hers, he hangs up and tries again. And sure enough, it is.

Rick is starting to get a bad feeling about all of this.

Chapter 75

ASHLEY

Without my ring I feel lighter. I head up to Gemma's room and exit the elevator on the seventh floor. Room 751 appears to be to the right. As I turn that direction, I see a commotion down at the end of the hall. The hotel manager is there, along with that FBI agent, a couple of paramedics, a very hairy man, the guy from the lobby with the iPad, the hater who accosted me outside the bathroom, and a woman with an iPhone who appears to be recording the whole thing. Is that Kylie? The woman I follow on Instagram? No, it can't be. She said she wasn't going to be in town for the Olympia.

I forget all about the Kylie look-alike once I realize the paramedics are wheeling a body out of a room. A white sheet draped over it.

My stomach drops. Somehow, I know out of all these rooms, that they are coming out of 751. I float down the hall toward them, like I'm having an out-of-body experience. The numbers increase: 737, 739, and 741. The odd numbers are on the same side as the room they exit. In a flash, the math is clear. There are four more closed doors before the open one. That would mean they are coming out of room 751. Gemma's room.

The thought stops me, and I float no more. My feet stick to the carpet.

I think of Lydia, roaming the hotel with a pair of scissors. Her eyes alive with hate. What if she killed my sister?

The iPad man's face is red. He keeps repeating, to no one in particular, "I don't know how this happened. How could this happen?"

I feel the same way. How could this happen? Maybe I made a mistake calculating which door is Gemma's. I run the numbers again, recount the remaining doors. I'm more deliberate this time, but keep getting confused. I keep coming up with 751. This can't be right.

Since my brain isn't working, I decide to forge ahead and see for myself the number on the open door. I unstick my feet and drag them along, like I'm walking on flypaper. The body is almost out the door by the time I get there. And there it is in shiny bronze: 751.

The iPad man says, "But how? What was she even doing in Gemma's room? And where is Gemma?"

I freeze. None of them notice me. All eyes are on the covered body.

Blood is whooshing through my ears, making it difficult to hear. Difficult to think. It's like some sort of karmic joke. Like I want the dead body not to be Gemma so badly that I'm imagining things.

The iPad man's phone rings. He answers, "Anita's dead. She's fucking dead." After a moment, "How should I know?" He hangs up and says to the Kylie look-alike videoing the scene, "Put that fucking phone away!" She swiftly complies.

Gemma's alive. My tightly coiled heart unspools. I know

whatever the fallout is from today, it will be okay. Lydia can dump me, my business can go bankrupt, the sky can fall. My sister is alive.

I discreetly walk back toward the elevator. Where in the world did Gemma go? Out of reflex, I pull out my phone and check my messages. There's one from her: "Hey, I decided not to go back to my room (long story, total nutcase outside it) and instead went backstage. It's almost showtime. Let's connect after Finals."

The paramedics are headed in my direction with the body, and that scary man with the iPad is still pacing around the hall. I'd bet money that he's the "total nutcase" Gemma referred to. I need to get out of here.

Not wanting to wait for the elevator, I duck into the stairwell and head downstairs to Finals, even though Lydia warned me to stay away. I can't miss Gemma's showtime.

Chapter 76

GEMMA

"Does anyone have an extra set of heels, size seven or eight, that I can borrow?" I ask the room at large. There are nine Bikini finalists backstage. Anita, our tenth, is not here yet. Everyone shakes their head or studiously avoids eye contact.

All except one. Kentucky Crystal's hand goes up. "I have a pair of sevens right here in my bag. They're a little big for me. I just brought them as backup." She digs through a yellow duffel bag and produces a pair of barely used, clear five-inch heels.

They dangle from her hand, glittering.

"Thank you so much!" I slip them on. "They're perfect." I feel like Cinderella.

A stage handler calls out, "Twenty minutes 'til showtime." My stomach starts to flutter.

Now that I have heels, I need to worry about the rest of me. I head to the tanning lady.

"What the hell happened to you?" she says, inspecting my body. There are so many streaks and blemishes covering it, I practically look like a topographical map. She shakes her head, squirts a dollop of Liquid Sun Rayz on her terry-cloth mitt and gets to work buffing me out.

"Since Prejudging, I've discovered my husband is gay, was chased by his lover, met my long-lost half sister, dodged my scary ex-coach outside my hotel room, and broke a heel and crashed to the floor."

"Oh, girl. You've had yourself an afternoon. Well, don't you worry. I'll fix you right up."

Thankfully, she does just that. After getting my tan straightened out, I get my makeup and hair touched up, with similar remarks about the state of affairs.

Kat is practicing her posing, but appears distracted. She frequently looks around like a lost duckling. Usually, Rick is right there in the middle of it all, consulting his iPad, barking out orders, adjusting hair. Tonight, he's nowhere in sight. Neither is Anita. I get an uneasy feeling.

My former teammates' group text starts to light up:

"Where the hell is Rick?"

"No idea. Maybe he was arrested for Megan's murder?"

"But where's Anita?"

"Maybe they're upstairs fucking?"

"They've been fucking for years. Rick would never fuck her before Finals. It would mess up her tan."

"True dat."

"My money's on: Rick's the Fit Girl Killer. Anita's his accomplice."

"This. OMG, this."

Finally, I'm called to the stage for my individual presentation. I numbly step out into the blinding lights, smile plastered to my face, and run through the routine that I've practiced thousands of times. I could do it in my sleep. In fact, it feels like I am.

Once all nine of the finalists have presented (Anita never

turned up), we're called back to the stage. We line up on two diagonals. Four stage left, five stage right.

This is the moment of truth. The announcer starts with fifth place. He calls a brunette in an emerald bikini. She brings her hands to her face in excitement. Wipes tears from her eyes. She steps out onto the center line and receives a bouquet of roses. A medal is draped over her head. It briefly gets tangled up in her hair, but she fixes it.

The whole process repeats two more times, until the announcer has fifth, fourth, and third place lined up.

"And now, I'd like to call our top two Bikini Olympians to the stage. One of these ladies will be your 2021 Ms. Bikini Olympia. The other will be your runner-up. May I get a drumroll please?"

Chapter 77

ASHLEY

"Ladies and gentlemen, your top two Bikini Olympians are . . . Gemma Jorgenson and Crystal Clancy!"

Around me, the audience erupts. Mechanically, I put my hands together. But unease snakes through my belly. My eyes keep drifting to the Bombshells Only sign that hangs over the stage. Something about it sets off my internal alarm system.

Crystal and Gemma walk out to the center line. They hug each other.

The announcer drops his voice. "Now, ladies and gentlemen. Are you ready?"

The applause is deafening.

Again, my eyes travel to the sign. And then I see it. The *O* in *Bombshells*. It's what the toolbox girl was working on earlier with her power drill, what I originally mistook for a zero. There's a black bomb in its center. I know it's not for decoration.

I look around the auditorium and see her off to the side, leaning against the wall. Despite all the action being onstage, her eyes are on the Bombshells Only sign. She holds her cell phone in front of her. Like she's getting ready to press a button.

I'm on my feet and rushing to the stage.

The announcer booms, "Your 2021 Bikini Olympia runner-up . . . is Crystal Clancy!"

Crystal covers her mouth and squeezes her eyes shut. Gemma and she hug again. Crystal receives a bouquet and medal.

The announcer continues, "Which means, your 2021 Bikini Olympia winner is Gemma Jorgenson! I'd like to call REIGN owner, Craig Higgins, to the stage to present the check."

I barrel up the stage steps.

Craig limps onto the stage at the same time I get there. "Stop!" I scream. I point to the Bombshells Only sign, which hangs over Gemma and Craig. "There's a bomb in the sign!" Everyone looks up. I charge ahead and knock Gemma and Craig out of the way, like a bowling ball knocking over pins.

A thunderous explosion claps above. My eardrums vibrate. The O, now afire, crashes to the stage, inches away, and splinters. More letters start to drop. Screams are all around. Alarms sound. The auditorium Exit signs start to flash.

The announcer declares, "Ladies and gentlemen. Please exit the building."

Gemma appears okay, other than a likely bruised ass. I reach my hand down to her. "Let's get out of here."

Chapter 78

GEMMA

Ashley pulls me up. "The nearest exit's backstage," I say.

We dodge falling letters and flaming objects, tottering competitors and trashed roses. One of my heels gets caught in a blond wig. We make our way backstage, where several people clatter toward the exit. Our hands are locked together, tight and sweaty. There's a bottleneck at the door.

I smell something sweet. Like the inside of a confectionary. To my right is a table, set up with champagne flutes and a white cake declaring *Congratulations Bombshells!* in red frosting.

Fat Gemma's laugh rings out in my skull. *Still here*, she says, *and now that we've won the Olympia, there's no reason not to treat ourselves.*

How can she still be here? After all this, how? It's like some sort of scary movie. The bitch won't die.

I squeeze Ashley's hand and press forward. Only it's not Ashley's hand anymore. It's much too big. I look down and see hairy knuckles. Follow them up, and there is Craig. Smiling. His whitened teeth gleam.

"Hi, Gemma, long time no see. You haven't been returning

my calls." He extends his other hand, and I think he's about to grab my wrist. But then my eyes catch something black, about the size of a flashlight, in his hand. There's a crackling sound, and an electric current rips through me. *It smells like rain*, I think. Then everything goes black.

Chapter 79

ASHLEY

I've lost her. Around me, people stream toward the exit. Could Gemma already have made her way outside? My gaze sweeps the area, and I spy her traveling away. That REIGN schmuck, Craig, is holding her up by the arm like she's drunk. He opens a door at the far end of the room.

"Hey, what are you doing?" I call and hurry after them.

Craig turns to me and says, "Oh, it's you," like we're friends. "I'm just helping Gemma out of the public eye while she wears this off. Looks like she took too many Xanax. This has become a bit of a problem." He shrugs, like it's no big deal.

"She was fine five minutes ago," I answer tightly. He seems to be favoring his right leg. His right hand is severely bruised. I don't remember these injuries earlier during the protest.

"That's been the pattern. She takes the Xanax before Finals for anxiety, sometimes too many. It takes them a bit to kick in. And when they do, this happens." He rolls his eyes.

"She can come with me." I reach for Gemma's arm. It's floppy, like an overcooked noodle. Her head lolls to the side. There's a string of drool hanging from the corner of her mouth.

Gemma smiles at me and slurs, "Ash. You're here."

Craig says, "Don't be ridiculous. She's in no condition to go anywhere." He pushes the door inward and starts pulling Gemma in after him. I hang on to her arm and step my foot into the room to prevent the door from closing. I look around for help, but everyone is near the exit, far away. He continues to try to drag her inside, while I attempt to pull her out. Eventually, we all lose our balance and tumble into the room. The door clicks shut behind us. Like a trap.

The space is dark and cool. It's some sort of storage room. There are wigs, racks of costumes, and props. Stacks of REIGN leggings.

Gemma says, "Ash, what's going on?" Her speech is marginally better. She looks around. "Craig, why are you here?"

Craig ignores her and calmly reaches for the deadbolt. His sleeve slides up, revealing a bite mark—full set of teeth, eyes through molars. A palette of bruises clusters around it. He smoothly twists the lock and reaches into his pocket, like he's about to pull out his wallet. Instead, out comes a black plastic block. It's about six inches long and has two metal prongs at one end.

Thanks to a website I designed for a weapons dealer, I immediately recognize it as a stun gun. Because I wrote product descriptions for all the website's products, I know that both metal prongs need to touch a person to stun them. The longer the prongs are held against a person, the more voltage is delivered, and the longer they will be incapacitated. A half-second touch may leave a person woozy, while a three-second touch can knock a person out for five to sixty minutes. I cannot let him touch me with it.

Craig lets go of Gemma, who slides to the floor.

He lunges at me with the stun gun. It makes a terrible

crackling sound. Electricity sizzles between its prongs and lights up the room with an eerie purple glow. His lunge is clumsy. He definitely has an injured leg. I dodge to the left and he wobbles, just missing me. From behind, Gemma manages to grab his ankle. He crashes to the floor but maintains his grip on the stun gun. "Clever bitch," he says to her.

I kick his hand holding the stun gun. He yelps and it skitters out of his grip. It banks off the wall and out of our reach. Craig gets to his feet, placing most of his weight on his right leg. He holds his damaged right hand back and strikes at my head with his left. Instinctively, I block his punch, bob and weave. My hands come up, guarding my face.

I step in closer, throw a jab and cross. But he weaves away, wincing, just out of striking range. Despite his injured leg, he's nimble. I reset. Again, he strikes with his left. This time, he catches me in the jaw. I stumble backward. In a blur, I see a braided wig, a pink feather boa, and finally the carpet, close-up. I land with a thunk, solid and heavy. Craig staggers toward me, but is yanked backward by the shirttails by Gemma, who is now standing unsteadily. He spins around, twisting the fabric from her hands, and smacks her across the face. She crashes into the wall and sinks to the floor.

I find my footing and get back up. Craig whirls back to me, but I'm ready. I jab to the nose, cross to the jaw, and land a right hook to his ear. It's the hook that does it. Craig catapults through the air. I note, with satisfaction, that his feet leave the floor. He lands hard on the carpet and doesn't move.

Chapter 80

GEMMA

I'm in a strange room with Ashley and Craig. Pink feathers litter the floor. Over a loudspeaker, a tense male voice is instructing everyone to evacuate the building.

I'm on my hands and knees and every muscle I have is sore. There are carpet fibers in my nose. My cheek is throbbing. My thoughts are fuzzy, and my tongue feels too big for my mouth. It's like I'm drunk and hung over at the same time. The last thing I remember is finding myself holding Craig's hand.

Ashley has just delivered a knockout punch so breathtaking that it sent Craig flying. He is now on the floor, out cold.

"What's going on?" I ask.

Ashley starts explaining about the stun gun and how we ended up in this room. I'm so busy listening, that I fail to notice Craig coming to.

Craig's hand lurches out and presses what I now know to be a stun gun against Ashley's calf. There is a horrible buzzing sound. Electricity lights up Craig's contorted face. His lips pull back, revealing purple pearlescent teeth. Ashley's eyes roll back into her head and down she goes.

Craig grins. "We never talk anymore." A chill slides through me. That Craig wants to hurt not only me, but my baby and Ashley, helps sharpen my focus.

He slowly starts to push himself up, keeping weight off his left leg, holding the stun gun gingerly in his right hand. He's still groggy.

Time is of the essence. I cannot flee and leave Ashley here. I can't allow him to get to his feet. His wingspan is longer than mine. With all my might, I kick him in the elbow. His palms skid out from under him. His torso and head connect with the floor. I stomp on his hand with my borrowed Lucite heels, three times in rapid succession. He releases the stun gun, and it hurtles across the floor.

From the loudspeaker: "Please evacuate the building."

I don't have time to retrieve the stun gun and figure out how to use it before Craig overtakes me. His palms come to the carpet, and he begins to push himself up again.

It's now or never. I straddle Craig from behind, like I'm riding him bareback. Grab hold of his ears and smack his head against the floor. Blood explodes—perhaps his nose? Red drops speckle my forearms. A stringy piece of mucus drips off my elbow.

There's a pair of REIGN Bad Bitch leggings on the floor next to me. I snatch them up. Wrench Craig's arms behind his back and begin to tie his wrists together.

He resists; the muscles in his arms bulge. I pull for all I'm worth. All those pull-ups, all those dead lifts, have resulted in some damn good grip strength.

Craig makes a growling sound. His arms tremble. Veins protrude. His hands grow white. Blood seeps around the leggings from angry gouges in his wrists.

He rolls to the right. Attempts to buck me off.

I roll with him. Wrap my legs around his torso, lock them at the ankles, and squeeze like a boa constrictor. I pull the leggings so tight that my biceps shake and my palms burn.

I struggle to tie the knot. My hands are slick with blood. Craig's and mine. Craig continues to thrash.

Ashley appears, looking groggy, with a second set of leggings and starts to tie his legs, but he kicks her in the solar plexus. She flies backward and lands with a thunk. I momentarily worry that I'm on my own. I don't know that I can beat him by myself.

But then Ashley staggers to her feet. She stands there a moment, swaying. Then drags her foot back. And kicks Craig in the nuts like it's the Super Bowl.

He yelps and reflexively curls up. We seize the moment and tie his limbs tight. Once he's secure, I leap up and retrieve the stun gun.

I zap him in the balls. As a precaution. I swear.

Chapter 81

DALE

This is bad for business, Dale thinks, as he surveys his lobby. DIET CULTURE SLUTS is written in five-foot-tall letters on the wall. Police and FBI agents are swarming the floors looking for rogue Fat Activists, who may be responsible for the bomb that went off at the Olympia. A dead body, possibly the victim of a serial killer, was wheeled out of his hotel's back entrance. There is extensive water damage to rooms 751 and 651.

Several guests have been brought to the police station for questioning, including Craig Higgins, owner of REIGN; one of bodybuilding's biggest coaches, Rick Schwann; some of the Fat Activists; the attorney from the lobby who scared Gemma earlier today; and Gemma herself. Dale understands that she zapped Craig in the balls with a stun gun. That girl is trouble.

Orlando's Nightly News is in his lobby, and Eileen Brachman is conducting a live interview. "I'm here with FBI Agent Sean Newman, who's been investigating the recent string of Fit Girl murders. Today we had another mysterious Fit Girl death. And in an unusual turn of events, a possible suspect was apprehended—tied up like a Thanksgiving turkey by a REIGN spokesmodel and Fat Activist protester working together. Agent Newman, what do you know so far?"

Newman says that it's too early to determine if the dead woman was actually murdered, if it's somehow related to the man who was tied up, and if any of this is related to the other Fit Girl murders. While he speaks, a blond woman, wearing so much mascara her eyelashes temporarily stick together each time she blinks, jumps around and waves in the background. There is a young man in a button-down shirt near her.

Just as Newman is wrapping up, the blond blurts out, "I was there!"

Predictably, Eileen heads straight over to her. "What's your name, please?"

"Kylie Erickson." Kylie doesn't look at Eileen. Instead, she looks straight at the camera, takes a deep breath, like she's ready for prime time, and declares, "I was there when two paramedics rolled a body out of the hotel room! I videoed it. You can see it at @queen_kylie. At first, I thought it was Gemma because that's her room, and I couldn't tell it wasn't her because the body was *covered with a sheet*! And Coach Rick was there and freaking out and told me it wasn't Gemma. Gemma's my coach, you see. She helped me lose fourteen pounds in six weeks! We talk all the time. We're super close, you know? In fact, I'm here today to support her and learn more about the sport of bodybuilding. I plan to compete—"

"Thank you, Kylie," Eileen interrupts, pulling the microphone away.

Kylie yanks it back for one last sentence. "Don't forget to follow me!" Then she sticks her lips out like a duck.

Post Show

Chapter 82

ASHLEY

"Does this shirt look okay?" Tony asks, exiting the bathroom. He's wearing a navy-and-gold plaid button-down. I've never seen him in anything other than a T-shirt.

"It looks great!" I assure him and smooth down a cowlick in his hair, damp from the shower. He had it cut yesterday.

We're meeting my mom for lunch (Tony's idea), and he's nervous. I'm not. Ever since I stood up to her, she's been much more accepting of me and my choices. I should have done it years ago.

Back then, I didn't think I was strong enough to fight back. I just took whatever the world dished out at me. Since taking up boxing, I've realized that that's not the way it works.

You don't fight because you're strong. You're strong because you fight. Every day now, I stoke that fire.

Sometimes it's hard for me to reconcile the person I was before the Olympia with the person I've become. I guess you could say I finally got my own "Transformation Story."

Looking back on my Before, I can't believe how far off track I got. How my desire to simply be comfortable in my own skin, and to encourage others to do the same, led me to reject those who wanted something different. How my goal of making society more inclusive somehow led me to follow someone who was making it more divisive. Who was killing people.

In addition to Lydia's toolbox woman being responsible for the Finals bomb, investigators picked up a Honda Accord traced to Lydia on a security camera in Rachel's neighborhood at the time of her murder. Another security camera caught Lydia's Continental speeding past a gas station six miles from the *Shrinking* campus shortly after Megan was blown up. Both Lydia and the toolbox woman have disappeared.

Bianca's murder, on the other hand, appears to have been committed by Craig, based on DNA evidence. Craig refuses to speak to anyone other than his lawyer.

The working theory is that Bianca's death by waist trainer spurred a creative streak of copycat killings by The Phoenix. I am so very grateful that I turned them in when I did. And that I heeded Anon's warning:

To the hacker who replaces me,

Lydia's dangerous. Get out while you can. She will let you take the fall. I would sign my name, but I'm about to disappear.

Anon

Before logging off the day I stumbled on Anon, I scrubbed all traces of my existence from The Phoenix's site and from the ransomware attack. Then I left a trail of breadcrumbs implicating Lydia, should I ever need it. Turns out I did. The Cyber Crimes unit of the FBI issued a warrant for her arrest last week.

A text comes through from Gemma, "Good luck! She'll love him!"

Gemma knows Tony's meeting my mom today and is enthusiastic about it. She's a huge Tony fan. He's a fan of hers, as well.

He met her when he picked us up from the police station the night of the Olympia. After recounting our evening to him, culminating with Gemma tasing Craig in the balls, Tony turned to me and said, "Stick with her."

Chapter 83

GEMMA

Identify the Body Part is my new favorite game. I look down at my belly, where something—knee, elbow, heel?—presses against its confines. Someone's running out of room. I rub my fingers lovingly over the bulge. Give it a little push back. I'm guessing it's a heel.

"All finished. Come take a look," Steve says, exiting our future baby's room. We get along surprisingly well, considering we're getting a divorce. It turns out Steve is my baby's father, which is probably a good thing, since Craig is in jail and his company mired in scandal.

The REIGN debacle has been all over the media since it blew up at the Olympia. It started with the murder of Anita and the attempted murder of me. It swelled to encompass the murder of Bianca. Then there was the documentary with its inside look at REIGN's deplorable sweatshops, complete with footage of preteens wearing rags in a dimly lit room, hunched over, elbow to elbow, in front of sewing machines, producing hundred-dollar leggings for rich American women. Next, lead was found in their protein powders. And arsenic. The factory was inspected and rat droppings were found. It should go without saying that their factories were *not* solar powered. Bizarrely, despite all his lies, it appears that Craig was, indeed, a vegan.

Todd is out of the picture. My home security system caught him sneaking into our home and opening the dining room window right before I returned from the Olympia. Apparently, he was trying to drive me crazy. Steve was appalled and doesn't want Todd around our child.

You know who else is no longer around? Fat Gemma. I finally defeated her. But not the way I thought I would.

Straddling Craig, pulling those leggings so tight around his wrists that my palms bled, my back burned, and my biceps shook, I realized that I am strong. Physically, mentally, emotionally. That strong is what I want to be.

And that's how I won the body war. By walking away. Fuck Fat Gemma. Fuck Thin Gemma, too. Their battle sucks. It's stupid.

I don't want to chase elusive beauty standards. I want to chase strength. There's nothing arbitrary about running a mile, doing a pull-up, or snatching one hundred pounds. You either hit it or you don't.

Strong is active. It runs up stairs, carries weight, pushes it away. Skinny just is.

Getting physically strong gave me the mental strength to dump shitty friends, quit shitty jobs, and just expect better. To believe I deserved better.

Somehow along the way, my Instagram account became more about losing weight. It became about shrinking. I want to shift the focus back to getting strong. Because that's the game changer. Once you do that, you no longer obsess about what you can't eat but focus on the fuel you need to nourish your body. Instead of fighting it, you embrace it.

Since finding out that I'm pregnant, I've become increasingly concerned about the world I'm bringing this life into. I want a world that's accepting. Encouraging. That builds people up rather than tears them down.

You know who's responsible for that? We all are.

I'm starting with me.

Steve gives me a hand and helps hoist me up off the sofa. I waddle to our baby's room. He stands back and lets me enter.

It smells like fresh paint. Sunlight streams through the windows. The walls are aglow.

In pink.

Acknowledgments

Jackson Keeler. Thank you. Jackson is the literary agent who took a chance on me, a complete unknown with a manuscript in serious need of shaping up. He worked patiently and tirelessly to help me mold it into what you hold today. Then he found the right publishing imprint, Blackstone, to bring *Bodies to Die For* into the world. I have learned so much from him about story development and this whole crazy business of publishing.

Thank you, Shane Salerno, for introducing me to Jackson and for giving me those early words of encouragement. They helped push me through some very trying times. Also, thank you for your insight: that if I could get the tone right (you were thinking "subversive"), I could have something. After your feedback, I wrote "subversive" on a Post-it and stuck it to my bathroom vanity, where it stayed for over a year. That Post-it is now stuck to the inside cover of my copy of *Bodies to Die For*.

Thank you, Daniel Ehrenhaft at Blackstone Publishing for seeing the potential in this story, your guidance, and unwavering belief. Thank you to so many others at Blackstone who have come together to help make *Bodies to Die For* the best

version of itself and to get it into readers' hands, especially
Josie Woodbridge for your enthusiasm, Madeline Hopkins and
Ember Hood for your keen editorial insights, Kathryn English
for the gorgeous cover that captures exactly what I envisioned,
publicists Tatiana Radujkovic and Nicole Sklitsis for your ded-
ication, marketing gurus Brianna Jones and Rachel Sanders for
your tireless efforts, and so many others. I am eternally grateful to you all.

Thank you, James Patrick, founder of FITposium (since
rebranded to Get Published LIVE). James not only helped me
break into writing articles for fitness magazines, but had it not
been for him, this book may not exist today. I had quit writing
Bodies to Die For during the pandemic when the media was re-
porting a possible link between Covid and obesity. I just didn't
think that anyone would want to read a book like mine anymore. When I told this to James, he said, "I'd still want to read
it. I think you should get off this phone and finish that book."
And so, I did.

Thank you to the magazines that have let me broadcast
my message to get strong from their pages: *Inside Fitness Magazine*, *STRONG Fitness Magazine*, *T-Nation*, and *D'FYNE Fitness
Magazine*.

I also need to thank someone who doesn't even know me:
Bret Contreras (a.k.a. The Glute Guy). I stumbled upon his
writing over a decade ago, after years in the body wars trenches.
Bret's emphasis on getting strong struck a chord with me, and
I read every article and book of his that I could find. I learned
so much from him. I am stronger mentally and physically because of it.

Special thanks to retired Winnetka Chief of Police, Marc
Hornstein, for responding to my very sketchy email titled, "Not
really in your job description, but . . ." and then generously

taking the time to let me interview him about how police investigations work. Any mistakes or flights of fancy (forgive me) are my own.

Thank you, Sri Achary, Cybersecurity Consultant, of Custom Cybersecurity Solutions LLC, for helping with cybersecurity insights, for turning around my questions quickly, and for putting some rather complicated matters into layman's terms. Also, thank you Karen Fellows, software engineering specialist, for helping with a few health software–specific details.

I'd like to thank my fabulous beta readers, all of whom I found on Goodreads. Sharon Umbaugh (https://thewritersreader.wordpress.com), Gabby D'Aloia (https://gcdeditorial.wordpress.com/), Anna Teal, and Shalini (digitalreadsmedia.com).

Enormous thanks to my parents, who raised me to be strong. Never doubting for a minute that I wouldn't be. I'm fortunate to have been raised by people who never commented on my looks, other than to tell me to go comb my hair (which was fair—you should have seen it).

To my husband, for supporting me on this crazy journey. To my kids, for their love.

And finally, to you, the reader. For picking up my book. For reading it. Digesting it. Embodying it. Strong women lift each other up.